THE SHORES OF OUR SOULS

A NOVEL

KATHRYN BROWN RAMSPERGER

TouchPoint
Press

D1611938

SHORES OF OUR SOULS
By Kathryn Brown Ramsperger
Published by TouchPoint Press
Jonesboro, Arkansas 72401
www.touchpointpress.com

Ebook Edition.

First Edition

Editor: Kimberly Coghlan
Cover Design: Estella Vukovic

Connect with the author online:
Website: shoresofoursouls.com
Twitter: @KathyRamsperger
Facebook: @kramsperger

I love you when you bow in your mosque,
Kneel in your temple
Pray in your church,
For you and I are sons of one religion
And it is the Spirit.
What difference is there between us,
Save a restless dream that follows
My soul but fears to come near you?

—Khalil Gibran, *The Prophet*

Dedication

To Brian,
For my happy ending.

We often lose ourselves in love; rarely do we find ourselves there.
Never do we see it coming.

QASIM

CHAPTER ONE
Civil War

April 13, 1975, Beirut

Gunmen kill four Christians during an assassination attempt on Lebanese Maronite leader Pierre Gemayel. Believing assassins to be Palestinian, the Christians attack a bus of Palestinian passengers, killing at least twenty-six. Civil War begins.

"Qasim, where are you, my son?"

I rifle through my papers, trying to complete my thoughts before my mother discovers me. I am wrestling with some legal details before sending paperwork to our attorney. This side of business has always been an anathema to me, and I have delayed dealing with it for far too long. I have spent *al Juma'a*, our holy day, working on my master's thesis in secret. I spent all evening looking over my shoulder. Had my mother discovered me working when I should have been praying, she would have given me, a grown man, a good thrashing.

"Qasim!" My mother swings the double doors open and stands in the doorway, sunlight filtering over her like a fluorescent bubble, hand on her left hip, head tipped to the opposite side. "Qasim, did you not hear me call your name? I was afraid I had missed you. The streets are explosive today. I heard reports of gunfire over by one of the camps. You didn't pass by it, did you?"

"No, Mama," I reply and reach to massage the scar that outlines my throbbing cheek. I ignore her reference to the camp. "I'm trying to complete something here."

"Work, work, work. That is all you boys ever do any more. Just like your father." She perches on the edge of the upholstery, her fingers tapping on her lap.

"That is what men do," I remind her.

"My youngest, all grown up," she says, half to herself. My mother is too shrewd for the boring details that occupy my days. I would be surprised if she did not spend most of her day plotting for all her sons, rearranging our future. Thus far, she has certainly met with success, leaving only a few skeletons in her wake.

Yet the conflict in the region has diverted even *her* attention outward. What happens outside our home is now of more importance than what happens within it. Still, one must keep up appearances.

These days, I am happy to forget my own assortment of skeletons. I forget my mother's face over mine in the hospital, willing me to live. I forget the shame that covered my father's entire countenance once I finally could breathe on my own. I forget my brothers' hasty comings and goings. I forget the imam's warnings. I already have known a kind of death; why should I fear nothingness? Most of all, I forget—I *will* myself to forget my wedding day. It is a haze, as is my life. I have money, prestige, my work. *One day I will have a mistress, I suppose.* For a time, I will hibernate in my fog. I hide any wreckage well, even from myself. *Who has time for one more irksome female?* I laugh, I joke, I am my old charming self. I am there but not there. Work has been my salvation.

I hear a rustling in the hallway. I walk to the doorway, thinking it is a colleague coming to get me, tired of waiting for me at the offices. Instead, Rasha sways on the bottom step, hovering above the landing, in her flowing white chiffon. "Qasim?" she says, her voice a blend of croak and whisper. She looks every bit a ghost.

"What is the matter, Rasha?" I ask. I am irritated at all the attention I am expected to bestow on females when they know I should be at my office.

"Qasim?" She repeats the question and sways some more. Her eyes seem glazed, and so I sigh, mount the staircase, and guide her by the elbow back to her bedroom. "I am not feeling well," she says.

"You rest," I tell her. "Rest is what you need."

She suppresses a whimper. "I should not bother you with this..."

"Perhaps I will send for your sister when I go to town?" I reassure her. "That would do you good." I dread having her sister in our home. Perhaps she will be gone by the time I return. *I will work late.*

She pulls her elbow from my grasp and flops down onto the coverlet. "Yes, that would do me good," she replies. "Thank you, Qasim. *Shukran*."

"Qasim!"

"Yes, Mama?" I am truly irritated. *Will I never be able to attend to important matters?*

"Qasim, I need you to take care of that spent ammunition today." My mother is in the hallway, holding a slim cigarette in a hand that trembles just enough for me to notice.

The ammunition was a curiosity at first. Tariq dragged it home one morning. That evening, Rasha yelled for me to go outside to see what he was bringing home. I leaned over the balcony first, as she is prone to fits of needless anxiety. Tariq's body, brown as a coconut, was bent over, walking backwards, towing it along, a cloud of dust making him sputter. He had broken a strap of one of his sandals, so he was limping, too. His dark, soulful eyes lit up with wonder. *How I love that boy!*

At first, I was merely bemused. He reminded me of a peddler who couldn't get his donkey to obey. I couldn't imagine what he was dragging that nearly matched his weight. When I realized his claimed treasure was weaponry, I became as agitated as Rasha. When I learned he had picked it from a gutter lining *rue Omar al-Daouk*, as innocently as he would have plucked a flower from a bush, I was frightened.

We had not thought things were so far gone that we needed to warn him about unexploded ammo. What would be next, landmines disguised as toys? Our Tariq would not need the excuse of disguise to investigate. His natural curiosity always gets the best of him. Sadly, artillery dots every neighborhood, begging for investigation from curious children. Tariq has never known this country at a time of relative peace. Weapons are more familiar to him than to me, his father. Perhaps not commonplace because we keep our war well hidden, but familiar, as familiar as the tooth he lost last month.

I brought the shell around to the courtyard immediately, wondering whom to call to rid ourselves of it. Tariq cried bitterly that he could not keep it. We brought our neighbor, old Ahmed, a veteran of prior wars, over to inspect it. He bent and rose, bent and rose, as though he were praying, as he pored over the still strange object. Finally, he pushed the glasses off the tip of his nose and squinted toward me. "Harmless," he pronounced. "A dud." With that, he turned and collapsed on the courtyard bench, fanning himself. He ensured us it would not explode in Tariq's hands should he not heed our warnings to look, not touch.

"What is it?" I asked. "What sort of weapon is this? I have never seen such a curious weapon."

"They're using some kind of ancient weaponry. Looks as old as the last World War. Must be some little-funded faction that launched it. If it hasn't exploded in thirty-five years, it's not going to go off in your garden." He laughed from his throat, and then his eyes drifted and glazed. He was back in his own world again.

The monstrosity sat in the courtyard for a few days while I searched for someone in the government who would retrieve it. They wanted nothing to do with it. There it sat: ugly metal, covered with soil and rust, a visible reminder of the war raging round us, while we went about our everyday business. Tariq treated it almost as a playmate or a pet. He actually talked to it but minded us and never touched it again.

A shower washed some of the mud away, revealing tiny scratches in the metal, like mosaic patterns, and when the sun glinted from the right direction, one could almost look on it as sculpture. It had a protuberance near the top creating a depth of field on its shiny, cylindrical surface that refracted light and shadow just so. I had once seen a water tower rising out of the desert sand in the middle of nowhere that produced a similar effect. I began to look on the cylinder as, at the very least, a part of our lives, and at most, a work of art. Our lives continued around it, at least until we found someone willing to take it away.

Oh yes, every now and then we overhear a burst of gunfire, syncopated with shouts of injury. Yet largely our lives are about money exchanging hands at my office, listening to Tariq recite his prayers and lessons, running the household, alternating weekend visits to our families, and winding our way down to the beach, filled with young starlets sporting bikinis rather than burkas, a recent, modern trend. Beirut moves forward even as the bullets fly, and so must I.

Long after evening prayer, I arrive home with news. Tariq lies on his belly under the same table I once used as a hiding place, reading.

"What is that, son?" I ask, and he grunts an answer. More than likely it is a book of riddles or a puzzle book. I wish he would read as I did. His dusty feet thump on the tile floor, and his straight hair sticks up at the crown like a rooster.

Rebuffed, I climb the stairs to my room. It is a day of heat, inexplicably stifling in this Mediterranean climate. My shirt sticks to me, the sweat entwined on every hair lining my chest. My tie, normally as comfortable to me as the neck it encircles, chokes me. I go upstairs, lay my jacket carefully on the back of my butler's valet, and loosen my tie. There, I can breathe.

I sit on the edge of my large bed, and I notice my wife has bought a new coverlet since the last time I sat here. I've told her I am not in need of new bed linens often. She feels compelled to replace mine when she replaces her own. I lean forward, rest my elbows on my knees, and take a deep breath. I am unprepared to break this news, but break it, I must. The offer is on the table, and I must answer soon. I am still undecided about which way I will go, yet the family has to know of my intent. I rub my eyes, hoping it will give me greater clarity, if not greater strength.

No one in my family will support me if I take this offer. My father and brothers will forever be wrapped up in manufacturing boxes and counting their money. Perhaps my mother will finally learn to live without me by her side. My wife is focused on changing coverlets every six months. My son is about to begin school. This is what is important to them, their day-to-day-to-day. They do not see what is in store for our country. They think it will end tomorrow, and if not tomorrow, then the day after. Over 100 killed, and many more wounded, and to us, it could almost be in another country. We are practiced at hiding things from ourselves.

Perhaps I should stick with the familiar. The pit of my stomach churns at the thought of leaving Beirut, even for a short time. I am adept at negotiation, even better with numbers. I have an agile mind, which could, in time, bring the family even greater prosperity than it already knows. Yet what will become of the coins my brothers and I spend our time counting, should this country destroy itself? Should my efforts not be toward saving all of

Beirut? I run my hands through my hair and prepare for battle. Better to win Rasha over before I tell my parents. I put one foot in front of the other, and down the stairs I go.

I find Rasha in the corner of the sitting room, folding linens for the party we will host tomorrow. She has drawn the shades against the sun, which blazes this time of year even in the early evening. She looks up at me, but I cannot determine whether she knows that I have news to share. Her round eyes are always so wide open that they could go no further even if they were pried off their hinges. I stand a moment longer, searching for words. This is the first time Rasha has stirred fear in me—unease, sometimes a familiar disgust, other emotions, yes, but not fear. I must choose my words with great care.

"Qasim?" Rasha's tone is at once expectant and resigned.

I decide that if I convey enough physical energy, I will win my point. I dance around a bit in front of her and grin, giving me further time to think. "I had a nice day," I say.

"Oh?" She begins to fold again, over once, over again, and then she pulls the napkin corner through to make a festive design. I wonder if she is even listening, which gives me courage.

"I have been offered a position, a very prominent position, entry level to be sure..."

I notice her hands have stopped folding in mid-air. She suspects something. I switch tacks.

"The family business is still uppermost in my commitments." I stride forward and sit down beside her. I take her hand; perhaps that will help. "I can do both. I have so much energy, and this country means so much to us all."

"What on earth are you speaking of, Qasim?" Her wide forehead furrows, and I know there is more work to be done. I forget sometimes that she knows nothing of the working world.

"I have been offered a temporary position at the United Nations."

"What?" She throws my hand away from her, rises, and lets the linens fall from her lap onto the rug.

I love that rug, the way it shines a different color depending on the light. "We will need to close the house for a while."

"What?" Rasha repeats. I decide to be quiet for a moment, let her absorb the shock. She paces over to the window, opens the shade, and paces back toward me. I clutch my own hands together. "Qasim, am I not a good wife to you? Is Tariq not a good son? Why would you want to move back into your mother's house?"

I gasp and then chuckle, for I realize she has again missed the point. "No, no, Rasha! Never worry about that. Under no circumstances are we ever to be dependent on my family again. No, we are going to move to the States for a time. I will be a diplomat."

She looks at me, and she struggles to contain herself. "I repeat — my husband, am I not a good wife? Do I not make you happy?"

The question sends me reeling for a moment. I was going one way with this conversation, and she is taking it the other. "Happiness is not the issue, Rasha," I snap. "We should speak about this matter when you are better able to grasp it."

She follows me to the bottom of the staircase and pulls limply at my wrist. Qasim... how? Why, this, all of a sudden? Who has offered you this job? This is our home, Qasim! Why would we ever leave, even for a month?"

She is blubbering now, and I have had enough. "As I said, we will discuss this later." I walk up the staircase with what I hope to be deliberation. Times like these, I wish I *had* time for a mistress. Yet, that would be just one more woman I had to pacify.

***

That night, an explosion rocks the house, and I turn over in bed. It is not yet dawn, and I am accustomed to the noise of civil war. Then consciousness takes over, and I realize how close the blast is to the house. I race to the back balcony. Fear clutches every pore of my body like the jaws of a great animal.

"Rasha," I shout. "Rasha!" I cannot hear my own voice over the rushing in my head. "Rasha," I shout, hoping she will hear me even if I cannot. "Where is Tariq?"

She strolls into the room, wiping sleep from her eyes. She throws a bright shawl over her shoulders as she approaches the window. "What are you talking of, Qasim? He is asleep in his bed, as you should be. Are you dreaming?" She touches my arm to wake me, but I am not sleepwalking.

I jerk my arm away from her and tear to Tariq. There he is, his arms stretched out over his head, his chest exposed, rising and falling, rising and falling in gentle, early morning slumber. Rasha comes round me, alarmed herself now, and runs her hands through Tariq's thick hair, assuring herself that I am the mad one. "You see, Qasim? He is here. Nothing is wrong."

"An explosion jarred me awake. It sounded close."

"I heard nothing."

I blink my eyes; in fact, all is silent except for the chirp of some distant insect.

Perhaps it was a dream.

I sit on the edge of Tariq's bed and rub my eyes, willing myself fully awake. Another explosion rocks the bedroom, sending Tariq's Matchbox cars careening off his shelf.

"Oh!" Rasha gasps.

I run to the balcony again. Tariq sleeps on. My eyes clear of sleep now, and the full moon sends its rays into the courtyard. I search its dim corners to make certain all is in order. *Something is wrong. What?*

A huge gash of terror rips through me. I realize that the mortar is missing. I stumble back, half in dread of what is to come, half because its disappearance makes no sense. *Who would make off with a dud, other than a child?*

I rush toward the front balcony, stumble over a broken vase that the explosion has jarred to the floor, curse, run back to my room for my lantern, and then head back to the balcony. It seems seconds have turned to hours. I vow silently never to have this threat of time hanging over me again. Moonlight spills over the balcony reminding me of long ago, the present more of a dream than the past. How strange that such beautiful light can still pour over a world where one's dreams are filled with the sound of explosions, where children bring home weapons instead of kittens, and where snipers hide in every shadow the moon caresses. I stand, letting my eyes adjust to the brightness.

Then I see him. Ahmed is pulling the dud up the alleyway across from us on an oxcart without any beasts hitched to it. His white nightshirt trails behind him in the dust. *He must have completely lost his senses.* Perhaps the explosions are getting to him. I want to call out to him, to make certain he is not sleepwalking, but I know that any sound could draw snipers. We are not in the usual lines of fire, but I cannot chance our safety tonight. "Go get something I can throw to warn Ahmed," I order Rasha. She scuttles away.

I wait, feeling my breath becoming shorter. Still no sound except the wheels of his oxcart on gravel. He is out of my line of vision. He must be at the corner of the neighborhood. "Rasha," I hiss. "Where are you?" Nothing. I see a flare light up the sky; I feel rather than hear the swish of it. "Rasha!" Nothing.

Suddenly, Tariq is there beside me, pulling on my pajama elastic. "Baba?" he gets out, and then the whole world rocks.

We cannot breathe. I feel myself pick Tariq up in my arms and carry him toward the center hallway, away from this infernal suffocation. *What could this possibly be? Some sort of gas?* I strip my pajama shirt off and cover Tariq's face with it, commanding him to take a few shallow breaths. I run and get my tie and wrap it around his head. Please God, let me keep him safe! Rasha is here by this time, and the servants come running up the staircase. I suppose she went to get them to throw something *for* her. She can never do anything by herself.

I grab all the clothes I can carry from my dresser. We race downstairs to the pantry, crowd into it, and I cover any cracks that would let in air with the clothes I have brought with us. Only then do I take my shirt from Tariq's face. He is breathing hard, but uninjured. "Baba," he chides me. "Were you trying to smother me in there?"

Outside I hear chaos. Screams from all around, and a particularly high-pitched screech, which could only be from someone who is wounded. Sirens call out from every direction.

"Must have been a live phosphorus shell," a servant mutters.

I ruffle Tariq's hair in relief. "Sit down, everyone. We must stay here until we get the all-clear in the morning." I still do not know if the shell exploded or a mortar hit somewhere in our neighborhood.

Phosphorus. What does all of this mean? All this time a phosphorus shell has been gathering dust in our courtyard? Why did Ahmed decide to drag it off when the crossfire began? Old Ahmed, our friend, our neighbor, who would not have hurt a flea. I banish the word "spy" from my mind. Perhaps he was a confused old man who had finally reached his limit. Perhaps he was sleepwalking. Perhaps he was dragging the shell away so it wouldn't be hit in the crossfire. Perhaps I will see Ahmed in the morning and bid him peace, express my gratitude. Phosphorus sticks to whatever it hits and burns, setting it perpetually on fire. My mind cannot help but fixate on an image of old Ahmed lying burnt—still burning—and disintegrating in the road outside our neighborhood, his glassy eyes staring out into the cold morning light. *Will we ever see him again?*

No matter the outcome of this terrible night, one thing is certain. It is unsafe here, and it is best to get out while we can.

I turn to Rasha. I feel my face tighten, ready for my own form of war. I am stone; I cannot be cajoled or swayed. "I am taking the job," I tell her. "You and Tariq are coming with me."

Dianna

CHAPTER TWO

Engagement

February 13, 1981, Lebanon

Lebanon's leaders adopt security measures to protect its embassies after the kidnapping of Jordan's charge d'affaires in Beirut. Snipers paralyze traffic between East and West Beirut.

February 13, 1981, New York City

Dianna scans the bar through strobe-lit smoke. A haze casts a film on the room's mirrored walls, hung to give the illusion of space.

Dianna hopes a night of companionship will prevent another night of reckless eating. She's dragged her colleague Sophia along to delude herself that she's here for some reason other than finding a man to fill her emptiness for a while. She wears a purple-and-navy Evan-Picone skirt with one pleat in front and a cream sweater. Before she left her office, she pulled her hair back from her forehead as her mother always advised. She recently bought new pumps, too tight, to give the illusion of height. Proper business attire, which belies her mission.

"Are you sure this is where you want to be tonight?" Sophia waves her elegant hand through the smoke and lights a cigarette. She feels a pang of guilt for dragging Sophia here. Two decades older, Sophia is more fairy godmother than buddy.

"Sorry," is all Dianna shouts over the din and shrugs. She catches her stomach sticking out ever so slightly in one of the mirrors and takes a deep breath to pull it in.

"Dianna, I'm afraid I can't stay much longer," Sophia says.

Doubting she has the courage to stay here alone, Dianna ponders her options. She looks up at the scum-covered ceiling and asks for inner strength. The subway will close soon, and she has no car.

Then she sees him.

He wears a European suit. An expensive watch with a black face and gold hands glints on his right wrist. Not much taller than she, but wiry, he seems at once exotic and familiar: olive skin graces distinct, proportionate features. His dark hair reminds her of her mother's, and his graceful stance, her father's. He moves with a purposeful gait, arms relaxed, head tilted slightly to the right. He seems part of a world she has yet to experience.

The man circles her, moving through the crowd, around chatting couples, each time drawing nearer, until he stands before her, touching her forearm. "Have you seen a woman...?" he begins.

Dianna misses the rest of his sentence because of the blaring music, his accent, and the word "woman." *He could be fibbing to make himself appear less threatening. Or maybe he has been stood up.* A half-minute passes before she relaxes and replies. "Look around you," she says and laughs. "Women everywhere. What did she look like?"

He moves in closer and speaks directly into her ear so she can hear him. Dianna shivers as she catches a whiff of his cologne. Her eyes catch his. With his tailored suit and self-possessed energy, he almost fits right in. Yet his eyes betray him. This man has suffered. She knows all about pretending. She's hooked.

"She has shoulder-length brown hair," he says. Then, "Never mind — how could you ever identify her?" He waves his arm upward in dismissal. His eyes shift away.

Sophia taps her shoulder, a silent question. *Can she leave?* Dianna wants her to stay, to keep her safe, and she almost follows her out the bar door. Her pulse thumps heavy in her neck. Then she gestures Sophia homeward and follows the man to the bar. She came here to meet a man, after all.

"What's your pleasure?" he asks.

She sighs — she will not have to spend her last few dollars to buy her own drink.

"Hello," he says, extending a well-groomed hand, as though he wants her to examine it. "My name is Qasim. And you are?" His fingers bear no ring.

"Hello. I'm Dianna. Thank you for the drink." Her hand lingers in his warm, dry palm for a moment before he lets it drop. Then she makes herself busy stirring the swizzle stick in her gin and tonic, squeezing the lime in.

"That's a beautiful ring," he says. "Your school ring?"

Dianna gazes at the green stone with a pang of pride. She doubts this man wants to hear much about her college days or the job that put her through school. "Yes," she replies.

"You work around here?" He takes a sip of his Scotch and looks around the bar, as if he might not get an answer.

She crosses her legs and steadies herself with her heel on the rung of the bar stool, and then she replies, "Yes, at the Metropolitan. And you?"

"The UN."

She raises her brows. "Ah, what do you do?"

He squirms on his seat before answering, and his eyes shift to the floor, then up at her face. "Oh, merely the regular diplomatic paper pushing. Have you been working at the Met long?"

His gaze makes her measure her words. "No, I moved here a year ago. This is my first job after graduation." Dianna smiles broadly, a vain attempt to closet her small-town naiveté. "I've wanted to live here since I was a child." She stops, not wanting to reveal more of herself to a stranger.

He seems to read her thoughts. "I am from Lebanon. When I was growing up, I too, wanted to live in New York someday. I always had a fascination with the Statue of Liberty. An American soldier once gave me a tiny replica." He smiles, and she feels its real warmth.

She relaxes and smiles back.

He clears his throat and adjusts his tie. "Do you know anyone from there?"

Her brain searches for her parents' friends' name and retrieves it: the Damuses.

Qasim beams and moves his bar stool closer. "The Met must be a wonderful place to work." He leans toward her.

"Oh, it has its ups and downs. I'm just a cataloger." Dianna feels a dreaded blush creep up her face. If only she could hide her emotions more.

"That's an important position for someone as young as yourself." He must have caught her blush, and he wants to make her feel better. His empathy tugs at her heart, and she leans toward him.

"I needed a job, and I wanted to be in New York." She blushes again; she hasn't procured the job she wants yet.

He ignores her embarrassment. "I'm here tonight celebrating!" He claps his hands together without sound.

"Oh." Dianna looks around for his companions but finds none. She wonders what he means — celebrating alone must be unusual, even in other countries. Perhaps the woman he was meeting was going to celebrate with him.

"I received my PhD this week. I defended my dissertation yesterday."

"Congratulations!" Dianna pivots toward him on her bar stool. She feels a tinge of her own empathy for this man, who must search for someone with whom to celebrate his life achievements. She uncrosses her legs, and the bar stool tips a bit with the movement. He reaches across to steady it. "What did you get it in?" she asks.

"Global Studies," he replies, those eyes measuring her reaction.

She takes care with her response. She surmises his self-image is linked to his education. "So you will miss school?"

"Yes." His eyes cloud, as though remembering all the classrooms, books, and grades. "I will miss it in many ways. Education is very important."

"Yes, I'll return once I have some money put aside," she says. "I'd also like to travel." She goes on to talk about the places that beckon her, forgetting her responsibilities in America. She begins with her chief lures, Paris and Venice, and continues well into her fantasies — African safaris and a cruise around the Greek islands. She's careful not to mention any place in the Middle East, lest he think she's hinting at a future trip with him.

"I can understand the desire to travel. To some of us, it is more than a desire; it is a need. I myself will always need to learn and travel."

"Yes, me too. That's why I came to this bar."

His laugh is like a tightrope wire, showing one crooked front tooth in a row of otherwise perfect, straight ones. He has caught her joke. The bartender brings two fresh drinks. Qasim takes one long gulp of his first Scotch and hands the bartender his empty glass. Dianna sips, wishing she had a better threshold for alcohol. She looks away, pretending to study the top-shelf bottles in front of them, feeling his gaze moving across her body. A ripple of excitement pulses through her. The alcohol is doing its job.

She has heard that diplomats listen more to what is *not* said than what *is*. She hopes he can't discern that she almost didn't complete college. She needs to support her mother — the mother who would have beaten her for being in this bar, let alone with a foreign man. No matter, her mother was in no condition to harm anyone these days. Funny how shame persisted; she should think of a joke about that.

Yet her discomfort dissipates with every word they exchange. She's surprised by this man's awareness of her, how he seems to hang on her words, and she becomes more at ease as he tells her of his country, his work, and when asked, about himself. Their surroundings become more raucous, but Dianna doesn't notice. This man, this Qasim, listens. Someone is listening to her.

He suggests escaping the rising noise and smoke to grab some Chinese food. "You've had Chinese, right?" he asks, and Dianna wonders if he's joking.

"Of course," she replies, her pride stiff. She goes to a pay phone to call her housemate Leah, and all she finds at the other end is an incessant busy signal. The phone eats her change.

The outside air smells of snow. They ransom his car, a late-model bottle-green Buick sedan, from one valet only to relinquish it to another ten minutes later. Qasim opens the door for her, helps her with her jacket, and orders for her. She will not remember the name of the delicious food they savor. Not so the conversation. She relishes every word he speaks, and his rapt eyes show she has his attention. Dianna marvels at the rarity of this bar-room-encounter-turned-date. Yet they linger, chatting about work, joking about chopsticks, bantering about Reaganomics and the new shops on Fifth Avenue. When the waiter brings tea and fortune cookies, Qasim offers her one, running his finger along the back of her hand. She shivers, unsure if she's feeling excitement or trepidation, but certain he has noticed.

Perhaps this is the beginning of something, Dianna muses and instantly snuffs the hope. What would he see in her anyway? This man is probably only here for a year or two since he has his degree, and she has a plan to remain uninvolved.

Qasim unfurls his fortune like a tiny scroll, glances at it, and then stuffs it in his jacket's breast pocket. The two movements — the first fluid, the second abrupt — bemuse her. It must not have been favorable. She slips her own minute piece of paper out of its broken shell, reading three inapplicable words: "HE IS LOYAL." She tosses the paper onto the tablecloth. Dianna does not believe in Chinese cookie fate.

"What did yours say?" She grins, Cheshire-like, and leans toward him.

"Dianna's future shines bright," he says.

Though she knows this is a line, she doesn't care. "That's very kind."

"Fortune cookie, very wise, very accurate," he quips, and she giggles. "Do that again," he says, and his voice trembles.

"I can't perform on command," she says, but she giggles again in spite of herself. "Really, what did it say?"

"Are you mocking me?" he asks and chucks her under her chin.

"No, just curious," she says, pulling his hand back and balancing her chin on his knuckles. She wants the sensuous sting of his touch to last. "What does your future hold?"

"I'll tell you later," he replies, motioning for the check. The check in hand, he writes a note on it, and then heads for the Gents.' Dianna succumbs to the temptation of reading it. It's a couple of sentences of gratitude in crisp, cropped script underneath a generous tip. She feels a bit chastened by her curiosity.

Upon Qasim's return, Dianna pushes back her chair, and he rushes to pull it all the way out for her. They stand there for a moment gazing at each other. Somewhere between dumplings and fortune cookies, they struck a silent pact. They are going to be together tonight. The bill settled, Qasim takes her to his home.

"What township do you live in?" she asks, hoping he hasn't noticed she isn't certain where they are.

He gives a name she has never heard of, and then he adds, "In case you haven't figured it out, we're going to New Jersey." His eyes twinkle, professorial, not the least malignant or patronizing. She's sure he's noticed her discomfort, and he is trying to allay her fears.

The last time she was in Jersey was with a man who bit her tongue when she wouldn't let him go any further. She wonders at the contrast of that night and this one. The lights of the city glimmer from across the river as they traverse the George Washington Bridge, and Qasim takes her hand. A few minutes later, they pull into a two-car garage, attached to a stately brick colonial and enter a table-space kitchen that gleams of white walls and stainless steel. Walking ahead of her, Qasim flicks on light switches. Each room displays a carpet more unusual than the previous one. He turns on every lamp in his den to show off the rug in there.

"Stand on the north side," Qasim urges.

Dianna gasps in admiration. "It's a completely different color from the south than from the north."

His expression turns gentle, relaxed. He loosens his tie, sits back on the sofa, and pats the seat. She joins him. They kiss — a simple but promising kiss. His lips are full and warm, a tad rough, and she wants to continue discovering them.

When he asks her to his bedroom, without prelude, she accepts, though for a moment, she wants to run. His differences that drew her in stand between them like a fortress wall. She is uncertain what she wanted from this night. She had wanted him to notice her; she did not mean for this man to move her as he has.

She follows him, off-kilter, remembering the last time she saw Danson, in a cemetery of all places. She remembers how the sun bounced off the etched stones, the crinkle of his leather jacket during their last hug, the rough texture of his fingers as he pulled away. No one has piqued her interest since. She's entertained some mediocre dates, even some flings, but nothing compared to tonight. She knew what was going to happen before she even decided to show up. She doesn't know if she wants Danson's image to remain or retreat. The image finally decides for itself.

As simple as his living room is elegant, Qasim's bedroom has bare walls, an armoire, a bed, and a hard, wooden chair. They strip off their business clothes: the ties, the tweed, the pantyhose that separate them. He urges her down onto the crisp linens of a king-sized bed. *Might he have a wife?* She locks this seed of doubt away for later. Sex is the one time she can let go.

Dianna looks scientifically at Qasim's body, as she does all men, deciding what pleases her: his curly black hair, meticulously trimmed, his scrupulous nails on long fingers, the curve of his mouth, the deep scar on the right side of his cheek, the baby-fine hair that hides most of his silken skin. His physique does not draw upon the depth of her passion; his eyes are her focal point. They remind her of a deep well of water.

He caresses her — her legs, her knees, the arch of her back, the hollow of her throat, the notch under her chin. Without hesitating, his hands glide fluidly over the red indentation that her skirt hook made. Dianna reflects on this only for a moment. She is drunk with gin and too much pent-up desire. She lets herself go. She takes herself down, down, down, murmuring that she does not do this often, not second-guessing herself or how he will react to her abandon. They fall into rhythm, and it becomes a dance. Later, the second guesses will come. For now, she is free, and he follows her.

He is speaking another language. It pours out of his mouth like steamy tea. Dianna is wistful, even in passion, that she cannot understand what he says to her. He interrupts the stream of words now and again with an English exclamation. He calls her "beautiful." He says it with an inflection of awe and surprise, as if he had been afraid of discovering some grave, cloaked imperfection that would destroy his first impression. She turns her head away, sadly, simply. She does not think of herself as beautiful.

She senses that Qasim notices her dismissal, the negative incline of her head. He takes his hand away, tentatively, for an instant. Her slight, dubious gesture hangs in the air like a "no" that has actually been spoken. It comes between them — a small echo of air — enough to let him know he holds the better hand.

CHAPTER THREE

Telecommunications

Dianna wakes to find Qasim on the phone, speaking rapid-fire Arabic, sometimes looking across the room, sometimes looking down. He laughs frequently, even in the middle of words. His laughter is quite the contrast to his punctuated speech—like water running over pebbles—melodious yet complex, complicit and implicit, not altogether a laugh of goodwill, yet infectious. When he hangs up, he doesn't share any details from the conversation with her. She wants to know but doesn't ask. It's too soon to meddle in his private business.

She's feeling a pang of remorse. She's never stayed with someone the night she met them, and he's so much older than she. In spite of her entry-level job, she's on a career track. She's finally sending some money home. She shouldn't have been so open. She shouldn't have had anything to drink.

Yet as she watches Qasim move about the room, she relaxes again into the magic they shared last night. *He certainly doesn't seem to be feeling any regret.* He's busy tidying up the room, humming a tune that's a little off key, folding the crease in his trousers, picking up her belongings from the floor and putting them in the chair beside the closet. He pulls a white terry robe out of his closet and places it on the bottom of the bed for her to wear. Then he chucks her under the chin. "Good morning," he says. "Ready for some breakfast?" He tells her to stay in bed. When he brings in a tray with tea and toast, her heart lifts.

"Mmmm. I can tell you're a bachelor. But thanks for the thought," she teases.

He laughs with her, that same, delicious, infectious laugh. "I am actually a gourmet chef. I don't have time to buy the food." And he sits down at her feet.

"You'll have to show me those skills some time," she says before she realizes that seeing one another again is an assumption they might not share.

Yet he reaches over the sheets and takes her hand. She settles back against the pillow in relief. "Any coffee in that gourmet kitchen of yours?"

"Well…" his eyebrows arch up in contemplation.

"Oh, I have to be a good girl to get coffee?" she teases. He clears his throat, and she can't understand why he's uncomfortable. "It's okay if you don't have any coffee," she reassures him.

"It is not that," he says, still holding her hand, but shifting his position. "It is that I only have what you would call 'Turkish' coffee. That is too strong for you, no?"

Dianna insists she wants Turkish coffee, not weak tea. When he leaves to make it, she opens his closet a crack to find it contains plenty of pressed shirts, jackets, pants, and ties, but nothing remotely feminine. Then she calls her housemate and best friend to let them know of her adventure, and her safety. Leah isn't home, but Heather answers.

"You won't guess where I am," Dianna says in a mock whisper.

"The bookstore," Heather guesses.

"Standing in the home of Dr. Qasim el-Kafry," Dianna says with a giggle.

"Who?" Heather cries.

Dianna leans back in Qasim's comfortable, ornate chair, bouncing on the springs to test it out. "I met him last night. His rugs look different from every angle."

"So you must have had fun."

"Oh, yes!" Dianna hears the enthusiasm in her own voice.

"Well, it's about time," Heather says.

"Time for what?"

"Time you got over that jerk Danson! But an Arab?"

Dianna studies the books on Qasim's coffee table, one in English, the other in Arabic, both textbooks. An annoyance creeps in. "I suppose so."

"Where's he from, so I can be sure?" Heather asks.

"Lebanon."

"All Lebanese are Arab," Heather says with authority.

Dianna starts to argue, to defend Qasim against Heather's tone, but stops at the fall of his footsteps. "I've got to go," she tells Heather.

"Be careful, Cinderella."

The opposite corner of the Persian's colors convey a hint of a particular and familiar, shade of peach—a Georgia Belle peach, like the peaches her father would peel for her from his family farm every summer. It's too soon to know what will happen next, after she rises from the chair, after her clothes are on, after he drives her to her apartment. She smiles at him, full of young womanhood. Qasim smiles back at her.

Then she follows him to his all-white kitchen, surprised by its light and space. She's never seen Arabian coffee made. His pot boasts engraved flowers and diamonds covering it from spout to base. The spout sticks out in a crescent shape.

"No sugar, please," she requests.

"Mostly cardamom," he says. "If you add spice, you seldom need sugar."

The bronze pot resembles the Arabian lamps she knows from childhood fairy tales. If she were still a child, she'd imagine the spices he adds to be some sort of magical brew. The pot seems to have traveled from another world entirely. She picks it up to pour and sees an Arabic inscription underneath.

"What does it say?" she asks.

"To Qasim El-Kafry. Best Wishes from H.E. Dr. Mohammed El-Sadi."

"H.E.?"

"His Eminence. Dr. El-Sadi is a former minister from Qatar."

"You mean clergy?" She furrows her brow.

"No, no, Dianna. Minister of Transportation."

She blushes, feeling schoolgirl foolish. "Oh," she says, rubbing her fingernail along the rim of the pot. Her Southern mother would not approve of her social blunders and naïve questions. Yet neither would she approve of Dianna being in an Arab man's robe.

"I told you I was a gourmet chef," he says. "My family has many happy customers. They've remained friends. That is the way in my part of the world."

"So they gave you coffee pots?" she asks, still perplexed.

"A token of affection." He pauses. "I have added to the collection in other ways." Another pause. "It truly is no matter. Come here, you," he says, and pulls her over to the round table near the window where the sun streams in.

She takes a sip from her cup. He compliments her on not making a funny face while making a funny face himself, puckering his lips in mock distaste. The nubby fabric of his robe caresses her skin. She rubs her cheek against its collar, and he brushes her other cheek, once only, with the back of his hand. No words. His touch tells her he somehow understands her, accepts her.

His neighbor has a bird feeder, and the late morning sun creates a kaleidoscope of color around a gathering of birds—jays, cardinals, even a goldfinch. The feeder itself is painted red, the color of the one her father built her when she was eight. How she wishes she had more memories like that, but he was always moving, and moving them. His death had come without warning, stealing any hope that she'd live in a real home, instead of a house. Still less hope that she could make her own home, her own life, with an ill mother and two siblings to provide for. The birds flutter up. She tries to find some perceived threat in the trees beyond her viewpoint, and a red feather falls onto the new-fallen leaves.

He's staring at her when she looks back at him. He moves toward her with that distinguished, floating gait she admired last night, and his kiss is long and powerful. When he pulls back, he looks appraising, uncertain, as if he too felt last night might be a dream that might not linger. They look out the window together.

"About time I got dressed," she says.

He still looks pensive, but he takes a breath. "If you must," he says, as he walks over and begins doing dishes. She grasps the tiny, white, porcelain handle-less coffee cup in both her hands, and chugs it down to the grounds.

CHAPTER FOUR

A Geography Lesson

On Dianna and Qasim's first true date, they rendezvous at an upscale pizzeria. They stand in a serpentine line, their breath blowing smoke through unseasonably cool air. The pavement shines with a rainbow of slick moisture from a storm that blew through minutes before. Qasim jumps up and down, pounding his feet on the pavement to keep warm.

"I was not made for this climate," he grimaces. "I wish I'd worn an overcoat."

Dianna smooths his wind-blown hair and notices the lights blink on at the top of the Chrysler Building. She glances at her watch. "It's later than I thought."

"Really? What time is it?" He hasn't noticed the city lights at all.

"Closing in on seven-thirty."

"It's getting dark earlier."

"No, the days are lengthening. We were supposed to be here at five-thirty to beat the rush."

"Oh, come now; it doesn't matter. I like the dusk, even if it comes early here."

She wants this date to be like their first meeting, full of giggling and exploration. She's spent two weeks imagining where he'd take her. Dancing? A show? What they'd talk about. Music? Politics? What would happen after they turned the lights out later.

In answer, more city lights twinkle on around them, and the cool air whips around her coat, dampening her daydream. She is amazed at how quickly she started to feel again, with intensity devoid of resignation, she who does not believe in fate. His devoted attention the day they spent together has her desire heightened. They've kept in touch with short, pithy phone conversations, but she sometimes has trouble with the way he runs phrases together.

He's whistling, like he's wishing away the cold. She still marvels at how familiar he feels in spite of his foreignness. The phone conversation has been full of wit and innuendo. Tonight, though, brings back memory of his touch and that depth of attention that he gives her, as if she's the only person he knows. It makes him feel almost like family, though she wonders if perhaps he acts this way with everyone. She's sure his charm must make everyone feel special. Yet as she seizes on this thought, he squeezes her hand, and there's that connection again.

How can he breed this familiarity in her? She's uncertain but wants to keep exploring. The fire behind his eyes is familiar, matching some unknown force within her, impatient to be born. Never before has she seen someone who echoes her hopes and hurts in this profound manner, with no words spoken.

"If talk is silver, then silence is gold," he says, though he looks like he knows what she's thinking.

"I'd love to do what you do," she answers.

"Be grateful, young Dianna. You are here in the land of the free, working at the nation's best museum!" He gives her shoulders a squeeze.

"You could at least tell me about it. What do you do when you travel?"

"I get people who don't want to agree to reach a compromise," he answers.

"So you're a peace mediator!"

"That's an idealistic way of putting it, my dear. More like getting people to share their toys on the playground."

"You establish trust, then. That must lead to peace!"

"It does to some fragile degree."

"You sit in negotiations all day? You don't get to see the countries you visit?"

"Not really."

"Well, I want to travel. Surely there's a way to balance travel and peace. Seems to me travel brings peace, at least inner peace."

"Let me know when you find it, Miss Dianna. Let me know if you find a way to dip your toes in the sea as well."

A tall, well-dressed American couple catches her attention, interrupting her intended response. The man has his arm draped around the woman. They move past the trattoria, obviously disinterested in pizza. Yet the man does a double take, motioning to his partner, and they hesitate for a slight moment, staring in Dianna and Qasim's direction. Dianna discerns a look of veiled disapproval on the man's fine features. She moves closer to Qasim. She needs to protect him from this bejeweled couple. Qasim puts his arm around Dianna. *Has he noticed too?* Then the couple continues on, leaving Dianna with an unsettled feeling. She hears the muted word "interracial" as they disappear into the night.

Qasim stares in their direction long after the couple moves into the distance.

"You okay?" she asks, and he hugs her close.

"Of course," he says, but his smile seems forced.

Did I misunderstand what they said? Dianna muses. *Is that what we are—interracial?* She's conjured up all sorts of other obstacles to a potential relationship with Qasim, but not race; no, not at all. She's not used to being the object of this sort of judgment. She hides her family's newfound poverty and her mother's ill health. That's what blue bloods—moneyed or not—do.

"One does not pay attention to slights from those who do not have the capacity to comprehend the slightest complexity," Qasim tells her. Then he changes the subject, talks about the wind, the weather, the hope of approaching spring. They round the corner, and the warmth of the wood pizza ovens spills out the flimsy door onto her cheeks. They are almost inside. She glances at Qasim and finds him studying her. She shifts her eyes to her feet.

"You remind me of a girl I knew in school," he says and traces her lips, then brings her face up to meet his fixed gaze. "Her cheeks and lips always turned rosy from the least amount of heat."

She smiles and acknowledges the oblique compliment. "Here we are," she says when they arrive at the doorway. "Come in before you catch cold."

"Ladies first," he redirects and guides her forward. They move like skaters on ice into the warm room with its comfort-food scent and bright noise.

The restaurant is as toasty as the night is chill. Qasim takes her coat and pulls out her chair. They drink lots of red wine and savor their deep-dish pepperoni. She notices he tips well, and he stands up when she goes to the Ladies' room.

On their second slice, Qasim gets a serious glint in his eye. It worries her, but he takes his time speaking. She squirms in her chair, not knowing how to keep the conversation going. Finally, he responds to her discomfort. *The man does notice things.*

"I must leave for a while," Qasim begins.

His face looks like he'd rather stay. "You mean you need to take me home?" she finally asks, knowing that's not what he means.

"I travel a great deal for work, Dianna. That will continue. If you continue to see me, you must learn to live with it. I will come and go, often with little notice. I hope you will continue with your friends while I am gone. I would like to continue to see you. I almost did not tell you, but that would be unfair. I want us to get to know one another better and better, yet I will be gone for extended periods."

Her eyes tear, but she holds them back. "How long?"

He takes her hand across the table. The lights flicker and dim, and loud music blares through the speakers. "Only three weeks."

"Where?"

"The Gulf. If I can get into Lebanon, I always try to stop there as well."

They have only just met; they are hardly lovers. So she stops her questions. *Never mind, never mind,* she prods her heart. *You'll have time later. What's the rush?*

"Will you send me a postcard?" she asks him instead.

"It is already done."

She half believes it is so. She imagines a prewritten card lying on his coffee table at home, waiting for him to pick it up and send to her. It's as though he is already on the airplane, he feels so far away.

CHAPTER FIVE

Absence

Dianna enters the museum with a cup of coffee and a bran muffin. Her breath comes ragged because she has run the entire distance. She never oversleeps, but the electricity was off today. Leah promised she'd pay it directly instead of mailing it. She probably will; Leah's curly hair needs electricity for a blowout. Dianna always pays the utilities, but the rate hike this month left her short. The end of the month always includes a hold-her-breath moment to see if she bounces a check or can afford a bill. The stock market supposedly rallied today, so maybe the economy is turning around. They've said that before. After taxes, she earns about $400 a week. Straight out of school, she knows she's lucky to have any job in this recession, and a job in New York City is some sort of miracle, no matter how bored it makes her. Thank God for Leah, whose parents send her a little extra to compensate for Dianna's little extra heading home each month.

She senses Peter Fox's eyes on her as she attempts a subtle glide into her seat. His gaze feels at once disapproving and invasive. She can't tell if he's attracted to her or not, but he certainly does not like her. Her coffee cup lid pops off, and a tiny pool of mocha-colored liquid forms on her desk. She'll have to go get something to wipe it up. Everyone else sits at their desks, clacking away at their typewriters, but she knows they've noticed she's late. Peter's the only one to cast his coy glance her way. "I see you," it seems to say. "I know the next promotion is mine, and mine alone." She hears her heart beating out the echo of a dumb blonde joke.

"How many blondes does it take to screw in a lightbulb?"

"Eleven."

"Why eleven?"

"One bleached blonde to do the work and ten real blondes to learn how it's done."

She shivers in indignation. It is difficult to live in a world that judges intelligence and sensuality on hair color. She wants to say something indignant to Mr. Fox, but the department's vice president, Mr. Grant, only allows conversation during the day's two breaks. Sophia has seen the shiver, though, in addition to the coffee spill, so she rescues her with a tissue dug from her bottomless desk drawer of necessary office items, in her usual maternal manner.

Dianna looks over her shoulder and nods a small glance of thanks. Then she looks down at her work and breakfast, now cold and soggy. She throws the muffin in the trash and pulls out typing paper and today's stack of little green cards. She's a cataloger, which requires a certain modicum of intellect, but also immense patience. The cards need the same description typed on them multiple times, and carbon paper has no effect on index cards.

"BRONZE AGE. (said to be from) Cyprus: Faience vase in form of a male head. Circa 1250 (?) – 1400 BC. Cat no. 19.14.73."

The first card always makes her mind work and breeds hope, yet the last card in any fifteen-card series leaves her exhausted. How she'd love to research this vase more, to find out who it is on the vase, the details of his story. They aren't even sure of the place and date it was crafted!

These days her boredom allows her mind to wander to Qasim. She wonders where he's traveling today. She knows he had multiple stops but forgot to ask where they were in his three-week voyage. He's probably forgotten all about the postcard; he's always so busy.

When she thinks of him, she sees desert and wind, but he told her he grew up by the Mediterranean. She needs to find out more about the Arab world, especially about Lebanon. It's been in the news due to conflict, not geography.

At last, her break begins. She fishes her muffin out of her otherwise empty trashcan and heads downstairs, outside, where no one can see that her appetite has gotten the best of her. She'll start by reading the paper, and if that yields little information, she'll head to the New York City Library. She sits on the front steps of the museum, trying to sit in the one beam of early spring sunlight to stay warm.

The breeze whips the paper about in her hands, and in the twenty minutes she has to read, the only information about Lebanon focuses on fighting in a southern city there. She'll need to find a map. She turns to national, then local, news. There's an op-ed about the fuel hike and a full-length article about Reagan's "protectionist" policies. Some West German leader has said Reagan will start an infinite spiral of international trade wars if he sets import quotas on Hondas and Toyotas. She rolls her eyes. She and most people her age adore Toyotas. She doubts Reagan can stop this economic tour de force, let alone topple the global economy, all by himself. It's much more likely that fuel will have an effect on the economy than Reagan. Her country needs to realize it must play its part in a much larger world.

She beats the rest of her coworkers back to her desk, and feeling sated and excited about learning more about the man who's opened up this new vista, she types away all afternoon, her pile of little green cards becoming two piles, then three. Sophia sends a green card with a gold star and a little note over her shoulder at 4:45 pm. "Great work, Dianna, goddess of the green card!" Dianna chuckles and covers her typewriter to head for home. Then she gives Sophia a good-bye hug of gratitude. What would she do without her in this dim, windowless basement she inhabits forty-plus hours a week?

The bus breaks down two blocks into its journey, sputtering malignant fumes as the driver cranks the engine, leaving her and other riders coughing. She decides to walk home. It will be faster than waiting for another bus. The leonine March wind bites around her wool skirt and through her stockings at her knees. The streets reek of urine and garbage in the one block she must pass through—a block that is going through gentrification, but still has many boarded, bedraggled buildings resembling crack houses. Walking faster makes the wind bite harder. She needs a car. At least that will give her some freedom. Maybe she could move to New Jersey, where it's cheaper.

The card drops through her mail slot a few minutes after she's entered her place. Leah's not home yet. It's dated the second week of his trip, but she's receiving it two afternoons before Qasim's scheduled return. She almost misses it because it's wedged between two pieces of junk mail. It shows a swimming pool with a cabana next to it. Palm trees instead of sand dot the terrain around the pool. She turns it over to see what he's written, reveling in the short sentences, the closely cropped script, the clipped verbiage bereft of prepositions:

Dear Dianna,
I arrived Riyadh last week. It is very warm here. I arrive Cairo tomorrow. Here I am really very busy. I will see you soon. Really.
Love, Qasim

She wonders what the small squeezed letters would look like if they were transformed into Arabic. She files this new information under "Handwriting" in a mental compartment devoted solely to this new man who is both lover and mystery. She has other filed items, gleaned from her dates with Qasim: he is wealthy, although she does not know how he acquired it. His expatriation seems not entirely of his choosing. He is a Muslim. He likes jazz. He likes her skirts to cover her knees. He does not like movies, but he loves literature. He is a gentleman of the old school, yet relaxed and casual, even in a three-piece suit. He's witty and loves to laugh. He discusses politics one night, only to be indifferent to it the next. He seems well versed in every subject she's brought up.

She wants to know more.

Dianna sticks the postcard within the pages of a picture book on the Middle East she picked up in a thrift store. Although the book contains vivid photos, she wonders about the accuracy of their representation: dhows on small aqua waves, alfalfa fields, minarets, prostrate men on prayer rugs, and women behind black hoods, which make her even more curious about what they look like. Are they beautiful? Wise? Full of joy or sadness? She searches their eyes for clues and finds none. They are, after all, only plain coverings, like scarves or shawls. Yet, she is a person who needs to see what lies behind the curtain. She wants to know more. To know more, she will have to travel there and meet them.

CHAPTER SIX

Rules of Conduct

They're traveling at a solid clip, Qasim's right hand on Dianna's knee, his left on the steering wheel, heading toward Wall Street to catch a ferry to Sandy Hook. Perhaps he also wants to make up for the afterthought of a gift he brought her, a souvenir from the airlines. She's hopeful, yet practical, trying not to fall in love hard, like she did the last time.

Qasim returned tanner and brighter, with a new Rolex on his wrist. He catches her skeptical expression, and his brow forms lines of concern. "You would rather not go to the sea today, Dianna?" he asks.

The skepticism recedes. She can't let her history or regret get in the way of what today brings. She's seen Sandy Hook from afar a few times and longed to go there. Plus, it's not quite warm enough to sit by the seaside, and she wonders why he'd want to go if not for her benefit.

"I was thinking perhaps it would be too chilly for you there. That's all." His warm hand covers her own completely.

"I miss the sea so, my dear," he says. "Especially when I return from the Middle East. I failed to dip one toe in the sea while I was there. All I saw was desert." His eyes redden. "I want to get back to my country."

She starts to speak, and if he were not driving with such speed, she would hug him. Instead, she scoots closer and lays her head on his shoulder. "I'm so sorry," she says.

"War is a difficult thing, but one must go on." He takes a deep breath as though to rid himself of any moodiness. "Better to be cold and by the sea than not by the sea at all."

The sun can't decide if it would rather be in front of or behind the clouds, and it's brisk for this time of year. Yet Qasim certainly is dressed for any weather. She mentally peels the layers that hide his wiry frame. She shivers when she remembers—his muscles, covered by a furry, masculine chest, covered by a white T-shirt, covered by a button-down, covered by a Ralph Lauren pullover, topped off with an artful tan tweed jacket. He would look like a professor, except that his tweed far outranks an academic's, with a finer weave and more refined design than any off-the-rack sport coat. It has a fine line of teal running through the browns and mustards. She's noticed he dresses like that—conservative yet with his own style. It's so subtle that people not looking for it would think he looked like every other academic in the city. Those willing to take a closer look would soon realize he's cut from different cloth, that he's his own man. Someone who needs to, rather than wants to, fit in.

She cups her other hand over his, and he smiles.

"Do you know your way?" she asks.

"Not really. We're on an adventure."

"What if we end up in Florida?" she teases.

"At least it would be warm."

"And we'd both lose our jobs."

"But we'd have toasty fingers and toes."

"There! The sign!" She waves him over to the ferry lot.

In actuality, she'd rather turn around and keep driving to Florida. She's never been to Florida. There, she'd have time to woo him, and he to court her, and he'd be hers. She wants to spend time with someone who appreciates, no loves, her. Does he love her?

She's never been on a ferry before. It's like entering a cave, full of dampness and oil, and gas fumes. Qasim has taken his hand from her knee, and his eyes dart about as they adjust to the dim lighting. She can hear the boat shift and settle each time a car enters across the gangplank. It's tight, and she wonders how they'll get the car out.

Once they climb a narrow steel staircase up, though, the vista above is as expansive as the car hold below is desolate. The ferry is already heading out over the choppy water, and she can see Battery Park and the bridges up close. Soon the New York City skyline looms in its majesty behind her, the imposing Twin Towers casting a deep shadow across the water.

"Let's go outside," she beckons Qasim, and he pulls on his leather gloves. The ferry is full of every sort of New Yorker, yet she cannot spot one dark-skinned person except for Qasim. Unusual, yet perhaps the Jersey coast is less integrated than the City.

It's one of those rare smog-free days, and she can see forever. She breathes deep, savoring the salt. She can almost see a lighthouse peering through the shiny sea air in the distance. It's all white, so the sunny background all but obscures it. She can barely make out its red-tipped beacon lamp.

"It's the oldest lighthouse in the States," she tells him. "The British occupied it, but George Washington turned it over to the state."

"Interesting," he murmurs. "You know a lot about New York history."

"I know a lot about lighthouses," she counters.

"Clever girl," he says, and she doesn't even mind if his tone is professorial.

They stand at the railing, pointing at the sights, gulping down the clean sea breeze, hands together to keep Qasim warm. Wind whips his thick hair around, and his face takes on a ruddy tone beneath its tan. He's never looked so handsome. They admire the ever-changing scenery, free hands gripping the railing as the ferry pitches to and fro.

His body stiffens, and hers follows. They're being watched by two men in down jackets.

"Pay no attention to them," Qasim whispers in her ear. "They're animals, heathens."

She can't help glancing back once. They do look like brutes, and they have foul expressions. *Are they Arab?* The tall one spits in the water. Qasim looks like he wants to spit in the water, but his manners won't allow it. His hand balls into a fist. "Animals," he hisses again under his breath. He takes her arm and guides her into the cabin area. "Do you mind too much?" he asks. "We're almost there."

She's actually relieved, even though all the white faces stare at them, too, more out of curiosity than animosity. The ship's horn blows, and it's time to go back and drive out of the ship's underbelly.

"Who were those men?" she asks when they're in the sunlight again. She's afraid he might know them.

"People we should not even deign to discuss," he answers.

She presses on. "So you know them?"

"I know of them, Dianna, sweet," he replies, his lips taut. "I believe you know them as well. People that want to make your decisions for you."

"What?" She frowns in confusion.

"I believe in this country you call them bigots, racists, supremacists? Do not think you have a premium on them because of your civil rights history. These people are everywhere. People with narrow minds. The secret lies in never letting them believe you think their opinions are just, or that you even acknowledge them."

She smiles in relief. She's been handling those kinds of prejudiced assumptions and misperceptions all her life.

She holds out her hand. "Come on, Qasim. Let's go climb the lighthouse!" When she looks back, the men are on the deck staring after them.

CHAPTER SEVEN

Introductions

"Hello? Mama?" Dianna holds the phone receiver between chin and shoulder. Her hands are busy stirring a pot of soup. "Can you hear me?" Dianna shrugs the receiver closer. "What?"

She can pick up the beginnings of annoyance in her mother's tone. "I said, I dreamed about you last night. It was so real. You were married, and you were pregnant. You were due in June. There was something wrong with the baby. Is it true?"

"No, it's not true."

"Are you sure?"

"Yes, Mama. I'm not pregnant. I'm not anywhere close to getting married."

"Well, I should hope you're not pregnant if you're not married. You're sure there's nothing wrong with the baby?"

"I'm not pregnant, Mama."

Dianna shifts the conversation into dangerous but necessary territory. "I'm dating a man named Qasim." Dianna blushes as she says the word *dating*. How she longs to confide in her mother like she did when she was a preschooler. About the boy who wrinkled her green sleeping mat. About the teacher who said her painting was perfect. About the girl who threatened her if she didn't trade shoes with her. Yet that sort of confidence ended long ago, before her mother's mind had become a muddle and before she hit Dianna. Confidences became a border between them instead of a bridge.

"Wait, let me sit down," her mother says. Dianna can imagine her mother swaying back and forth. If she doesn't sit down, she'll fall and break a bone.

"Did you sit down, Mama?"

"Yes, of course I did. Spell his name for me."

"Q-A-S-I-M. Qasim el-Kafry."

"I meant his last name."

"Mama! His name doesn't matter!"

"The hell it doesn't! Is he Turkish or something?"

"No. Lebanese. Like the Damuses."

"Oh. Is he handsome?"

"Yes, mostly."

"Dark?"

"Yes."

"From a good family?"

"Yes, Mama."

"Dianna?"

"Yes, Mama?"

"Why hasn't your father come to visit me?"

"He's dead, Mama."

"Oh." Her mother quiets, processing this new information, which has to be recounted anew in every conversation. "Dianna?"

"Yes, Mama?" Dianna can hear the nurses talking in the background. She starts to unload the apartment's archaic dishwasher and put the silverware in its accustomed space.

"You've never taken anybody to have an abortion, have you?"

"No, Mama."

"You know it's illegal."

It's no use to tell a woman whose mind is trapped in the 1950s that abortion has been legal for more than a decade. "Yes, Mama."

"I love you, Dianna."

"I love you, too, Mama. I hope you're okay. Bye."

CHAPTER EIGHT

Home Base

Dianna has worked for a week on the meal. She has straightened the house, even cleaned out drawers. The filet mignon sits marinating in her refrigerator, and her Gran's famous cheese potatoes simmer in the oven. A puddle of hummus is plated in a sea of black olives, and the smell of eggplant fills the kitchen. She spent the weekend shelling pecans, imported from her last trip south. A day's salary purchased the bottle of Chateau Haut Brion on the dining table alongside a complex flower arrangement of dahlias and gladiolas, Leah's contribution. For dessert, Dianna will serve homemade pecan pie, the kind her grandmother used to make. She's pleased with her east meets west menu.

Between the filet mignon, the wine, and a "new" used car, she's totally broke. She wants Qasim to approve. She gazes out at her new ten-year-old pockmarked Toyota Corolla, parked in a place of prominence. Owning a car makes her feel she can leave at a moment's notice, though she's never driven a car of her very own. Still, she realizes Qasim might be ashamed of it for her. The car has no front passenger seat, no heat, and no air conditioning. It leaks oil, and its hood flies up at speeds exceeding fifty miles per hour. She's gathering tools for her trunk, in case she breaks down. She paid $200 for this transportation, her entire savings, an extravagance in a city like Manhattan.

Initially, Leah balked at joining them for dinner, objecting to being the proverbial third wheel, but Dianna insisted. She wants them to meet. So here they are, drinking a glass of wine in anticipation, putting on the finishing touches.

"I can't believe I'm finally getting to meet him," Leah says with genuine glee.

Dianna is glad to see Leah has forgiven her for not getting her call the night she met Qasim. She has stopped sniffing and turning her head away every time Dianna mentions his name. It's nice to be sharing a drink and speaking without tension.

"I'm glad you two will get to know each other." Dianna picks up today's newspaper from the floor and stows it in the basket by the couch.

"Save the *Style* section," Leah requests. "Where is he from again?"

"Lebanon. Beirut."

"We should have a lot to talk about." Leah takes a last sip of wine, then pours herself a large glass of iced tea, and makes herself comfortable on the couch, one of the few pieces of furniture in this post-dorm room.

"Yes. It's been invaded repeatedly because it's a strategic trading location on the Mediterranean. It's been an ethnically and religiously diverse refuge for millennia."

"Boy, you've been doing your research." Leah takes a sip of tea and sets the glass down.

"Oh there's a lot more. Qasim says it has true seasons—that it's lush along the coast and arid near the mountains. You can swim and ski the same day. It has the most beautiful cedar trees in the world. I would love to go there someday." Dianna hands Leah her cosmetic bag. "Can you put that in your purse, please?"

"God, I can't imagine you in a war zone," Leah interjects and gets up to search for her purse.

"I want to stand under those trees someday, but I guess it's too violent right now," she says. "Every time there's new violence, Qasim seems so far away and sad. I want peace to come for him, and I want it to come so I can visit. It must be terrible not to be able to return to your native country."

"I suppose so." Leah draws a deep breath, finding her purse in the coat rack by the door and dropping the case inside. "Do you think he's really ever going back for good?"

"Oh, I haven't thought about that." Dianna blushes. "We're taking things slow, enjoying each other's company."

"Seems he has it pretty good right here anyway," Leah says. "He's lucky he got to leave. What did you say his surname is? Spell it for me?" The buzzer zings, and she goes down the steps to the street to meet him.

He is almost on time tonight. His hug lifts her from the ground, causing one of Dianna's shoes to fall off. She doesn't care.

"Spell your last name for me," she says. "I want to get it right to introduce you to Leah. She's a stickler for these sorts of things. It doesn't sound like it's spelt."

He laughs and spells at the same time, "Yes it does! E-L-K-A-F-R-Y."

"No, it doesn't sound the same when you say it as when I do," she says, squeezing him. "Let's go up. How was your trip? I got your postcard."

"It went well. Quite well."

She hesitates at the door and grasps his hand. "What happened?" The question bears both her desire to start small talk before introductions are made and genuine concern.

He tips his head to the left, raises one eyebrow, and purses his lips, then shrugs. "The usual."

She's wearing her cords and clogs, and Qasim, for the first time, is in jeans and a yellow cotton pullover with some sort of emblem on the chest, not one she's seen, and designer loafers. It's nice to be low-key with him.

"Look at my new purchase!" Dianna points to her dilapidated but proud car, wedged into a nearby space, its bumper nudging the Oldsmobile parked in front of it. She tells him how she maneuvered for ten minutes to get it properly parked. She laughs at her rusty driving.

He looks past it, his eyes landing on a new dark BMW.

"No! There!" She points again, and this time he spots it.

"That's not a car," he laughs. "That's a roller derby special. Sure you didn't go all the way to Beirut to buy it?"

She laughs with him. It *is* after all a quirky little car, and she can imagine it sitting on a corner near a bombed out, smoking building. *Trusty little war machine.*

They turn and walk up the steps in the cool evening air, full of the smell of boxwoods and hyacinths. She buzzes into the building and holds the door for him, but he twists, almost stepping on her toes, and reaches round to hold it for her.

"There's no need to do that every time," she says.

"I am incapable of doing it any other way, my dear." He grins. "I know you young American women want to do everything for yourselves, but you will not take the politesse out of me. It is…"

"Ingrained," she finishes, and laughs.

"Something smells wonderful," he says as they enter her apartment.

"I'm glad you came."

"I said I would hold you to it."

Leah stands at the brown corduroy sofa. The few pieces of furniture in the living area are hers: the couch, a couple of plastic end tables, a standing lamp, a weathered coffee table, and an oblong dining table with chairs. Dianna contributed the framed Met posters on the walls.

A year ago, Dianna drove a U-Haul to the city from her parents' old home, glad to have a sold sign in their yard. She'd taken what was left that she called her own. The truck was laden with her girlhood bed and dresser, Gran's old porch rocker, and a stereo, all installed in her bedroom. If she'd had to furnish the entire apartment, they'd still be sitting on the floor.

Dianna introduces Qasim and Leah, and she catches the approval on her roommate's face.

"Dianna tells me you work for the mayor," Qasim says once they are seated.

"Yes. I do." Leah has on her political, go-get-'em face.

"Quite challenging work, that."

"He keeps us busy. I enjoy it." Leah's face opens and turns pink.

"Keeping up with his media exposure is challenge enough, I expect."

"He has his own personal media consultant."

Qasim raises an eyebrow. "And you?"

"I handle the constituents, the community."

"A challenge, as I suspected."

Leah's eyes widen, and her face remains rosy. "That's kind of you."

"Just being truthful—the truth as I know it."

"Shall we?" Dianna motions Qasim to the head of the table. Leah moves her bouquet closer to Qasim, who takes a deep breath of its fragrance. "Did you pick these yourself?" he asks, and Leah glows.

The dinner goes well. Qasim eats everything. This is one of the few full meals Dianna has shared with him. When they dine alone, he usually declines and watches her eat, a pattern Dianna deplores. She has enough trouble eating in front of someone without his staring at every forkful of her food. His hearty appetite relaxes her, translating as acceptance of her own.

The three of them linger at the table, the candles burning low. Dianna serves dessert and Turkish coffee, found after a thorough search of the city markets.

Leah shows no signs of retiring to bed. "Come on, Qasim," Dianna says finally, and pulls him from the table. "Let me show you my jazz record collection." This is a first, but a necessary first. She is glad for the wine; it blunts her discomfort at asking him to bed in front of Leah.

They troop upstairs: one, two, three, four, five steps into the small, beloved space. She crosses around her white four-poster bed, too young for her, but all she has of her past. She reaches into a cardboard box and pulls out a Billie Holliday album, one of her favorites, puts it on the turntable, gently placing the needle down on a track. "All of Me" fills the small room.

He moves beside her and nuzzles her neck. She notices he's wearing American-manufactured briefs instead of his usual unisex boxers right before she dims the lamp. Then his kiss and the feel of his body against hers take all her attention.

CHAPTER NINE

Light

Dianna cuts the edges of the newspaper picture with care. Snip, snip, go the long scissors' blades. Her nose is close to the blades to ensure she has complete control of this project. When she finishes, she holds the picture up to the flat overhead light. Sweat has broken out on her temples, and her hands are stiff and moist. She turns around, asking wordlessly for Sophia's opinion. Sophia's stare penetrates the pixel dots of the front-page photo, then moves to meet Dianna's gaze. "A handsome couple," she admits.

It is early morning—long before their co-workers shuffle in with Styrofoam cups full of frothing cappuccino. Dianna spent the night at Sophia's. They had tickets to the play "Beyond Therapy." The play seemed interminable, too much like the people Dianna already knows: full of angst, humorous angst, but angst nonetheless. Leah. Heather. Even Sophia. Especially Dianna.

Yet Dianna welcomed the chance to drop by Sophia's apartment for time away from Leah. Sophia's on flex time, coming in and leaving early to beat the rush to spend more time with her teen-aged daughter. Spending the night means coming to work with the sunrise. It's not all bad. The office is peaceful, and the museum reminds her of a book she read long ago about two children who run away from home on a whim and end up at the Met. It's like a huge, hollow house with lots of empty rooms but no people.

After showing it off, Dianna slips the photo into a blotter in her desk's long middle drawer, which already holds the complimentary airplane slippers Qasim gave her and the postcards he sent. The postcards all have some exotic-looking sky on them, superimposed on a homogeneous high-rise hotel, usually with a swimming pool surrounded by palms. Even the London postcard has a swimming pool with a palm tree in the middle.

"Anything else?"

Sophia reaches her hand out, asking for a second glance at the newspaper clip, which shows a seated King of Jordan and his American-born wife, Queen Noor. "Yes, Dianna Apassionata, she looks like you."

"Qasim is no king. He's a diplomat."

"Could you live that kind of life?" Sophia asks, starting to type again, her brow raised ever so slightly.

"I've never thought about living there." Still, Dianna's mind drifts, wondering what it would be like, starting over, an ocean away from her family. New people, new territory. What could she do there? She could imagine herself a diplomat's wife about as much as she'd imagined herself a princess when she played dress-up in her mother's shoes. A fantasy. A Muslim diplomat's wife?

"Sophia, from what I've read, I only have to say I believe in God and that Mohammed is His Prophet to convert to Islam. Islam is derived from the Arabic word for 'peace.' I love that! I've read about their beliefs, and they're not that different from my Christian beliefs. In fact, they reject the belief that God's word and God's works are in conflict; they believe that there's no disconnection between science and religion. I like that notion. It's just the radicals that frighten me. They seem to take things out of context like radical Christians, but then they still fight wars over it. That's not peace."

Sophia smiles. "Seems to me we recently finished a war that tried to wipe out a whole race and culture because of religion. World War II. Hitler."

"I'm sorry," Dianna says. "I tend to forget that religion was a huge part of that World War. Do you think I could live in Lebanon?"

"You're getting ahead of yourself. You'll have to wait and see if your mind and heart agree." Sophia pats Dianna on the shoulder and goes to the filing drawers. She moves like a dancer; she could be part of an Impressionist painting. Dianna wishes she could imitate her movements and her wise self-reflection.

Could Dianna really do it? For life, until death? Change her religion and her country? Leave all family and friends behind? All of her doubts rush in like seawater, submerging the closeness that creeps around the edges of her relationship with Qasim. She takes a long, deep breath. She thinks not. A move overseas does not daunt her; it excites her. The permanence of marriage confounds her. What happened to Cinderella and Snow White after the glass slipper and the waking kiss? Everyone gets swept up in the romance of fairy tales, never asking about the princesses' ten-year anniversaries. Qasim seems to be two people, and she cannot commit to him until she sees him in his own country. She cannot see his country without some form of commitment. A paradox.

"Sophia's right. I'm getting ahead of myself," she whispers to herself, and turns to her typewriter.

CHAPTER TEN

Rumblings from a Distance

Dianna walks with her acquired New York gait toward the UN's newest rental building and Qasim's relocated office. Her steps have a spring in them as she marches toward his new quarters—with a door to a private office all his own. She's meeting his friend and colleague Jamal today.

The building is another skyscraper ablaze with windows. Last week when Qasim told her of his recent promotion, he smiled and looked down at his desk blotter in a rare moment of humility. He explained his new job description, but her mind switched off. She can tell it's a big assignment.

Truthfully, Dianna can't understand why there needs to be so many titles in so many divisions filling up so many shiny windows to perform one simple task: to help people get ahead in life so peace can prevail. Yet Qasim's usual contagious animation causes his hope for peace to infiltrate her and become her own. She is happy that he is happy. She cares deeply for what he is trying to do. Dianna believes any organization that holds a person like Qasim must be worthy, and so she closets her cynicism.

Dianna wears a gray calf-length skirt, navy blazer, and a red bow tie beneath the collar of a light blue button-down shirt. The skirt is neither new nor expensive, but its pearl-coated triangular buttons run down all the way to its hem. She replaced the original ones with buttons from an old blouse. Although the blazer is from a consignment shop, she's sure she looks "put together," even chic enough to step into these lush, new offices.

"Let's go." Qasim stands up as soon as she enters his office. "Jamal will be waiting for us."

"He will meet us there?" Dianna asks. She is surprised Jamal left work and Qasim is still there.

"Of course." Qasim walks out his office door and looks back with impatience. "You coming?"

"Yes." Dianna grabs her purse and rushes to catch up with his stride. Jamal is the first person she will meet whom Qasim considers a friend. Both

Lebanese, they began working at the UN at the same time. They have mutual friends in Beirut. Dianna is further encouraged—Jamal's wife is Christian.

"Why is Jamal's wife not coming?" she asks when Qasim punches the elevator's lobby button.

"I am sure I do not know," Qasim says, his expression piqued. "She may be with her parents, or perhaps back in Lebanon."

"Oh," Dianna says. "She's Lebanese."

"Yes. What did you think?" Qasim asks and then hums out of tune.

It is a sultry evening, with stale air wafting in from the river. The buildings obscure the clouds that surely must hem the sky above. "It is probably going to storm," Qasim says. "Perhaps I should go back up and get my umbrella."

"No!" she says. "I mean, we're late, aren't we? I want to meet your friend."

He squeezes her to him. "Okay, we will take the chance." He squeezes her closer and really looks at her. "You look melancholy."

"It's my father's birthday."

Qasim squeezes her even tighter. "Yes," he murmurs. "I do understand."

She basks in his understanding but does not reply. She hasn't thought of her dad all day. Seeing Qasim brought back childhood memories, some good, some not. She is very close to tears, and she can't speak without her eyes overflowing. She doesn't want to ruin their dinner.

His arm still around her waist, they head to a popular New York City chophouse. She wonders why they haven't ever been to a Middle Eastern restaurant and ventures the question.

He takes his arm away slowly and brings it up to push her hair from her face. "Because, my dear, I make better Middle Eastern food than any restaurant around here."

"Oh, is that true?" She laughs. "In that case, we have to find some time, so you can show off your skills."

"I am afraid it will not be soon, Dianna. I travel again in two weeks." The restaurant looms in front of them, and the conversation is over.

Jamal's hair is gray and receding, and his suit a little wrinkled. His smile is warm, though, and he shakes her hand with a firm grip, telling her that Qasim has spoken of her. He doesn't say what he's heard.

The maître d' leads the three to their table, surprisingly still available. "How are you this evening, Mr. El-Kafry?" he asks, and Dianna realizes Qasim's suggestion that she book reservations at this restaurant was based on other meals here. The men order cocktails, and Dianna orders a white wine spritzer. Her hand shakes as she brings the drink up in a toast. This meal is more than food; it is a trial—a trial she will pass despite her nerves. She is a progeny of the South, a baby who was fed breeding in a bottle, a child who learned dinner manners and conversations before she knew how to ride a bicycle. She is careful to order the appropriate appetizer and entrée—tasteful but not too expensive. There is only one thing that may betray her, and that is her growling stomach. She is starving; it is closing in on nine o'clock.

"How long do you think Assad will tolerate Arafat's presence in Beirut?" Jamal is asking.

Her back prickles with interest. Some newspapers are saying the civil war of the 1970s hasn't ended; others say that a new war has begun. Israel's Sharon and Syria's Assad seem on the brink of joining the internal strife. Israel has bombarded a refugee camp this week. Twice Qasim has aborted trips to handle family business. A citizen and UN representative, he still has been unable to enter his own country.

"Assad and Arafat loathe each other." Qasim sniffs. "They are like caviar and beans. I cannot imagine Assad will be silent about his remaining there. He was the one, after all, who detained him in 1966. But Assad cannot intervene with Lebanon unless invited."

"So you think Gemayel is asking for more than that?"

"Bachir is smarter than that. He remembers his history. His Maronite pride will not allow a Jewish or a Muslim neighbor to come in and run his show."

Jamal shakes his head slowly, side to side. He strokes one eyebrow. "I am not sure I agree with you. I wish I could."

"It would be political suicide for Gemayel to ask Assad to come to his aid."

Dianna wonders how any leader in Lebanon can escape political suicide, being wedged between Syria, Jordan, and Israel, with maritime access.

"Yes, it would. Yet it's been done before. The Gemayels are risk-takers. They are known to be a bit ruthless and reckless in their judgment. That's what got them into office."

Qasim scowls but defers to the older man. It is the first time Dianna has seen him defer to anyone, and she can tell he has argument left.

She's impressed he knows the Gemayels. She's seen the handsome Bachir Gemayel in American newspapers. She knows he's a decorated military leader and that his family is Lebanese political elite. "Isn't Assad a Muslim?" she asks, hesitation already gripping her throat.

"Yes, Dianna." Qasim touches her hand briefly, motioning her question aside.

"Wouldn't he come to the aid of another Muslim?" she persists.

Qasim looks as though she has burned him. "One Muslim does not another Muslim make, my dear."

She frowns but continues. "So Assad is not a Shiite?"

Qasim drums his fingers on the table, starts to speak again, and then hesitates. "We shall speak of this matter later," he tells her.

"So you aren't a Shiite?"

Thunder crosses Qasim's forehead, and she can tell he is counting to ten. "No, I am Sunni... Sunni, understand?"

Jamal keeps himself busy arranging his napkin. A slight smirk plays at the corners of his lips.

She pushes her spine against the back of her seat. The food has come at precisely the right moment. Everyone picks up their drinks to cleanse their palates and their minds of her faux pas. She has flunked Southern Breeding 101. She chose the wrong question at absolutely the wrong moment. She vows not to mention religion and politics in the same breath again.

CHAPTER ELEVEN

Night Goggles

"Qasim!" she screams.

Dianna wakes. Her heart races underneath her right ear lobe. *Just a nightmare,* she tells herself. Darkness invades the room. She doubts she can return to slumber. She looks over to the digital light of her clock radio: four a.m.

She dreamt of a strange, frightening place—a place at once filled with smoky sand and sunlight and the dread that daylight cannot erase. She closes her eyes, trying to recapture the details. There, there he is.

The dream boy trudges behind a glowering man who is tall, dark, with a dreary melancholy on his brow, creased in a perpetual frown. He is thirsty and oh-so-sick to his stomach. He wants to run, but he is too weak.

Whack, his captor's heavy vine leaves an immediate welt on the boy's back. "Get up, boy! There's work to be done!"

The boy groans but does as he is told. They arrive at a stable. The man throws him a brush and gestures toward the stalls. The boy begins brushing a roan. This beast is huge, the stench incredible. The horse's eyes remind him of his captor's. He feels blackness engulf him and searches for something to hold onto. He catches sight of the man's eyes.

Dianna switches on the overhead light and prepares for her shower. *Why did she scream Qasim's name?*

The pall of the dream follows Dianna as she dismounts from the bus and enters the Met's employee entrance. Smiling mechanically at the security guards, she mulls over the dream like she would an archaeological puzzle: Does the dream reflect her deflected desire to go to the Middle East? Does it mirror her unsettling relationship with Qasim? Does it point to her overall despondency at feeling trapped in a job she doesn't like and a family she doesn't fit into?

The phone rings at her desk, bringing an abrupt ending to her thoughts.

"Hi, it's Leah. I'm back from Ramallah. This trip was better than the last one."

"It seems you left so recently."

"Doesn't seem that way to me."

"So it was exciting?"

"Guess you could call it that. It was no joy ride."

Dianna bites her lip. She despises her friend's lack of appreciation for her good fortune. Only twenty-something and on her way. Who would have thought working for a mayor would lead to this kind of international travel?

"I'm going straight to the office," Leah continues. "Want to meet for a drink tonight? I'll fill you in on the details."

Dianna is uncertain she's up to being around Leah tonight. The dream makes her realize she needs a heart-to-heart with Qasim. "I'm not sure," she responds. "I'll need to check in with Qasim. He was in Washington for a few days, but I think he's back."

"Oh, good God, girl! You're still waiting around for him?"

"Not exactly. I've been going out. I just haven't found a more appealing alternative."

"We'll have to change that tonight."

Dianna bites her lip again. Leah is usually the one who ends up captivating any audience, especially an audience swilling beer. Her slim figure and confident demeanor arrest most men's, and some women's, attention. "I'm not sure I want to," she murmurs.

"Well, call him then, you big lug," Leah says, then takes a sip of something. Dianna can hear her swallow before she says, "He probably has religious commitments. When is Ramadan over, anyway?"

"I have no idea," Dianna replies. She hasn't thought to ask Qasim.

"Well, he won't be able to come if it's near the big feast day."

"No, I suppose not." She depresses the button to end the call, feeling uncomfortable, wondering if she'd be interrupting some sort of religious meal, like her own Christmas Eve dinner. She waits a half-hour to ring Leah back.

"He's not back." She grimaces at her fib. How can she let Leah know she's uncomfortable calling her boyfriend? *Boyfriend*, now there was an American assessment of her situation.

"Great!" Leah's enthusiasm ripples and is infectious. "Around eight?"

"I'll see you then!" Dianna puts the phone down for good this time and turns to her typewriter. She rolls a little orange card into the carriage and begins to type. She is cataloging, or so her bosses have told her, some very important artifacts. She remains unimpressed with the necessity to catalog any antiquity more than twice. Although she sometimes retypes the same article description twenty times, she's forced to pay attention. She may need to edit the description, depending on the file for which it is destined. After card fifteen, she switches subjects. On card seventeen, she finds herself thinking of other words to replace "small earthenware jug, most likely from the tenth century B.C.E."

Trance-like, her fingers type away:

I sit at a desk in a room full of desks,
Counting invisible grains of sand.
I wish I were myself enough
Not to need to think of you,
Not to think of time and space
Between us.

She hears footsteps and jerks the card out of the typewriter roll. She already envisions the glare of her supervisor over her left shoulder. She rips the card into tiny pieces and puts it into an envelope to discard at home. Then she places card eighteen into the typewriter carriage and pecks away: "small earthenware jug. . ."

***

The wind blows some dry, brown leaves past her on the sidewalk as she reaches the bar in the Village. She missed tonight's last bus and had to walk. She sees Leah chatting up the bartender. She motions Dianna over. She looks happy enough to see her despite her avid conversation, so Dianna slips onto the bar stool next to her and gives her a quick hug of welcome.

"It's good to see you again."

"You, too! Glad good ole Qasim is still out of your hair."

Dianna feels her pale skin turn pink. "He's not in my hair."

Leah flips her long locks behind her and laughs. "Enough about him anyway. We have the bar to conquer."

"I don't want to conquer anything. I want to hear about your trip."

"I'm not sure you'll want to hear after I fill you in on the details."

"Yes, I will."

"You want to see my pictures?" Leah pulls out a manila envelope. "I've never seen anything like it before, but I guess I will again. Ever see a dead body?"

Dianna opens the flap with her heart in her throat. The only dead bodies she's ever seen have been those of embalmed relatives. She wonders if bullet wounds and bomb shrapnel leave their victims' faces distorted, or worse, their bodies torn apart. She is relieved to see several young men and one child, all with their eyes open and their bodies contorted, yet with very little blood and no organs visible. "It's very sad," she murmurs.

She sees a flicker of water around Leah's eye rims. "As soon as I get a way, I'm going back there to help those people," Leah says. "We'd be doing something if their skin was whiter."

Dianna remains silent. She's not sure this is true, but she is in no position to argue. She is dating an Arab, and she didn't even know it was Ramadan. Instead, she takes in a deep breath of smoke and beer and says, "I wish there were a position for me there, too."

Leah exhales, reminding Dianna of the horse from her dream. Her eyes narrow then widen. "Oh, yeah, art history majors are everywhere, rolling bandages, Di. You should have had a different major if you wanted to be in relief."

"You know my scholarship was for political science," Dianna objects, but Leah is off on another tangent.

"We're dating the wrong men; that's what! We should switch. I should be the one with Qasim, and I should introduce you to my artist friend."

Dianna's gasp is audible, and the man sitting beside her turns his head to investigate. Leah continues unabated. "I need somebody to get me back there. Those people need help. I'll get there by hook or by crook, but the sooner the better. Think Qasim would pull a few strings?"

"No," Dianna says, and turns to the bartender to order.

CHAPTER TWELVE

Obsession

The waiting this time is almost too difficult. She's heard waiting may be the most important part of any negotiation. She holds off calling him again and decides to focus her attention on something more constructive. She decides to lose weight.

Weight loss is not a new initiative for her. How many times has she tried, succeeded, failed, and tried again? Weight—the gaining, the losing, the maintenance, the hunger—it has begun to frighten her.

Oh, how she wants to control her weight. She wants to wear a sleeveless garment without shame. How she wants to dance without self-consciousness. She wants to sit without adjusting her suit coat. How she wants to be held without holding her breath and pulling her abs in. Yet she does not seem to be able to muster up enough discipline to control her most personal, most intimate possession. Her body expands, contracts, expands again, seemingly of its own accord.

It doesn't help that most people are always offering her food. How can she eat carrot sticks when people are piling her plate high with pizza and cake? Qasim seems the only one who doesn't. Indeed, he almost withholds it. He seldom eats. They sit in restaurants and drink, and her stomach calls out for dinner.

So she looks forward to a long weekend alone without temptation. Leah's away on a another business trip, and she has the apartment—and the refrigerator—to herself. On Dianna's first night alone, she eats only green salad with vinegar. She skips breakfast the next morning. For Saturday lunch, she cuts an apple into tiny pieces and takes an hour to finish it. Saturday night is an extravaganza: a fish filet and an unadorned, baked potato. On Sunday evening, she is frying a plain omelet using water in lieu of oil, when Leah returns bearing Chinese take-out –for two.

Dianna wants to run upstairs, but her feet remain rooted in front of the stove. "Omelet?" she offers in a quiet, steady voice.

"You don't want Chinese food?" Leah asks, as she pulls food laden with the smell of soy out of two paper bags. "Come on. It's good for you."

"No, thank you," Dianna declines, putting on her best Southern smile. She has seen her mother perfect this smile to an art form, yet it always eludes her.

"I bought it for you. I can't eat all this food."

"Neither can I, Leah."

"Please. Please. I'm feeling down. Charlie hasn't called me all week. Come on, Dianna. You don't have to worry about weight. You look fine."

Dianna wavers for an instant. She turns her head one way, then another, and that is enough for Leah. She gets out tableware and spoons chicken delicious onto a plate by Dianna's right hand. Dianna picks up the fork and eats, and eats, and eats. It seems she will never stop eating. Leah smiles, and Dianna eats more. She eats all the fortune cookies and takes a bottle of beer out of the refrigerator to cap off the experience. Then she says she is tired, that she is going upstairs to read. She sits cross-legged on her white, little-girl bed, her head cupped in her hands.

She quietly cries for thirty straight minutes, timing herself and cutting herself off at precisely eight thirty p.m. She doesn't want anyone at work the next day to suspect she has been upset. She washes her face and half-heartedly brushes the soy taste from her teeth. She looks around the bathroom like she's searching for something that's missing. She doesn't dare look in the mirror. Then she climbs into her nightshirt, goes to her bedroom, and climbs under the smooth cotton of old sheets. She lies there in quiet victory. She wanted to get rid of the food, but she didn't! Her mouth tastes only of spearmint. Her stomach isn't churning any longer.

She looks over at the clock. It's only nine thirty.

Dianna's finger trembles as her nail glides down the long list of Arabic names in the phone book: *El-Debes, El-Haddad, El-Khawas, El-Mesry*. She's skipped over it and has to doubleback. There it is: *El-Kafry*.

She tosses back and forth until her sheets surround her like a shroud. She pulls the hall phone into her bedroom and calls Qasim. Miraculously, he picks up his phone.

"Hello, Qasim."

"Hi, sweetie. What's new? Tell me."

She imagines him there at his elegant table, eating whatever he chooses. "What are you eating?"

"How did you know I was eating?"

"An educated guess." She climbs back onto her bed and twists the edge of her sheet in her hand. The butterfly design becomes gnarled and pressed, as though she is trying to press the free blue butterfly back into its sticky cocoon.

"I picked up some couscous on the way home. Want to come over and have some?" She hears the click of utensils.

"It's too late. It's Sunday. We've both got work tomorrow."

"Dianna. Always the responsible one," he teases. She wonders if he has been drinking. He sounds a little too happy. "So, what are you eating?" he asks. She can hear his teeth click together. Heat permeates her blood vessels, a response to holding in her anger. "I already ate. Leah made me eat Chinese food."

"I thought you liked Chinese food. That's what we ate the night we met."

"I didn't want it tonight." *I want to save that food to eat with you*, she wants to add, but she hesitates, and her chance is lost.

"Why?" She hears the suppressed laughter in his voice. "Did she destroy your three-course dinner by bringing home Chinese?"

"No. I wanted an omelet. It's still half-cooked on the stove, as a matter of fact."

"Ah, yes. An omelet reduces Chinese take-out to food for the masses."

"You're mocking me."

"No, sweetie. I would never, never mock you." He is laughing openly, a big broad laugh that usually makes her laugh along with him.

"You are," she says, her voice breaking between the words.

"Tell her you want your own food, Dianna. Don't eat something you don't want to eat."

Her anger swells up like oil under pressure. She trembles, trying to tamp the pressure down. She changes the subject. "I went to that movie with a friend," she tells him. She doesn't want to give him the satisfaction of knowing it was Heather. "We enjoyed it."

"Good!" he says. The vigor in his voice annoys her. "I want you to have fun! You're young and single, and you should have fun. What was it again?"

She doesn't tell him. "Don't patronize me, Qasim. I may be young, but I can handle my life."

He takes in a breath. "Come now, Dianna, sweetie, I'm teasing. I've had a good day, and I want to share my good humor with you."

The pressure rises in her veins again, and she clenches and unclenches her jaw.

"Dianna? It needn't be so stressful, this phone call. Take a deep breath." His voice caresses her, but the anger has gone on a moment too long for her to retreat.

"I don't need a breath to know you're patronizing me," she says and takes in a deep breath all the same.

When he speaks, his words are clipped. "Whatever you want, Dianna. Why did you call?" She hears remnants of laughter when he says her name. She suspects there is still a chance to salvage this conversation, but she is not certain she wants to.

"I don't know. Believe me, I don't know. Have a good week."

"You, too."

Click.

CHAPTER THIRTEEN

Confessions

As she waits for Qasim outside the museum, she ruminates about the unfinished work that lies on her desk. She's made too many secret forays to the Metropolitan's library and taken time off for job interviews of late. Each day sitting in front of a typewriter with no correction button, preparing the museum for computerization, is becoming more mundane. She longs for adventure.

A bright crescent moon seeps back into the skyline. The passing traffic on Eighty-Fourth and Fifth stirs up the wind, and she stuffs her hands in her blazer pockets, peeved at herself. Her prospects are presently dim. She interviewed at the National Organization of Women in Washington, where she was told she is overqualified. The American Petroleum Institute offered her a job, but Dianna declined. She cannot imagine working for any organization that deals with oil, even one with an alluring salary. An application for a position at NYU resulted in a photocopied rejection slip. Dianna wants to travel, but she knows of no occupation that would pay off the loans she took out for her family—and get her out of the country, too.

Lost in herself, she doesn't notice Qasim's car pull up. Coming out of her reverie, she sees Qasim waving frantically to her, and she runs to get in the idling car. Horns sound behind them.

"I wanted to beep my horn, too," he says, "but I didn't want to startle you."

She laughs, amused. She gives him a kiss. "Hello, Qasim. Why would you be afraid to beep in a place like New York?"

"It's that – that it's rather uncouth, don't you think?" He fidgets, then fiddles with the radio, turns it on, then off. "Beirut is full of beeping horns these days, not to mention the rare explosion. You can no longer hear the sea."

Dianna beams at him. *He is such a gentleman.* "Let's go."

He smiles and touches her knee. "Want to go eat?"

"Will you eat with me?"

"No, I am coming from a party for the Egyptian ambassador."

"Then let's go have a drink at your house."

They glide through the city streets and slip through the Lincoln Tunnel, bereft of rush hour traffic. It swallows the car like a cement cocoon. They leave the lights of the city on the other side. It is already eight thirty—a typical late night for this, dare she say, couple? They have, after all, weathered their first major disagreement.

"You know, I wouldn't have minded going to that party," Dianna ventures.

Qasim stops at the light and gives her a stern look. "You? You wouldn't have enjoyed it at all. Those parties are deadly boring."

Dianna bites her lower lip. "It's just that I want to know more about you, and what you do is who you are. I want you to know about me."

"What do you want to know, Dianna?" he asks. "I am an open book."

Qasim takes his hand from her knee to hit the automatic garage door opener as they approach his house. He parks his car in one smooth movement. He reaches over her to open her door. They walk hand-in-hand as he fishes for his key; he mumbles Arabic words she likes to think are curses. He finds his key, turns the lock, and they stand in a place she has come to feel as refuge. He takes her jacket off and hangs it in the foyer closet. She sits on the living room couch at first and then decides to head downstairs to his den. She wants a chance to look through his bookcases, but he soon follows her with two drinks.

"So tell me about your day," she demands.

He brings her little finger to his mouth. "No, you."

"I'm looking for a new job. I've done administrative work for a couple of years now. I want to help the world, not type."

"But the Met—"

"I know, Qasim, the Met. Everyone envies me, except other people typing little green cards alongside me day in and day out."

"You're young, Dianna. Give it time."

"The best time is now, Qasim. I am young. I can travel. I have lots of energy and ambition to help others. Typing helps the historians, not the history makers."

He smiles with approval.

"What about your day?" she asks.

"Another busy day. My boss asked me to head another task force."

"Congratulations!"

"Yes. I am young to be getting this kind of attention."

Dianna beams at him and kisses him on the cheek. He pulls her close and strokes her hair.

"I like being with you, Dianna," he says. "It has been a long time, really, since I have had a good time like this. I like you, Dianna Calloway. I like you."

"I want to know you. I want to know all about you, Qasim." Her breath catches in her throat. Her trust hangs, ambivalent as a half-dry sheet hanging on only one clothes pin. She waits for rejection.

He does pull away. He looks down and touches his fingertips together, reminiscent of the game she played as a little girl of opening the church doors and seeing all the people. She smiles. The image is a Christian one, and it is difficult at this moment to see him as anything other than a kindred spirit.

His voice jars her when he speaks; the silence has gone on for so long. His words spill out like water from an urn, and she drinks them up like a person too long in the desert. "I was born during your last World War," he begins. "Lebanon was as complex a place then as it is today. I was born in Cairo, but my mother wanted to move near the sea. She was Lebanese, and she missed the lap of the waves, the snow on the mountains, the cedars. Lebanon has the most beautiful cedar trees in all the world. You will see them one day. My mother also wanted to get away from the violence." He stops to chuckle.

"Why is that funny?" Dianna asks. She hasn't missed his comment about her seeing Lebanon.

"Dianna, my dear, conflict is part of this world. It is never far away. You cannot escape it." His smile is tight, and he pats her hand. "That is why you must wait for the right time to see it, once it is again at peace."

"It sounds idyllic without the war," she says.

He takes a sip of his drink. "Beirut is a port city with an aquamarine coastline and nearly unceasing sunlight. In summer, the light bounces off things, like a ball. It bounces off the tops of minarets and the mosaics beneath them every morning at the call to prayer. It bounces off high-rises and hotels, churches and banks. The only places it cannot reach are the alleyways of the souqs. I spent many a day there as a boy, trying to keep cool. I also remember lying at the top of one cliff and watching the dhows bring in their catch and the cargo ships unload. I come from a family of traders, and I always long for the sea. I have not seen Beirut in a couple of years, but I dream of it when I sleep. I want to go back, always."

"It must be difficult to be so far away from home, not being able to get back," she murmurs. She does not reach out for him, afraid any interruption will end his story.

"It is the most beautiful place on earth—beautiful, so different from Europe, so different from here. I was the youngest in a family of boys. I had an older sister. We lost her at a young age, when I was five." His eyes mist. "Infection. My parents were good to me. I went to mosque and prayed, but I went to a Quaker school during the week. I was quick; I received good marks. I met a girl there; I cared for her. I believe she cared for me. She was French. My parents did not approve. I never even thought of going against their wishes. I was a good student, a scholar even, and so they soon arranged for me to go away to boarding school." His eyes redden again.

"And the girl?"

"I have no idea what became of her. I never saw her again. Civil war was already brewing. Many foreign nationals were pulling out. Your Marines landed in Beirut in 1958, the year before I began university. Things got better for a while, not for long."

Dianna can feel the tears forming behind her eyes, but she is determined not to let them drop. She learned long ago that tears spell doom in a relationship. His parents had forced him to leave their love to prevent his love. "You were both so young," she says, not believing the words herself. She knows all too well that age has nothing to do with intensity of feeling.

"Yes, yes," he nods, then smacks his palm flat against the coffee table top, jarring the glass decorations there. She pulls back, startled by this physical motion of violent air and noise that comes between them.

Dianna doesn't know what to say, so they sit in silence. His voice startles her again, this time with a question. "Would you tell me about yourself? I don't know much more about you than you know about me. Do you have family here? Do you have an ex who's going to beat me up?" He laughs, to make sure she knows that he is joking. "Tell me. Tell me." He reaches over, and his fingers tighten around hers.

She moves her shoulders from side to side. She hasn't expected to answer his questions tonight, yet turnabout is fair play. "I was born in Virginia, but my parents were from the Bible Belt South." She pauses, trying to figure out how to explain the meaning of this phrase. "They didn't believe in evolution." He frowns, and she adds, "I do."

The lines on his forehead give way.

"My father was military, and we moved around every two years, and then settled in the North Carolina Mountains."

"You had mountains, too?" Qasim's eyes dance across her face. "We had one each of everything—sun, sea, mountain…" His tenor voice deepens into his chest. "Go on. What about your mother? Did she work?"

"My mother was very smart. She was a teacher when she could find the work, what with all the moves. The rest of the time she was home torturing us. My mother and I didn't agree on much."

The light leaves Qasim's eyes. "Never speak ill of your parents. Never. They are to be obeyed."

Her mouth screws up in a rebellious little ball. She waits for his flat hand on the table trick.

"Go on," he says, surprising her again.

Dianna hesitates. "My father is dead. My mother is very ill. My younger sister takes care of her. My brother is in college. We keep in touch, but we're not close."

"I'm sorry." He seems penitent about his earlier judgment.

"It's okay. I'm okay. People always think I'm not, but I am. I wish I could have done better by my family. I wish I could have done more for them. I wasn't strong enough."

"Look at what you are doing, Dianna."

"What?" she asks, confused. A moment ago, he was disapproving; now his eyes radiate gentle warmth.

"You're obviously sending money home. Otherwise, you wouldn't have to watch your budget so tightly." He cups his hand over hers as though the motion will give her the good luck she hasn't ever had.

"Oh, that." Dianna blushes, pulls her hand away, and examines it.

"Oh, that. Your humility amazes me." He pulls her face up to meet his. He stares at her for a long time. Then he draws a breath and walks over to the bookcase she was eyeing only moments before. He takes out a thick, white photo album.

He opens the first page. Dianna's heart quickens when she recognizes a tuxedoed Qasim, smile on his face, dancing with a skinny woman with long dark hair piled high on her head. Around her thick hair, she wears a tiara. A white, Western wedding dress drapes what little there is of her. Others, dressed in evening attire, smiling and clapping, form a semi-circle around the couple.

"This was my wedding," he says.

"When?" She should have known. She probably did know. The king-sized bed that first night. The impeccable interior design. The hot air balloon that once contained her hope plummets to the ground.

"I was in my twenties. It was an arranged marriage. My parents' choice."

"She's…pretty." Dianna shortens both words, knowing they ring hollow. She is simultaneously jealous and curious. She waits for one to win out. Pride overcomes them both. She won't let him see her jealousy, that she fears this woman is still in his life. That would mean the end.

"I suppose." He sniffs, taking a quick bite of air. "You see this scar?" he asks her, and he takes her middle finger and traces it over his cheek.

It is his sexiest feature; she noticed it the first night. She simply nods yes. She feels dizzy. She desperately wants to kiss the scar.

"I drove my convertible off a cliff the month before the wedding. An accident, of course. But they almost had to postpone the vows. My face was a mess for some time after."

She stares at him, waiting for the courage to ask. "Are you still married?" she finally queries, and her hands turn clammy.

Qasim throws his head back in laughter. "Is that what you have been worried about? No, no. I do not have five wives stashed away in my closet. I am divorced."

"Yet how..." she begins, and he cuts her off.

"Divorced. Period. D-I-V-O-R-C-E-D. Divorced."

Silence again.

He clears his throat and shifts his weight. "There is one more thing you should know," he says. "I have a son. He is in Beirut with his mother, but he spends his summers with me."

Dianna's heart leaps. "You have a son! How old?"

"Almost ten."

"May I see him?"

Qasim walks over and pulls another album from the shelf, flips through the pages. "Here, here he is—his name is Tariq—about a year ago. He loves it here. His mother hates it."

A boy in a jogging suit and sandals stares back at her. He has his father's lips and smile; he has his mother's nose. His ears stand out from his head, unlike either parent. His hair is unruly like Qasim's. His stiff posture overshadows the laughter in his eyes. This is a boy who has overcome, who is happy in spite of, rather than because of, his history. "A little Qasim," Dianna whispers. "You have a son." She flips through his wedding album again, reaches up, and caresses his cheek. Then she traces the scar on his photographed face. "You're smiling," she asks rather than states. "Were you happy?"

He sighs, shifts, sighs again. "I guess so."

CHAPTER FOURTEEN

Standoff

Dianna dials with her thumb: 545-2328. Qasim's answering machine comes on with an electronic, English recording.

"Hi, Qasim. It's me. Call me back when you get in, okay?" She hangs up and begins her vigil by the telephone, switching the television on, then off, then on again.

The phone rings the next evening.

Dianna's heart leaps. She restrains her impulse to grab the receiver on the first ring.

"Hello?"

"Hi, sweetie. What's new, eh?"

"Same old, same old. I submitted an article to a journal."

"Oh? I didn't know you wrote." He sounds both proud and skeptical.

"There's a lot we don't know about each other."

"Not true. Not true. You know everything significant about me. You can always ask if you want to know something."

"Really?"

"Really."

"Do you like plays?" she asks.

"They're fine." His response surprises her.

"Would you like to join me some evening in the next two weeks to see *Evita*?" She wonders if she should offer to pay, or if that would offend him. She could always put off paying her school loan for a month.

"The next two weeks? I don't have my calendar in front of me. I know I'm quite tied up the next two weeks. They need me. I may need to travel. "

"Oh. Maybe I should have consulted your secretary instead," says Dianna. Even she can hear the wry tone in her voice.

"No, no." He's laughing, but she hears strain in the cadence. "I want to go with you. I want to spend time with you. It's a matter of when."

"You're working too hard again." She sucks in her breath. "I miss you."

"I know. I know. I need to get through this one last year, and I can pull back a bit."

She searches for incentive. "The crowds are dying down for this play. You won't need to stand outside in the cold for long." Dianna loves the cold: the way it tickles at her nose, the layers of clothing, the way the street lights twinkle when the wind blows.

"It's not the weather…" She imagines his eyes, shifting from side to side as he battles between desire and duty.

"So. No play?" Her heart sinks down to the ugly shag rug beneath her feet. "If you're too busy, we need to give peace a chance." She tries to put a laugh in her voice. She's conflicted, too. She wants to spend time with him, and she understands the demands of his work.

"No, no. We'll go. We'll go. We may need to wait until next month. Definitely between Thanksgiving and Christmas. I have plans to dine with two charming little old ladies on Long Island for Thanksgiving. They've adopted me. You know, I've never had an American Thanksgiving dinner in all the time I've been here."

The tears begin to pulsate, traveling, starting in her belly, moving to her chest, but she steels her heart against weeping. She refuses to resort to such feminine manipulation. She has never, ever shown him she is weak. She will not begin today. "So you'll call me when you know a time?"

"Of course, Dianna. Of course."

She can hear his smile over the wire, and she relaxes, lets her breath out.

"When will I see you?" he asks. A touch of melancholy in his voice tweaks at the tears trapped in her chest.

"That's a question only you have the answer to, Qasim," she says, and she puts the receiver back in place. "So long," she mouths to the thin, limp air.

***

She wonders for the next hour why she hung up prematurely, what would have been said next if she had jerked the phone back up to her ear before she broke the connection. Then she rehashes what she should have said, what would have turned the conversation around. Perhaps she should have been more business-like. Perhaps she should have stood up to him—

convinced him that she was more important than a bunch of papers on a desk. Perhaps she should have invented some little old men who were taking her to a Thanksgiving banquet.

No, none of those options would have felt right. Perhaps she should purchase a day-of-the-play, cheaper balcony ticket for herself. Perhaps she should resign herself to her canned turkey breast and her second-rate rendition of Gran's dressing. She jumps almost to the ceiling when the buzzer rings.

"Yes?" she says to the intercom box, her fingers pushing the button so hard that they are numb.

"Dianna, let me come up." Qasim's voice fills the room. His voice seems deeper, gravelly, full of electricity.

"I was just going out," she fibs. She looks at her watch. It is almost ten p.m.

"Let me in." His voice comes through with physical force this time, and she pushes the door button, her breath fast and sharp.

His face is ruddy from the wind, even though he is wrapped to the hilt: scarf, gloves, overcoat, and a jacket underneath. His frown lines look deeper than the last time she saw him, when she had chickened out of opening a real conversation. Yet here he was before her, and he was already upset. She might as well let it all out.

He takes his coat off and throws it on the couch, then takes her in his arms, pushes her head down to his shoulder. "Oh my God," is all he says.

"What?" she asks.

He takes a breath to speak, but she decides she must intervene before he has a chance to change her mind. "Look, Qasim, things haven't been right between us since that night we saw Jamal. It feels like you're covering up anger at me. I can't have you losing it in front of my friends, and I need to know more about you to trust you. Do you trust me?"

He pushes back from her. The furrow deepens as though her comments are rain drops that have flooded a stream and caused it to overflow its banks. Yet, he says nothing. Finally, he says, "Continue."

"Please," she says. "Sit down."

He remains standing.

"I need to know who you are and what your intentions are." She is amazed at her own candor. *Where did those words come from?* Her father used to use that word, "intentions."

"I'm sure I don't know what you mean." He looks so comfortable there, hands at his sides, feet parallel, torso holding his entire body erect. He gets like this when he is nervous—still instead of frenetic.

She sits down instead. "I'm not sure what I mean either. I know we're from different cultures, different worlds, but that makes no difference." She flinches. In truth, she hasn't decided whether it means something to their future together or not. "I don't understand why you have outbursts that seem to come from nowhere. I don't understand where you go when you are here, in town, but don't call me. I don't have a clue about the vicissitudes of your family situation. In fact, I can't get it out of my head that you are still attached to your former wife." She stops for a moment, for she has no breath left.

"Dianna, I am divorced. I have told you that." He paces in the small room, folding his arms behind him.

"Then where are you?" she cries. She thinks of his wife's moon face in the wedding photos; she thinks of Leah's long legs and her words of disdainful reproach. She thinks of her mother.

"Muslim men have responsibilities to ex-wives, and I believe even you Americans have responsibilities for your children, is this not true?"

"Well, where are they?" She looks down. She is embarrassed by his intent gaze.

"My wife and son are with my father. I told you my son visits in the summer. He was with me this summer. He was with me recently for a week."

She begins to ask why he did not allow her to meet his son, but she squelches this protest. Many divorced fathers wait to know a relationship is serious before introducing women to their children. It made sense, even though it hurt.

"I have responsibilities, Dianna. Some of them are obvious. Some are not. My country has been at war for some time, and we may have some small chance at a peace. I have a responsibility to my country. Part of this responsibility is fulfilled through my work; part of it is not. I also have a responsibility to my family business. I cannot leave my brothers to handle my duties there."

"What is your family business?" Dianna asks, her embarrassment turning to curiosity. "Oil?"

"Why do all you Americans think every Arab has oil fields? I don't understand why *you* can't understand that there are more people in my life besides you. Stop being so narcissistic!" He is almost hissing, flailing his arms in front of him and waving them wildly through the air. She dares not repeat her question.

Her curiosity turns toward shame. "I'm sorry," she says. "I know there is plenty I don't know. I've tried to read, but it's difficult to find current material that isn't about conflict. You have to educate me. I'm sorry I didn't realize your responsibilities were so legion." She pats the space beside her on the couch.

He looks at her with the craggy gaze he usually reserves for business conversations.

"Come on, relax. Come sit with me."

He remains standing, a rigid yet elegant figure.

"Qasim? What were you going to say when you walked in?" she asks.

"I was going to say..." He pauses and looks around the room like an animal would its cage. "I was going to tell you I had missed you. I was going to tell you that you looked as beautiful as the day we met. I was going to tell you I had a way to join you at the play next month."

She doesn't know whether to believe him or not. The key turns in the lock, and Leah bursts in.

"Well, hello there, Qasim. You guys been on a date?" Her smile is wide and receptive.

"Of sorts," he replies. He gets his coat, twists his scarf around his sturdy neck, and puts each glove on one finger at a time, all the while staring at Dianna and she at him.

"Please don't leave," she implores.

He turns and goes to the door. Leah bustles in the kitchen. Dianna hears the microwave beep.

"Qasim, please."

He puts his hand on the doorknob. It stays there, like a heavy weight. He turns back toward her, his ruddy face paler, stricken. He throws off his winter clothes as if on fire. Then, in one swift move, he is across the room, sitting beside her, holding her hands in his, kissing each finger. When he speaks, she can hear torture in his voice: "Look what you do to me, woman," he says. His hands run up and down her throat, and his fingers are as cold as mercury. "What am I to do?" he asks.

"It's fine," she says. "Work. Travel. Do what you have to do. I need to know I mean something to you."

"I must go."

He turns again to leave. He kisses her, and his lips are as cold as his fingers.

QASIM

CHAPTER FIFTEEN

Liberté, Égalité, Fraternité

I walk to my sedan after giving Dianna a quick kiss at her doorstep. I can't feel badly that I did not spend the night. I need some space before my busy day tomorrow. I reach unconsciously into my pocket for a cigarette. Almost fifteen years since I quit, and I still reach for a smoke when stressed. Perhaps I shouldn't have shared as much as I did. Maybe it's too early. Maybe nothing will come of this liaison anyway.

Still, I grudgingly acknowledge she needs to know more about my past to trust me. Why is the past so important to a woman? I wish to walk away from my past, toward my future, and here she is, pulling me back. I stomp my cold feet and stuff my hands in my pockets to warm them. I don't find the desire to smoke often these days. She has a way of dredging history up before I realize it. I remember things I thought I had long forgotten.

There's a vague sense of recognition, of nostalgia even, each time I see her. Nostalgia beckons, and memories flood in, not many of them uplifting. There's the moon, almost bright enough to be a half moon, and I can hear the sea. Impossible here in New York City, yet I hear the rhythm of shallow waves hitting the shore, as though I am standing in front of them. I fish for my keys, unlock the car door, climb in, and start the ignition. There it is again, the sea nudging me back in time to another such moon, another time, another place.

What was that day? It couldn't have been a holiday. Perhaps it was the first day home from school for the season. My brothers were home, so summer it must have been. That crescent moon high in a sky still pale in the dusk's remaining light. My father standing at his car, high up on the hill, motioning the rest of the family toward him across that great expanse of beach. My mother standing, shaking the sand from her skirt, folding the blanket, telling them to hurry.

***

Today we are to go down to the water. Each trip is a special occasion. I can already feel the aquamarine surf as it breaks on the sand—not quite waves, more than placid ripples. It will hit my skinned knees and take the sting away. It will cool my body for the first time all day. For now, I wipe the hot droplets of perspiration from the back of my neck before they can fall onto my vest, which I am expected to wear year-round—except when we are down by the sea.

My mother packs a long, straw basket with good things to eat: hummus, bread, cheese, honey, lots of olives. I pop one in my mouth as I pass the table. She smacks my hand, and I run out the door. How nice it will be to feel as cold as this olive is. Its briny taste sits in my mouth long after I spit out the pit.

My brothers play football in the courtyard. I watch the ripple of muscle on flesh as they vie for the ball. "Move, Qasim!" Saif yells, as he dribbles the ball with one foot and steps on my toes with the other. I back away, laugh at him to hide the tears biting my eyes. Eight years my senior, Saif is already almost as tall as my mother; soon he will be as tall as my father. I wish I could be as tall as he. This does not seem to be my fate, though. My pet name is 'Goat:' small, compact, rugged, hopping from place to place, all horns and hooves. That is who I have become because I would not want to disappoint them.

I swing around the fig tree and scratch the itch on my neck the wool vest creates. I kick some pebbles up in the air and watch them fall to earth. "Stop, Qasim!" yells Rayik. I kick some pebbles in his direction and run back into the house.

I scamper into my father's library. There he sits in his leather chair, reading. A dim light tries to shine through leaded glass from the Tiffany beside him. His library is the only dark room in the house, otherwise full of light. I crouch behind the table at the far end of the room, breathing in the dust and mold of old books and trying to become the shadow beneath me. The fan rotates its dull full circle above. Baba raises his head and inclines it toward me. I wonder if he has seen me, but he picks up pen and paper. He is working again. He is always working, it seems. He rubs his chin and adjusts his reading glasses after he finishes each thought.

"Baba?" I whisper, and when I receive no answer, I say it with conviction, "Baba!"

He looks up, his expression a bit startled, a bit perplexed. "Qasim?"

"Baba, can we go to the seaside now?" I whine.

"Qasim, you need to ask your mother that question."

"But Baba..." I want to stomp my foot, but I know better.

"Let me finish this, habibi." He dips his fountain pen and begins to write once more.

I sigh but run out of the room back toward the kitchen. "What time will we leave, Mama? Are we almost prepared to leave?"

"Qasim, your questions delay, not hasten me." My mother smooths her apron along the detailed seams of her full skirt and pushes up at the silk sleeves that run down to her slender wrists. She pushes a stray strand of thick, wavy black hair behind her ear and runs a delicate hand across her forehead. She begins to roll a yellow damask tablecloth into a perfect cylinder. "Go outside and bring me some figs. We could use some figs."

I roll my eyes but make certain she cannot see me in my insolence. I run out again, banging the door behind me. "Qasim!" my mother reprimands me.

"Qasim!" my brother shouts. "I thought you were gone!"

I shimmy up the slender tree trunk before he can catch my sandal, and I begin to pluck figs. If he catches hold of me, I know he'll muss my hair to incite my mother's wrath. I throw a couple of pebbles from my pocket down at him, and he runs back to his game. I reach for the tree's top branches, where I can savor both figs and sunlight. The secret is to eat only as many as will not be missed. The tree bends with my weight, and I grab one last delicious morsel. I dread the day my weight should become too much for the tree. I would dare not break a branch from this tree; it is my father's favorite, planted when he was but a boy.

"Qasim!" my mother calls. "Where are those figs? We're ready to leave!"

I jump the last few feet to the ground, upsetting a few figs. My brothers rush to grab them and thrust them into their mouths. My mother waits at the door, her hand on her hip.

"But where is Baba?" I ask Mama.

She swings her heavy basket over her arm and gives each of us a bundle to carry, beasts of burden, all of us. "He will join us when he can, Qasim. Hurry!"

We step from the cool mosaic tile of our home into the bustle of the narrow street. My mother catches hold of my hand as we scurry down the alleyways on the edge of the West side, her heels clicking on the rose-colored walkways as we pass through our neighborhood. There's the green grocery, the cafe shop, where we sometimes sit and drink chocolate glaces; there's the little man who sells coal in the winter and ice in the summer. My mother pulls me past the midday clamor of the souqs, and finally, just as the red tile roofs of the Ottoman section of the city come into view, we can catch the scent of the sea. It overtakes the lingering aroma of cardamom and myrrh as we step on the trolley that will take us down the hill to the seaside. I can make out other children running up and down the sand below.

One boy has a white cloth on a string, but there is not enough wind to carry his makeshift kite to the azure sky. It catches a breeze, tilts to the right, to the left, and then topples on its side, defeated. The boy does not give up hope, though. He is already running against the wind again. I find myself cheering him on under my breath. "Come on! Let go! Now! Let it catch!" No matter the reason, over and over again, the kite catches, flags, and dies.

After our day in the sun and sea, Rayik and I lie back on our blanket, as the cool trade wind whips through our hair. We are sated from food and play. Saif sits with my mother nearer the cliffs behind us. She reads to him from a book that looks boring enough. I pull my sandaled toes out of the sand and then dump sand on them again to cover them once more. "Mama won't be happy you are getting your new sandals so dusty," Rayik warns me.

I hear the smooth engine of Baba's car before I can see it. It makes a great whir as he shifts down an incline. He drives a big, black cavern of a car with a silver hood ornament that reminds me of a horse but is probably meant to be a dog. My mother hurries to gather our belongings into her basket and run up the hill so Baba will not need to wait long. Another day over with Baba just getting here. I love him, and so I hate his work. I vow I will never take life so seriously that I cannot come down to the sea.

***

Papa, always hurrying us, never in a hurry for us. He was a good provider, though. A man doesn't have time for beach outings when he is building his family business, a business that belonged to his father, and to his father's father. He was trying to keep the business profitable—trying to keep the family from hard times, times that crescent moon had yet to witness. What year could it have been? 1947? 48? Definitely before 1950. I was so small then I thought the beach was big. I had vowed never to work so many hours I could not go down to the seaside. Yet here I was, working too many hours. But for peace. That was the difference.

I jump. A horn blares behind me. How long have I been sitting here at this green light? It is late, but not late enough for impatient drivers in New York City. I frown into my rear view at this American in a hurry. An American woman. I have a mind to get out and lecture her on the art of driving but then think better of it. One can never predict how these Americans would react to an accent, to a foreigner with dark skin.

I rev my engine once to let the impatient female driver share my annoyance, sit until the light turns yellow, then proceed on my way.

What can Dianna know of what war can do to a family? To a man? I think back to that day shortly before I left Lebanon, the arguing, the name-calling—all because I wasn't taking sides. What difference did it make what label one put on one's forehead, as long as he believed in one God? No, no, I am a good Muslim, a good provider, a good man.

The memories flow by me again like a river.

CHAPTER SIXTEEN

Bridges

April 28, 1957, Bhasmana High School, overlooking Beirut, Lebanon

I perch on the school's balcony, and I gaze out over the courtyard. Somewhere a rooster crows. A peddler calls out his wares. The lines of students in their wool vests, plaid skirts, and navy knickers wind like six snakes below, each grade forming its own living, sinuous "S." I move the branch of a mulberry tree to attain a better view. A mild breeze knocks the green shutter back and forth behind me, and the sun glints off the red tile of a roof across the courtyard. The school anthem is about to begin. Usually, I am part of snake number four, but today I have other plans. I plan to show my school chum Fouad, once and for all, that it can rain when the sun is shining. I also hope to win Marie-Amelie's heart.

I am a student with high academic merit, Mlle Bertrand has told my mother. It is quite a compliment in a Quaker school. My mother shakes her head and puckers her mouth. "Mlle Bertrand does not understand your misbehavior of late. It is inconsistent with what seems to be a high desire to learn. Why, Qasim? Why must you make trouble? This behavior has been going on for two years—*two* years—since you turned thirteen. And now you're fifteen! It's time to think of your future. All your excellent marks will not make your way in this world if you are sent to detention more often than you sit in front of a blackboard."

"It's funny," I mutter.

"What?" My mother strides toward me, one hand on a slim, silk-covered hip, the other cupped to her ear, feigning deafness or expressing incredulity, I cannot tell which. "There is no place for 'funny' in the schoolroom. Do you realize what an honor it is to attend one of the most prestigious secondary schools in the Middle East? You are there to learn. Save your pranks for those who do not hold your future in their hands." She whisks her own hands together, as if she is ridding them of dirt.

"I do learn," I mumble under my breath. I dare not tell her that I am bored beyond measure, that I make up my own equations in my head to pass the time, or that I translate the teacher's French to Arabic to English and back again before I answer her questions. I do not want to irritate her further, and besides, there is an advantage to hiding the level of one's mental agility, especially when one is the youngest in a family of boys. You can get away with more.

"When you are bestowed an honor, a responsibility comes with it! Have you no sense of responsibility? No family honor?" She shakes her head and clucks her tongue. "Your brothers would never have…"

I stand there looking at the ceiling. *What does she want me to say?*

My mother throws up her hands. She walks to the kitchen, her thin heels clicking against the tile. She returns, hand raised in the air with a large wooden cooking spoon. "Come here, Qasim," she says, in a voice so soft I can barely decipher the blurred intonation of her Arabic. *Ah, she is angry.*

I turn my sullen face to the other wall, but she stays put. I finally accept my fate, walk toward her, and extend my hand for punishment. The spoon comes down five swift times before I hear her heel turn away. Only then do I have the wherewithal to look up. I can never look in my mother's eyes when she is using that wooden spoon. I am taller than she is now, and broader, but I still dread her wrath. She has the strength to do what my Quaker teachers cannot: teach me a lesson using corporal punishment. I respect her for that.

I know I will get the wooden spoon again tonight, or the next, when she finds out what I am preparing to do. It is plainly too funny for me to restrain myself. Life is so deadly dull without finding a little fun. Fouad deserves it, the dense little coward. "Oui, Mlle Bertrand." "Choississez-moi, Mlle Bertrand." Always puckering up to that old maid, who probably never had a lover in her life. Fouad, with the willowy physique and the wavy hair. Fouad, who could get by with murder, even in this pacifist school, if he so desired. Capitalizing on his looks and his "Oui, Mlle Bertrand's." *Oh, how I loathe him. How I loathe people who receive commendation strictly on the assessment of the length of their lashes, the resonance of their voices, or the breadth of their shoulders!*

Today, and for all time, Fouad will realize that I have the upper hand, that intellect combined with a sense of humor can conquer the looks of Adonis or the brawn of Hercules. The words and wisdom of Thoth, Egypt's god of Letters, are on my side, and he will see that this little pipsqueak pays.

Yesterday, Fouad and I placed a wager. I said water could fall from the sky without a single cloud above. "You will see water fall from the sky when the sun is shining," I said again.

Fouad, as I might have predicted, disagreed with me. He always disagrees with me. Each boy in our classroom puts in a pound, and whoever wins the wager will receive it all. Besides, everyone will laugh. When people laugh, Marie-Amelie looks my way.

I first saw Marie-Amelie two years ago, in eighth grade, standing in snake number two, waiting for assistant headmaster Mme Al-Alami to come out and ring the bell that signals us to file into our classrooms. Three months of the school year had already come and gone, and I was getting bored. Fiddling with the binding of my Biro, containing my conjugations of English verbs, I was seeing how far I could detach it and still reattach it with its existing glue. I took it a little too far and then feverishly attempted to paste it back. As I had to hand the Biro in once a week, it was essential that it was all in one piece. My grade depended on it, and competitive achievement appeals to me. My wool vest prickled my neck, and my hands became hot and wet.

I looked up, and there she was. Her flaxen hair, the color of sand dunes, was tied away from her forehead, and the sun shone down upon the fair skin of her face. My eyes trekked toward hers and were surprised to find that, although her eyes were the shape of almonds, their color matched the aquamarine of the Mediterranean. Her features were delicate save for a prominent Roman nose. Her laughter rose above the fracas of the schoolyard. I knew I must meet her, but I did not know how I would manage. She was in a different queue, and she was obviously new to the school. The intensity of her smile and her laughter, the density of her eyes, the texture of her hair frightened me. Suddenly, the condition of my Biro didn't matter.

I began to resort to all sorts of pranks and jests to gain some notoriety where before I had none. The bookworm turned jester, I had heard that laugh in reaction to my shenanigans at least four times. Today I was sure I could prompt a laugh again.

A very few people stay with you even when you do not realize they are there. Marie-Amelie is one of those people. They spur your imagination in your dreams; they inhabit your mind as soon as the sun rises; they are your last thought as you fall asleep. They find a hidden corner of your heart and hide there, appearing seemingly out of nowhere when you least expect it. Marie-Amelie has taken up residence in my heart, and I will not stop until she agrees she belongs there, until she emerges from her hiding place and calls my heart home.

I do not worry that she is a Christian. My chums tell me I have a screw loose in my head. They say a prominent family such as mine will never allow me even to dance with a Christian, let alone take her to dinner. I tell them it doesn't matter; I don't dance well. Food is far from essential when conversation is stimulating. We can take a stroll along the sea instead, or we can listen to jazz on the record player. We can sit at a coffee house and sip our drinks, nibble on our Arabiscos. Rico is a snob, and Fouad is simply jealous. He wants Marie-Amelie for himself, and I am here to show him he cannot have her.

And today, she stands in my line. Somehow, she has skipped a grade level. They tell me she mastered two years in one year's time. She is not the first to raise her hand in class, but Mlle usually calls on her, and if she answers, her response is not only correct, but also incisive.

I was thinking about the Suez War when Mlle called on me recently. I was wondering how the Egyptians had traded without that canal, since it has been closed to them since the war. I doodled a ship passing through a canal, when Mlle caught me off guard. She asked that I recite a poem, and the contrast between verse and sword left me mute. Marie-Amelie sat still as a vase in a painting, watching me. My throat constricted, and I could no longer get air in, let alone get words out. Mlle whirled around, disgusted by my inattention.

"Mlle L'Armand, can you recite the poem for the class? Monsieur el-Kafry seems to have no recollection of such a verse."

Marie-Amelie looked at me, looked down at her hands, and took a deep breath.

"Mlle? We are waiting." The professor strode about the room, her focus now on someone else she could shame.

Marie-Amelie looked straight at me once more and began, in her melodious French accent, reciting in Arabic:

> They cross the bridge at dawn, light-footed,
> my ribs stretched out before them as a bridge.
> From the caves and swamps of the old East,
> they cross to the East of the new,
> my ribs stretched out before them as a bridge.
>
> They will pass away while you remain,
> an idol left by the priests
> for the wind to lash and burn.
> A relic—empty-handed, crucified, alone,
> in snowy nights with horizons of ash,
> with smoldering embers and dust for bread,
> with frozen tears in sleepless nights(...)

The entire class seemed to be holding its breath, as Marie-Amelie was not quoting Homer's *Iliad*, but Al-Hawi's "The Bridge" from his collection *Nahr ar-Ramad* (*Rivers of Ash*), a poem both current and political. I followed her gaze and then noticed I had distractedly sketched a canal with a bridge on the back of my Biro, echoing the bridge in the poem. Was Marie-Amelie citing these lines for my benefit? Her voice almost made the cadence romantic. Still, her eyes fixed upon me, and I matched her gaze.

Mlle stood, transfixed—her lips pursed, her face like wood—and we waited for her to react. Her lips finally came together in a hard, thin crooked line. Then, she picked up her English book and began conjugating a verb at the board.

I rouse from my reverie to check the trajectory of my plan one last time as the six snakes begin to curl and sway, and then a voice rises up in our school song, a vague mélange of French bistro music and Arabian rhythms. I pick up the tin bucket I have slaughtered with 100 nail holes and swing it on its rope, up, over my perch. I check the skies to make certain that no errant cloud will arrive to obscure the sun, and then I pour the rainwater I collected on my balcony at home into a ceramic pitcher. I immediately send the water from the pitcher through the bucket and—voila!—instant rain in the sunshine. I aim for line number four and Fouad's pompadour.

The period following the anthem is to be a time of silent reflection and contemplation. We are supposed to be focusing on "the inner light that dwells in the spirit of the ordinary." This is as sacramental as a Quaker School gets because Quakers observe no special sacraments, and the school "embraces all faiths in their interdisciplinary education." They stress instead humanitarian activities, peace education, racial equality, and individual responsibility. I could quote that in my sleep. This morning I take my individualism quite seriously and, in the process, ruin even this subtle, spiritual ambience. My aim is exact, and Fouad looks up and shows me his fist just as Mme Al-Alami comes out to guide the first line indoors.

Mme walks directly under my line of fire, or stream of water in this case. Her perfectly coiffed hair, which always looks too stiff to comb, hardens like meringue, then droops into her eyes. Mme tries in vain to sweep the dripping, straggling clumps of coarse hair away from her eyes, that she might see the culprit.

"Look! A rainbow!" someone cries. Indeed, the sun shimmers in iridescent hues on the pavement below. I pull the pail back over the rail. It's too late. Mme has seen me.

Amid much sputtering, Mme looks up at the balcony, and I avert my eyes, but I cannot hang my head. "Monsieur El-Kafry," the grande dame intones.

Too triumphant to run or hide, I stand grinning on my balcony. I hope the smile is contrite enough for Mme but not too contrite for my schoolmates. Einstein says, "Nothing happens unless something moves." Well, at this very moment, I made something move. Nothing anywhere will be the same for me after today. It does not matter what the consequences of this movement brings—at least from Mme. I have won the wager. My eyes fix on Marie-Amelie.

Every snake gyrates with the pulse of irrepressible laughter. Marie-Amelie looks up. At first, her mouth forms a perfect "O." Then the muscles in her face recognize the joke, and her expression becomes light and airy, full of mirth, and yes, perhaps of joy. I love the giggle that signals I have made her happy. Our eyes meet, and I know I have won her.

CHAPTER SEVENTEEN
Curfew

July 13, 1958, Fort Bragg, N.C.

Mr. and Mrs. Robert E. Calloway proudly announce the birth of their first daughter, Dianna Lynn, blue eyes, blonde hair, seven lbs., eleven oz.

July 14, 1958, Beirut

President Dwight D. Eisenhower dispatches U.S. Marines to the bikini-clad beaches of Beirut. Several thousand Lebanese have already lost their lives in civil war.

July 5, 1958, Beirut.

Funny. Until the 1950s, Maronite Christians and Sunni Muslims, like me, were Beirut's primary inhabitants. Why then, the distrust between us? Perhaps it is a matter of geographical habituation. The Maronites surrounded Mount Lebanon, and we Muslims stayed down here near the ocean, which makes it all the more compelling that we join together since this bizarre Civil War has broken out. I don't totally blame the Shiite refugees from Palestine, but I long for the day when I can be comfortable in my own homeland, without looking over my shoulder. I am even more anxious that Marie-Amelie and I can come out of hiding.

Such are my thoughts as I look into the sky at my eldest brother's wedding reception. The night is filled with a million stars. They shine down on our courtyard as Saif and his new bride take their first dance as a couple. Saif gazes down onto her face, which glows, whether with love or anxiety, I cannot tell. She is beautiful enough, by society's standards, and she knows the newest dance moves. She has probably taken all the traditional steps to prepare for this long-awaited evening. Yet what are groom and bride thinking underneath all of this outward ornamentation? They barely know each other. Marie-Amelie and I, in a few conversations, know one another better than Saif and his new wife.

Wife. Tonight they will caress each other. Tonight they will kiss, and *in'sh'Allah*, their bodies will meet. My parents will be watching through some sort of imaginary crystal ball, to ensure their grandchildren. Love will grow, they assure us, as theirs has. Theirs was an arranged marriage, and look at the love they have between them.

I cannot help but wonder if they are not two of the lucky ones. Lucky enough because love is definitely part of our home, a cool, marble love offering shelter that points the way for all five of us. A well-worn path. Love, yes, but where is the romance? I have yet to see it—the sideways glances, the clandestine brush of his hand on her arm when they think our attention is elsewhere, the joking uplift of my mother's lip, the arch of my father's brow. I have seen them exhibit these mannerisms to others, but not to one another. Aren't these romantic gestures supposed to be shared with the one you love?

My parents must understand my reticence for an arranged marriage. I will bide my time and await the proper moment. Eventually, if they know what I feel in my heart toward Marie-Amelie, they must let us pursue a romantic courtship. Time will tell if it is meant to be more. We know each other only superficially, and I acknowledge our youth. Yet, yet...

I startle when I realize time has passed while I stood here in this corner, daydreaming. It seems only moments ago my family was at the door, offering a thousand welcomes to our guests: "*Ahlan wa sahlan,*" they were saying repeatedly, like a chant. Until it became a mantra, lulling me into my daydreaming. Until the dancing is winding down, and the wedding is nearly over. I may be able to make my exit soon. I have my schoolwork as a pretext; I am working on a summer project so I may graduate next May. I must return to school tomorrow. Such is the life of a boarding student, something I used to resent but now see as a kind of freedom.

Tonight, Marie-Amelie is in Beirut. The cobalt sky whispers in conspiracy. We are to rendezvous after the wedding, or as near to its end as decorum will allow. We have read to each other, shared tea and Arabiscos, even tried that American invention, a malted shake, drunk out of the same straw while holding hands under the cafe table. Yet, after a very long year, filled with unspoken opportunity, we have not kissed. A year is a very long time. Perhaps this evening is my chance. You never know.

I walk along the darkened avenues of Beirut, toward the jazz club with a brightly-lit neon sign beckoning me toward its dim interior. It was surprisingly easy to make my exodus from the wedding; the revelry was at its height with all eyes on the newlyweds.

I am young and agile. I shimmied down the drainpipe and dropped the remaining two meters to the ground. The jasmine wafted through the late dewy air, and my step quickened down our walk and out onto the dim alleyways of my home city. Not toward the Mediterranean this time, but inward, toward the Christian section. I kept track of my direction and took care turning corners even though these streets are part of my childhood domain. It is almost time for curfew. I shouldn't have let her come; it's not safe.

I walk in and find her. A warm breeze replaces the moist air. Her almond-shaped eyes look down at some sort of fountain drink, expensive to most, but probably not to her, the daughter of a diplomat. I stride toward her, quick steps at first, then slowing down to hide my exuberance.

She glances up, knowing I've been there all along. "I ordered you a cup of tea, the British kind, the flavor you like so much." Her smile is at once demure, derisive, and expectant.

"Sorry I am so late," I stutter.

All she does is turn her head on her long neck side to side, and I swallow hard, caught between knowing I've kept her waiting and wondering if she is going to punish me for it.

I am overjoyed when I hear the words, "It was your brother's wedding after all. I have another hour before my carriage turns into a pumpkin."

"But the curfew?" I manage to mouth.

"Another hour." Her laughter flows like water over smooth shining stones. "What do you do with that expensive watch you wear on your wrist? *C'est un bijou seulement,* or do you ever glance its way?"

I turn red, and I am happy to know she won't notice because the sun has bronzed my face. I take the watch off and wrap it around the decrepit bud vase full of wilting flowers sitting in the middle of our cafe table. "My time is yours entirely for the next hour, your highness," I say, and I put my hand over hers.

It is her turn to blush, and unlike my embarrassment, hers is a beacon of light under pale, iridescent skin. I congratulate myself on my quick rally. The band strikes up over the clamor of evening dinner conversation. A hollow-eyed woman dressed in a silk evening dress with fur bracelets at the end of each see-through sleeve begins moaning out a Billie Holliday tune.

I extend my arm, in what I hope to be an unaffected gesture of gallantry. "Shall we dance?" I ask.

Her eyes radiate the mirth that I remember from that day a year ago in the courtyard, and I remember her lips forming a perfect "O." I imagine my lips on hers, and I immediately chastise myself for my overexcitement. A dance may lead to a kiss; it may not.

"What have you heard about the war?" she asks, stepping onto the dance floor.

I heard that since the Shiites have set up camp on the outskirts of the city; suspicion has turned its evil head against the Christians. That it is not the sect of Shi'ism that has been our traditional nemesis. However, I don't say that. Instead I say what the papers say, "It's a just cause—for pan-Arabism, for a stronger, united Arab presence globally."

Her lips turns to a smirk. "How can this bickering, this chaotic vengeance bring about any kind of unity? I see it as nothing but divisive. It seems that sooner or later, everyone will be against everyone."

"Perhaps," I reply, not wanting to think of war, but of love. "The factions in this country need to find a way to understand one another and get on with living."

Marie-Amelie leans her head toward mine. She is quiet as her finger traces an ill-defined letter on the shoulder of my tuxedo jacket, and I congratulate myself on not taking the time to change into clothes that are more casual before joining her. She sighs, and then drops her head down on my chest, and we dance out the set in this position.

Three-quarters of an hour pass almost imperceptibly, and I make myself look toward my wrist and then realize my watch is still on the table.

I guide her to our seats in the corner and look out of the corner of my eye at the second hand tracking a worn path round and round, a constant reminder of our imminent departure. Most of the café's patrons have already made their way out the door. I squeeze Marie-Amelie's hand, and miraculously, it squeezes back. I look down at her lips, unable for once to clown myself out of my rapture.

"Marie-Amelie, I am going to kiss you," I state and wait for the rebuke.

It does not come. Her almond-shaped, Mediterranean-blue eyes trek up toward mine, and she offers her lips in a perfect small circle up to mine. As my lips touch hers, I travel to a place beyond reproach.

As I move away, I come back to earth, half expecting an adult to come and snatch one of us away from the other, but nothing happens. Her lips brush mine of their own accord a second time, and her dress rustles as she turns away. "I must be getting back home," she murmurs. "Curfew." For once, her eyes send out a sincere beam of feeling, no trace of mockery. I know at this moment that if she will have me, she is the one.

The last of the wedding revelers are still in full swing when I tiptoe up the stairs to my bedroom, the remnants of Marie-Amelie's scent still wafting up from my jacket. I am taking the steps two at a time when I feel long nails sink into my shoulder.

"Studying outside, Qasim?" my mother asks in her stern "I know where you've been" voice. I notice her eyelids are ringed with red, and I wonder if she is tired or upset. Perhaps she has been worried about my whereabouts, and I feel instant remorse.

"I am sorry, Mama," I say, penitence flowing out of every pore of my body. "I decided to take a walk before curfew."

"Qasim El-Kafry," she says, no trace of anger in her melodious but weary voice, "Watch yourself, my son. The Americans will be here, and then God help us all."

I have no idea what she is talking about, but I deduce it has something to do with Marie-Amelie. Yet Marie-Amelie is French, not American. I hope beyond hope that she does not know, but I know all the same that she does.

"Never forget, Qasim, that we are Arabs." Her face is hard, like the rock on the cliffs that lead down to the sea, years of the waters beating against them. Her red-rimmed eyes make me afraid that there is no way of escaping my destiny.

I want to argue, I do. I want to explain that I am of a new generation, that times are changing, that I am in love, that race and ethnicity are of no consequence. I cannot argue with destiny. I am only sixteen years old, and already, my fate is sealed. My soul shouts out that I will continue seeing Marie-Amelie. What harm will it do? My brain knows there is no way we can maintain a long friendship, let alone a romance. The world is too large.

I trudge up the steps, no argument left in me. My mother, a product of this Eastern world, and I her byproduct, will be obeyed.

CHAPTER EIGHTEEN

A Certain Kind of Peace

September 28, 1961, Damascus

Syria withdraws from the United Arab Republic after a military coup. An initial step to creating a pan-Arab union, the UAR previously combined Syria and Egypt into one country, with Nasser as its president.

I turned eighteen yesterday—a special birthday—a bit of a Western concept, admittedly, but special, even by Eastern standards. *Eid Milad Sa'eed* to me. For yesterday, I became my own man. I am proud and expectant, waiting for something to take hold, showing I am changed. Today, I am still receiving my father's tuition checks and my mother's advice, but they must let me fly on my own soon.

Without knowing a thing about my recent rite of passage, Marie-Amelie will arrive in Beirut tomorrow. Her timing always was spot on.

True, Marie-Amelie and I were never allowed to become close, and distance has run its course. True, we have moved on, to separate universities, to other people, to separate lives on opposite sides of the Mediterranean. First, we stopped holding hands under café tables, then our eyes turned downward each time we passed one another in the school hallways, and then she moved back to Paris. My brother still teases me about my bout of "puppy love," especially now that I have lost my "puppy fat." Yet, she is coming back to visit a school chum, and she sent me a letter requesting an audience. She is like that—regal, demanding, and haughty. Most of the time, I forget she is even alive, but I will meet her, most assuredly, after I spend a few days fortifying myself against her pull, like the way waves push against the tug of the moon.

I stroll across the green campus square, toward one of my economics classes. I dread the class today, not because of an exam but because of a woman. I am seeing Latifa today, and she will want me to join her and the gang tomorrow. Latifa and I are an item, but I cannot bring myself to feel for her, even though I know it would probably be best for me. She is Muslim, from a good family, with a quick wit. It takes a special sort of woman to major in economics. Her eyes are full of mirth, and her face is pleasant. My mother and she would get on, I can predict without having introduced them. Yet where is that spark I felt before? Is it presumptuous to wish for that ardor again someday?

All the women I meet come and go, like breath inhaled and exhaled, almost without a second thought. Perhaps love is supposed to be this way. Breath is not supposed to linger; perhaps love is meant to be as fleeting. My chums here at university and I have a pact: we will never let women come between our success and us. Life has taught me this philosophy to be the wisest. I would love to reclaim that lost feeling I had in my youth, but perhaps that is all it was: youth. Youthful impertinence and impulsivity. Yet they all have women chosen for them; I wait. I will choose. She has to be the right fit, and only I know the right fit. I am good at waiting.

I scoot into my desk and await the professor's call to order. He writes an algorithm on the green chalkboard, and I wonder how he will use it in his lecture. It is not a stratagem that I can correlate with the subject on my syllabus. Latifa slides into her seat beside me and turns her raven lashes in my direction. Her blouse hangs on her narrow, inward-turned shoulders, and she smells of Ma Griffe, which makes me cough. I wonder if the perfume is hers or her mother's. I am already thinking of an excuse for tomorrow.

"Qasim, are you joining us?"

I give her a side-glance, continue underlining my textbook, although I have no idea what the marked text says, and clear my throat.

"Qasim?"

"Yes?" I grin at her. "Sorry? I didn't catch what you were asking." She looks like a rabbit in a hutch, with some sort of furry hairpiece twisted around her thick, tied hair. The lengths that women take to avoid looking human! She really ought to cut her hair into one of the new bobs; it must take her hours to wash and dry. She needs to wipe off some of her make-up.

"What are you reading, Qasim? We didn't even have an assignment."

"Didn't you know? We have an exam today."

"No!" Her eyes widen, and I remember what attracted me to her the first day of class. She is relentlessly trusting.

"Oh, yes." I look back down at the blurry words on the page I've haphazardly turned to. It takes fortitude to hold my serious expression.

She begins rifling through her notes. "I don't…there's nothing in the syllabus to… Where did you get this information?"

I feel the merest flicker of a sneer on the corner of my upper lip, but I manage to suppress it. "You must have left class early last time."

Her eyes widen more, and her jaw drops. "I did not! Qasim El-Kafry, you little liar!" She turns away from me, and I feel guilt at my delight at her discomfiture. She annoys me to no end at this moment. Perhaps she won't speak to me for a few days, and I can rendezvous with Marie-Amelie without even needing to offer an excuse.

The professor marches to his desk and begins shuffling papers. I shift my posture and begin to listen. The algorithm on the board relates to a new economic theory, and my professor is writing a paper on it. I wonder if undergraduates are allowed to co-author articles. I ignore the air of disdain coming my way from the desk beside me. A cool breeze blows through the window. I await the night and my tomorrow.

***

I watch Marie-Amelie as I walk toward her, hoping my stride contains swagger instead of hesitancy. Most people would say she looks precisely the same. Her back faces me as I cross the campus, zigzagging: I am late. I got involved in a conversation with a professor. It followed a fascinating lecture on macroeconomic theory. I take long steps, reminding myself to ask about undergraduate co-authors. I have at least six more years of school before I can finally do something with my life! Even more should I pursue a PhD. I should like to become a professor, but I should also like to try my hand at business.

Marie-Amelie's hair is cropped short, and I am pleased to see that she is thin without being gaunt, and her dress is quite chic. I will shop in Paris for my wife one day. She seems to sense me, turns, and there is that mouth again, that perfect "O" of pleasure, surprise, recognition. She pushes her hair behind her ear, and her earring glints in the sunlight, lighting up her face. I almost stumble, so swept away by it all. After all, I haven't seen her in two years.

She watches me advance. At rest, her mouth still curves in a sardonic smile below her straight Roman nose. Her eyes retain the sparkle I remember. I walk toward her, kiss both her cheeks, and take in the smell of French-milled soap and a shampoo smelling like lavender.

"*Ca va?*" she asks, a wry smile playing on the corners of her mouth, her perfect teeth grazing her bottom lip.

"*Ca va bien,*" I reply. "*Tres, tres bien.* All goes well."

"What are you doing these days?" Her eyes, like crystal Mediterranean water, blink a few times in expectancy.

I don't know what she wants to hear, so I repeat myself. "All goes well. My studies, my life. Already there is talk in my family that I should go into the family's business. And you?"

"More of the same." Her eyes shift up to the sky. I can see she wants no more questions, and her friends prevent any further discussion.

Introductions ensue, but I cannot even remember faces, let alone names. I only recognize one girl, a mutual friend of ours from high school. Her friends mill and disperse a bit to give us space. I wonder what she has told them about me.

It's not the same; I want it to be the same, but it's not the same. I am still drawn to her, but we have become different people, and the gap is more than geography. She is Grace Kelly smooth, and I still have my rough edges. I touch her shoulder, and she angles away from me. She looks my way, and I am uncomfortable returning her gaze.

A young man from Kuwait is speaking to a crowd of students, and Marie-Amelie moves closer, perhaps to hear him better. "Yes, we are very, very exuberant," he says, as he rolls his watch back and forth on his wrist. "We are finally free! We have been under British control for nearly a century!"

"But isn't having British troops based there also bad?" Marie-Amelie interjects and moves still closer. "It can't be much different."

"Oh, but it is," the young man says, and his eyes get wide, his feet shift as though the energy he possesses inside is trying to escape. The man is much too intense for me. "The Iraqi invasion keeps them there," he continues.

"I would feel a bit uneasy, even so," Marie-Amelie sends her steady gaze into his darting eyes, trying to pin him down in the moment, trying to see what is behind his fervor. I know, because she has done it countless times with me, tried to see behind my words, sometimes even my thoughts. "Iraq on one hand, and the Brits on the other."

"Oh, Iraq will always be with us." He laughs. "We go back a long way. But these are booming times for Kuwait. Iraq has been thwarted, for now."

"Aren't you worried about your size and small military budget?" another man interrupts. He has a much darker complexion and is very tall. Who knows where he was born; it is difficult to guess.

"Iraq won't dare do anything now," the young man says, brushing the question off, and the conversation is over. No more questions asked. I have several, but all I want to do is get Marie-Amelie away from this crowd. I have a gift for her, a gift I bought when she lived here, but I was never brave enough to offer it to her.

We walk along Bliss Street, amid the smell of water pipes and strong coffee and spice. The day is beautiful; the sun is strong enough. "Want a bite to eat?" I offer, but she shakes her head no. We walk on, glad in each other's company, but I can't help but concentrate on her leaving. "Let's sit over here, in the shade," I suggest, and wave my hand toward a large crepe myrtle. I push my hand deep into my trousers pocket and turn the leather box over and over. We sit without conversation for a while, and she seems perfectly comfortable.

Finally, she speaks. "I heard your father wants you in the family business, even before you mentioned it." She turns a ring around on her right hand, still not looking at me. "I heard it all the way in France."

"I am still not certain I will take him up on it," I answer.

She looks at me with those sea-eyes of hers, and her look is that of parent to child. "Oh, I believe you will," she says. "It is the sensible thing to do." She laughs then, not a full laugh, but a melodious one, and her eyes become moist. I am not aware of the joke.

"And you?" I try to take her hand, but she pulls it away.

"Oh, I will marry a French nobleman, and he will take me away to his *chateau*, where we will live happily-ever-after. *Bien sur,* only after I spend the proper amount of time earning the wages of a French schoolmarm." We both laugh; the picture she has drawn is not that of a life either of us would wish for her, but right here, right now, it seems a viable one.

I pull the box out of my pocket. "I have something for you," I murmur.

"A souvenir?" Her eyes have a mocking quality, but I push on. I open the box, and remove a delicate silver chain. A circle, studded with turquoise and garnets, hangs from it, entwining a Christian cross. I knew it was meant for Marie-Amelie the moment I saw it. She stares at it for what seems eons before she takes the cross in her hand, turns it over, examines the back, and turns it over again. She raises the cross, pressing its silver against her lips that form a perfect circle. When she looks up at me, her eyes are tear-filled, more of the sea in them than ever. Never looking away, she puts the chain round her neck and fastens the clasp.

"Oh, merci, cher Qasim," she whispers. I begin to speak, to start an ordinary conversation, much like the one we had two years ago. I even begin, but I don't get very far. We sit and look at each other. I try to memorize her face, but I know I will forget. "I can't stay, you know," she says, simply, sadly. She brushes the air with her hand, a resigned gesture. "My family is waiting dinner for me."

"I know," I say, and I touch her lips, then the circle at her neck. She rises, places a kiss on my forehead, between my eyes, then one at my right temple. Then she turns, and in an uncharacteristic motion, races down the road. Once, she turns back and waves. I raise my hand, but I haven't the strength to wave back. It hangs, suspended in the air like her whisper.

She is gone, and I will never, ever forget her.

CHAPTER NINETEEN

Surrender

June 5-10, 1967, the West Bank, formerly the Directorate of Palestine

Following the build-up of Arab troops on Israeli borders and the closing of the Strait of Tiran, Israel attacks. After six days of war with Syria, Iraq, Jordan, and Egypt, Israel declares victory and occupies the West Bank.

I never noticed the brightness of the moon before I began my private rides up the steep sides of Mt. Lebanon. Its light glints off the windshield of my bright red convertible, making it a dull black next to the luminosity surrounding it: the glow of the desert in this otherwise verdant countryside. I wonder if the sands of the moon resemble the sands of Arabia. They say soon the Russians may walk its surface. They are racing to beat the Americans to see these lunar sands. I wonder if it will all be worth it in the end. Gliding through space would be enough for me. I have seen sand, touched it, sniffed it before. It has run through my fingers and crunched beneath my feet. I doubt sand is the reason for this competition. Strange how they think they can rule the earth by conquering the sands of the moon.

I come up here when I need to think, but the moon has distracted me tonight. I close my eyes to banish its seduction. Oh, how I wish I were on my way to the moon tonight, a place with no precedents, no rules. I shall always have the need to return here to these sands, these rules, these expectations. I feel tears sting my eyes, and I will them to be gone. I must do what is right here on earth, not dream about the moon. I am only human, pulled down by the earth's gravity. I cannot escape it on my own.

One deep breath, deep from the caverns within me, and I must return. My engagement will be announced tonight. I cannot shame my parents with a late arrival. How would it look in the society column if the future groom should arrive late?

The woman and I have spoken several times, and she seems pleasant enough. We have similar backgrounds and plans. She is a bit skinny for my taste, but I cannot argue that the match is not an advantageous one for my family. It is difficult to get to know a woman when chaperoned, though, and she seems ill inclined to get to know me before the wedding night. She looks down when I ask her a question; she pulls her hand away when I try to touch it; she wants to speak of decorating instead of life. She seems pliable enough, however; and perhaps, *In'sh'Allah,* I can shape her into something more. She is younger than I, and again, God willing, we will bear a son. My mother assures me my future wife desperately wants to please me and that her blushes and downward gaze indicate she is smitten with me. I wish I could share her feelings. That should come also. God willing.

The kitchen has the familiar scent of roast lamb. The wind blows the door shut behind me, and I wonder if tomorrow will bring rain. Our former nanny turned housekeeper, Haneefa, sits at her familiar place at the table, preparing part of tomorrow night's mezza. She beams at me as I enter but cringes when the door slams.

"Careful, Master Qasim," she intones.

"Come now, Haneefa," I chide. "That door has withstood almost thirty years of three boys running in and out of it. Why should it collapse in a little wind?"

"It is not the wind that concerns me." She frowns. "It is you. You are not with us; you have been in another world all week."

I stride toward her, wishing I could hug her waist as I did when I was a boy. That would not be proper. Instead, I cover my eyes with the palm of my hand, making sure they are smiling and impish when I remove it.

"Dear, dear Haneefa, what will you do without your little boy to worry about? Is it not normal for a man to be preoccupied when he is betrothed?"

She shakes her head up and down, then side to side, as she stirs with her wooden spoon. "Come now, Master Qasim, talk with me. Tell me. What is it that is on your mind?"

I stroll over, sit at the table across from her, and shrug, first one shoulder, then the other.

"What is it?" she repeats.

"I am sure I do not know," I reply. *What's gotten into her?* I wish she would stop staring at me.

"Qasim," she begins, but purses her lips as though she is trying to find words for what is bothering her, or perhaps she is trying to spare my feelings. I almost chuckle at the thought of this. Haneefa does not usually mince words. "Remember when you were a boy and you asked me to read your coffee cup?"

I laugh. Leave it to Haneefa to come up with some supernatural explanation for my behavior. "Of course," I reply, "but it was not my coffee cup. It was Baba's. You would not let me drink coffee then. I had to sneak it."

"No, what it said was meant for you," she says and screws up her wizened eyes. "Do you remember what I told you?"

I grin, search for my lighter, light my cigarette, and sit down with her at the table. I try to determine what the rest of her face looks like underneath her veil. How has it changed from the face I held dear ten years ago? It is difficult to imagine after all this time, but to know would give me more information about her thoughts. "You told me I was destined for greatness. You told me that I would travel afar. You told me that I would find true love. You see, Haneefa, I never forget a thing."

"You indeed have a good memory, Master Qasim. So why do you not use your keen mind to help Allah map your destiny? Have you found true love, Master Qasim?" Haneefa ceases her stirring and looks through her wrinkled eyelids, waiting and watching for my response.

I feel wetness behind my eyelids once more, and I struggle to banish the burgeoning tears and to meet Haneefa's penetrating gaze. We are silent for a long time, she waiting and me trying to balance composure with the wisdom that is hitting me hard.

"Haneefa, you are a good woman, a good Muslim woman. You know sometimes one has to do something for the end result. My parents have told me that love will come."

Haneefa shakes her head, back and forth, back and forth. The rest of her body remains motionless. "For most of God's children, I would agree," she says, and there is not a trace of a waver in her voice. "You are different, my Qasim. The coffee grounds bear this out. Yours will not be a traditional life." Her eyes smile, and I imagine her upturned lips and the openings where teeth once were rooted. "You will follow your destiny, Master Qasim, whether you marry this woman or not. Master Qasim, let me tell you a story."

I sit back in my chair and wait to savor her tale, another memory of me in her lap, with her stroking my thick, damp hair, before sleep. "Continue," I advise her.

"Listen, my ward, and I will tell you a *zajal*."

Haneefa stops stirring, letting the long spoon fall with a thunk against the side of the bowl. She leans across the table toward me, and for a moment, I believe she may reach for my hands, but then she folds her hands, which have grown smaller with age, in her lap.

"There was once a merchant who had a prosperous business. His only son, who was dashing and possessed *kayr*, was eligible for marriage. The merchant began serious contemplation of the most suitable wife, and he knew he could negotiate a perfect union because of his successful business and his son's charisma. He prayed each day at morning and evening prayers for divine guidance, and for his path to be shown, so he could make the right decision.

"After much deliberation, his eyes chose two women deserving further contemplation. One was a beauty, with braids down her back and a waist the size of a thimble. The other was matronly and loud, but her family was renowned and prosperous. Just after *'isha*, the man made his decision. He would ask for the matronly bride first, but he would tell his son it was *al-mut'a*, temporary. Then the merchant would make his new daughter-in-law so miserable she would sacrifice her dowry and demand divorce. His son would then be free to pursue the beauty of the village, and in the end, the family would gain two dowries in place of one."

I rub my hands together, impatient to get on with the story. "And then? And then?" I ask and lean forward over Haneefa's folded hands.

"And then, nothing," Haneefa sighs. "The father was mean, evil even, but the new bride either didn't care because of her improved circumstances, or because she was ashamed of *talaq*, her reputation, or because she and the son were truly happy together. The marriage—and the dowry—stuck."

I clear my throat. I am uncomfortable with this story, but I want to hear its ending nonetheless. She must be telling me that I should be sure of what I'm doing. Marriage is irreversible. "Go on," I command, and feel my throat closing again.

Haneefa's eyes twinkle over her veil. I wonder if she is laughing at me. "The father could not understand why his efforts had come to nothing. He had concocted the perfect plan; he wanted the best for his son. Yet, he finally gave up hope. Then, one evening, he went up the stairs to his son's dwelling quarters, and he found the two of them. Never had he witnessed such passion! Never had he even imagined what was taking place under his own roof every night. The old man chuckled. Only God's will is destined! He had prayed, and Allah had answered. He had unwittingly done for his son what he had hoped to do, with God's help." She stirs again. The spoon clinks the sides of the bowl. She ends her tale as she always has: "Then this story is ended. They stayed there, and I came here."

I unfold my fingers and rub the new shadow on my chin. *The woman confounds me.* "What are you saying? That I shall be happy or unhappy? That I should follow my heart or no?"

Haneefa rises and takes the bowl to the counter, her eyes smiling but with little mirth in them. "I am saying neither, Qasim." She shifts to remain standing on her elderly limbs. "I am saying no one—not even you—can escape Destiny."

I do not want to pursue this matter further; she has shaken loose some part of me that I struggle to contain. I get up, walk to the doorway, turn as if I have something to say, but I cannot find it. She stands there stirring, and I know I will remember this moment, too. It is a curse to remember everything, never to banish a single memory. I turn once again. Does she believe that I have a choice? How can an old woman who had no choices herself dare to tell me that I can escape when she never could? I have no choice. I have no choice. There are no words to express my desolation.

***

The guests begin to arrive, the women in sparkling long gowns, every color of the rainbow, the men forming their own circle on the room's outer edges. They stand, smoke, and drink in their stiff black and white. They crowd even our large entertaining area and spill out to the garden. Tables covered with delicate lace line two walls. A dancing area has been cleared, and a sax sends out its tempting invitation to take to the floor. Smoke and noise veil every corner of the room as the guests puff and chatter. The noise transforms itself to an amorphous buzzing in my head. I long for a cigarette, reach into my pocket, but feel only the square of my lighter. I've left my cigarettes upstairs. I begin to perspire; my only thought one of nicotine, and the room reels and pitches.

I vaguely greet, smile, and try to maintain a superficial equilibrium. This is the first time in my life I have felt I might faint. The room is close and steamy and strangely still despite all the noisy guests. *Who are all of these people anyway?* I recognize only a minority of them.

My bride-to-be arrives, amid much clamor. Inside of me, everything is still, and I lean against the wall. My mother casts a glaring eye in my direction. This is a double infringement of rules—I am not greeting our guests, and I am contaminating the wall.

My bride—her name is Rasha—turns her dark, full moon, chinless face toward me, and her eyes give me a shy acknowledgement. I return her silent salutation, contorting my leaden lips into a wide smile, showing all my teeth. I feel my eyes crinkle at the edges. *Well done*, I tell myself. We seat ourselves. The guests mill and flow round us, greeting each other and kissing the hands of their elders. Servants bring trays of grape leaves stuffed with rice, thyme, mint, caviar, and flutes of the best French champagne, a conciliatory gesture by the bride's family, which is of a more conservative bent than my own. I thank God for the alcohol, which may be the only way I can quell the panic rising deep in my belly.

I must admit my bride is more becoming than I've ever seen her. Her cheeks take on a rosy tone, and the scarf that drapes her neck accents the darkness of her eyes. One can almost get past the roundness of her face, if only it didn't look like a pumpkin on a scarecrow's body. I walk toward her, hoping to speak to her before the women begin their traditional dancing.

"You look lovely," I stammer.

"You are too kind," she answers, her cheeks flame, and she looks at my shoes.

I twist my hands together. "I hope this is all to your liking, what my parents have arranged."

"Oh, yes," she replies and gazes at her shoes. "It is truly magnificent. You have a beautiful home." The band strikes up in a song, half jazz, half nomadic. The rhythm is off kilter. They must not want the dancing to begin just yet. I want to know how she feels, if we share the same fears, but I dare not pursue it. I can think of no more trivialities, so I turn on my heel and walk to the wall again.

My parents look positively royal tonight, standing with Rasha's parents, marrying off their youngest. My mother is dressed in peach chiffon, and my father stands stiff in his perfectly tailored tux. My mother beckons me to join them.

"Rasha's parents were expressing their joy to us, habibi," my mother beams. "We thought they should tell you themselves."

"Ah yes," I reply and shuffle my feet.

"Well?" My mother raises an eyebrow. My father puts his hands behind his back and sticks his chest out.

"We are so very happy for you both," my future mother-in-law says. She has a squeaky voice like a Disney character, some woodchuck or something. Or perhaps it is a chipmunk.

I usually love suits, but I would give the world to take off this tux. I, who am never at a loss for words, search for inspiration. What does one express when wished joy? Gratitude? Agreement? Yet this is no mutual decision.

"Qasim." My mother's voice is sharp, and I recall the wooden spoon days. I know I must find words.

"It is a pleasure to join your family," I finally blurt out, and I see all four sets of shoulders relax, although Rasha's father gives mine a look of begrudging concern.

"My son will see that he brings as much joy to your daughter as she is bringing all of us tonight," my father says. "Another drink?" He leads

Rasha's father over to the bar, and I am left with the two mothers, mine small and insistent, the other stodgy and judging. They look at me, then at each other. My mother opens her mouth to speak.

My brothers save me. They come, clap me around my elbows, and practically carry me to the bar, where the fathers are finishing.

"A man's work is never done," Rayik jests. "Why were you standing there mute, Qasim? Cat got your tongue for once?" They laugh at me, hearty laughter, at my expense.

I still have nothing to say.

The music picks up, and the women begin their gyrations. It is time for the men to retire to the next room.

The rest of the evening passes in a blur. I receive congratulations from every side of the room as I express my condolences to myself.

Why me?

Love will come.

What can I do?

Be patient. All will right itself.

Why must I do this?

I love my family. I love my country. This must be my backbone, my Rasha. Love will come.

I am drawn to the conversation on the most recent regional war in the opposite corner of the room. Two men sit in my father's leather chairs smoking cigars. "Don't you think they will continue to advance?" one man asks.

My uncle, hands gesticulating back and forth, spits into the air. "They wouldn't dare! They would be backed by neither superpower."

"I am uncertain that they care, or even that they had such backing in the first place. It matters very little. They have the firepower, the capital, and the religious zeal."

"Firepower given them by our Western friends."

"Oh yes. Mark my words, brothers; we are but pawns in the great scheme of things. Little jewel of a country, much coveted, much maligned, but always claimed by others. We will need to fight to maintain our independence."

"Do we stand a chance?"

"Of course we do!"

"It would help if the Palestinians wouldn't launch their incursions from our southern borders," I manage to interject, before I regret having spoken. I do not want to call attention to my demeanor tonight. I want to bring my parents pride, not shame, and I cannot stop perspiring. In fact, I am beginning to shake. I take another long drink.

"I do not believe in the end the threat will come from Israel. Look at how our streets have changed. Beirut is not safe as it once was. Israel is but the catalyst in our house of dominoes. The ultimate threat, gentlemen, comes from within," a man in long tails intones.

I can stand it no longer. Ordinarily, I would have been the first to cast myself into the fray, questioning, disputing. Tonight, talk of war from within is too much for me. I stride toward the door to take my leave, remember the betrothal harem in the next room, stop in my tracks, trapped. I consider climbing out the window. I smile to myself, remembering my mother standing at the edge of the drainpipe shaking her head with folded arms, a recurrent image from my childhood. Only this time I would be a betrothed adult guest of honor in a tux. Sweat pours down my face and drips down inside my collar, adding further discomfiture. I must find a way out.

The music stops. The women retire for refreshment. I dash through the room and outside through the portico. The moon looks down at our land from its high cloud. Is it mocking me or signaling its complicity? Perhaps it is showing me how little things change in one fleeting lifetime. I imagine sand seeping through an hourglass. Each grain represents another moment gone. Each time I blink brings me closer to marriage. I never think of time as concrete, as sand. Time is fluid, an elastic continuum, flowing in every direction. *What has gotten into me?*

I wipe my brow, run my finger around the inside of my collar. Continue to breathe. This is what I shall remember most from my engagement night: the moon.

The next thing I know, the party is ending. She and her extensive family are departing. Congratulations all around, a light touch of felicitation, a sympathetic eyebrow raised, a bear hug as I join the league of men. A knowing, envious gaze acknowledges my newfound identity, my increased status. Betrothed. I am marrying into a political dynasty. Who knows what my future will bring with the merger of these two families?

I know I must see the moon again. I need the wind blowing on my skin, and I need to be above the city, to gaze out upon the sea, the slow gossamer mist of gentle waves cast in moonlit bronze. I nearly catapult into my convertible, and I become more at ease at every shift of the gears. I speed out of Beirut to the hills.

It is not much different from earlier in the evening, but I have changed. I jerk the car to a halt at the top of my favorite ridge and pat my pocket. Still no cigarettes.

My breathing quickens, and I close my eyes to still it. What shall I do?

I do the only thing that makes sense. The champagne, the nervous energy, the lack of sleep over the last week takes hold of me. I close my eyes and sleep.

When I waken, my legs tingle, cramped under the steering wheel. The moon has moved high and distant in the early morning sky. The wind has quickened. The shimmering sea beckons me, and I decide to answer its call. I head up higher, ridge after ridge echoing the cresting waves below. "May God forgive me," I whisper, as I speed faster and faster. My vision is blurred, whether from the champagne or emotion, I care not to know. On and on, the speedometer climbs with the altitude. Soon, soon, I will be on my way, the only way, my only answer.

I realize I am praying, reciting the ninety-nine names of God. I long again for a cigarette and laugh. Funny, how that is my last thought. Then it is done, before I even realize it. I am careening out into space toward that round, sandy moon in its perpetual orbit. I sense a jolt, and then I am flying. Serenity hits me like a wall, stopping all thought and emotion. I blink. I seem to be able to fly forever. Perhaps I *will* reach the heavens.

Then my head jolts against something very sharp, jagged, and I feel a seeping at my scalp. I attempt to raise my hand to determine its cause, but I cannot move. The moon still shines, moving ever forward on its trajectory, but I close my eyes to it, too weary to keep them open. The blackness seeps into my eyes, my heart, my very soul.

So begins my prenuptials, and my marriage is much the same. My hospital stay lasts months, and my wedding comes quickly on the heels of it. I survive one coma only to walk in a daze, yearning for unconsciousness to overtake me again.

CHAPTER TWENTY

Little Soldier

February 1982, New York

"You know, Qasim, the market's quite competitive at the moment. We might be able to renegotiate those contracts." Jamal sits in front of me, his hands between his knees. "Qasim?"

Jamal's tone runs up my spine like harsh electricity. *How dare he? How dare Jamal speak to me as though I have the ability to make any changes now? He knows I have a new boss.* I must pass any strategy through him. It would be scrutinized.

"Look, Jamal," I point out, trying to hide my anger, "I prefer to stay out of all this."

Jamal smiles, not altogether an unpleasant smile, but a knowing one. "Qasim, you will need to take some risks to get through this career. Think of yourself, your future. Think of your country."

I do think of Beirut. In fact, it has been an obsession lately. I wonder which buildings still stand along the Green Line. I wonder if the pharmacy in my old neighborhood still has that pharmacist I liked, or whether he has left along with everyone else. I wonder if my old playground remains since children must stay indoors. Most of all, I wonder about the cedars.

"Let me think on it," is what I say instead.

When Jamal leaves, my thoughts turn from Beirut to Dianna. I have nothing to offer her. I shouldn't have let myself go last night. That night before I knew all of this was about to unwind. It was unlike me to act impulsively. How can a woman as sheltered as Dianna understand my dilemma? I cannot even form the words in Arabic. How can I present an acceptable argument in English? No, she can never understand the workings of my world.

Yet she continues to beckon me. She has changed me, somehow. There is something familiar about her, her scent both sweet and unsettling. I would love to take her along the Ponte Vecchio, buy her some gold for her long neck. I long to have her beside me at events, on my arm when I fish for the right words. Next to me in bed during those long, cold nights when I search for inspiration. She gives me hope.

Of course, I must keep up appearances. I cannot tell her the real story, or I will lose her. No American woman is going to play second fiddle to an ex-wife, nor can I imagine Dianna interacting with my brothers. My father would most likely cut me off for a time, if not disown me outright. I cannot tell Dianna how a young woman, a young *American* woman, will be viewed by those in power, to those whose help I need to help me further my goals for the world, for peace. That is what is real. That is what needs to be focused on. Not the way she touches me. Not the way I feel when I sit beside her, when I take her coat from her shoulders, when I hear her voice on the other end of a phone.

Just yesterday at the embassy, a young, Arab woman stepped out of her car, and all eyes turned on her in disdain. She wasn't wearing the right clothes, the right makeup. Her hair wasn't right at all. And she was all alone. I felt ashamed for her. It was only an instant, and then I turned away as the attendant asked if he could take my coat. What if that had been Dianna? Could I have withstood the scrutiny? Could I have stood by while those men looked her up and down? Could I have remained silent while they whispered under their breath, picking her apart? The way she showed her teeth when she smiled? The way she looked men straight in the eye? All those things that make me desire her and yet make her unattainable.

Dianna will undo me.

A family of influence has differences, I will start to explain to her. But she wouldn't listen to that. It means next to nothing to her. I can already feel her disdain for the hypocrisy I will begin to describe to her. She is a woman who believes in honor and integrity and naively believes the world to be pure. I won't be able to persuade her that things are different when one deals with countries riddled with poverty, ignorant because of lack of education and opportunity, and decimated by war.

Besides, every time she comes into my view, the words fail me, and all my prepared speeches evaporate. I will myself to stop thinking and return to my desk with the sun shining on the work I have yet to look at today.

I sift through the pile of papers my secretary has left me. A dam in Bahrain that will bring water. A negotiation in Gaza. Nothing yet about a resolution in Lebanon.

I press my head into my cupped hands, eyes closed, and feel the sun on my back. For some reason, I see my mother's face. How long has she been gone? Six years? Seven? I am not one to notice time lapse. I miss her so. What would she say? Duty? Or love? If it even *is* real love. What is that anyway?

Divorce is the same all over. War is not. Dianna is a nice girl, though she runs rather hot and cold. I need more time to know what my future brings. I need more time to see if she fits in it. I need to find some sort of peace before I can tend to love. Yet the war has been going on since I was four or five.

***

My mother tells me we are "at war." I am uncertain what this means. I wait to see bombers flying overhead, the ones I've seen on the Allies' newsreels. The only different thing I can see is that we turn off all of our lights at night. Sometimes they go out all by themselves. Sometimes Haneefa goes around snuffing them. My brothers and I hide to frighten each other, sending delicious, blood-curdling screams down the hallways.

Hours pass, days pass, and still, not one bomber overhead. I go out on my balcony first thing after waking and before prayers at dusk and then again right before I climb into bed. Yet I hear nothing save the calls of the night birds. I see nothing save the twinkling lights of ships loading from the port. The same stars send out their constant light; the same cobalt sky canopies our garden.

Then one morning, a week after my mother has made the pronouncement of "war," I amble into the kitchen to find her sobbing. Her head rests in her delicate palms. Her elbows rest on the long, marred table that Haneefa also uses as a cutting board. Her tears flow out of the corners of her big, dark eyes, hanging for a moment on her lashes, then drop to the mosaic tile below. I notice they create a crescent pattern—well, almost a crescent—each tear improperly formed, asymmetrical. Not closed like a true crescent, as though someone has taken a bite from its tip, as I do from my crescent roll, strolling home from the boulangerie, hoping not to get a scolding, but savoring the fresh butter taste on my tongue.

I snap myself out of my reverie, both fascinated and shaken by this unusual scene. I have never seen my mother weep. I did not even know she could. "What is it, Mama?" I go to her and run my fingers up her arm. She would normally brush me away, but for now, she lets my hand linger. She does lift her head and wipe her eyes, which still overflow with unshed feeling. Then, a long moment later, she caresses my cheek, turns her head, and rises.

"Do you want sahoor?" she asks. "This is your last chance to eat an early breakfast. Dawn is almost upon us."

I had forgotten it was the first day of Ramadan. This is the first year that I am to fast, about which I am of two minds. I am flushed with pride to be mature enough to pay proper homage to God, but I am worried my stomach will get the best of me. It is strange to eat breakfast before getting dressed, but I consent.

"But Mama," I persist as I begin spooning my yoghurt and honey, "why were you weeping? Is it to do with the war?"

"In a way, habibi," she says and touches my cheek. I love when she does that, and it is not often enough these days. She turns away from me and begins chopping vegetables, a task reserved for Haneefa except at Ramadan.

"But it does not seem as though we are at war," I wonder aloud while I sip my yoghurt.

"Do not slurp, Qasim," my mother scolds as she chops. "We are part of the Arab world, and the Arabs are at war."

"With whom?"

"It is very complex." My mother frowns. I wonder if she understands and is trying to explain or if she herself does not understand the reason for this invisible violence. Then she continues, and I see that she does understand. "It has to do with land. Land that someone once had and lost, and then wanted back, but now, someone else owns the land, and they are being chased off it."

What if soldiers arrive at our door, order us out of our house, out of the light-filled rooms, the mosaic tile-floor kitchen with pots and herbs hanging above our rustic table, the dark wood of my father's study, the shutters that open onto the balcony from my bedroom, the fig trees and jasmine in our garden? Will they let us take our playthings, or would we be forced to leave them behind?

"These people—the Palestinians, most are farmers, some are wanderers—are fleeing from Jaffa and Haifa," my mother continues. "Thousands are flowing over our borders.

We are a small nation—a welcoming nation, yes, but this is too much. Where will they live? They're in tents and shanty villages right now," her voice rises. "And who knows? We may be next. The people—these Zionists—who want to conquer the land, they may want our land next. And we've only just established our freedom." She stops herself and looks at me.

"Go ahead," I prod. She has my devoted attention; this is quite a story. I am afraid I won't hear the end of it. She may think she has said too much already.

My mother breathes in deeply, as though she might continue, but she does not. Her frown remains, though, and that worries me. My mother is the strongest person I know. "What land have they taken?" I ask, twirling my spoon in the honey, and feigning a certain disinterest. I am at once not the least bit hungry. Jaffa and Haifa are not very far.

"It is still in Palestine, habibi, don't worry. That's several hundred kilometers away," my mother clucks as she chops and chops.

"Then why are you crying? Lebanon is not at war?" I flick a crumb onto the floor, and she slaps my hand, diverting my attention, but then my eyes come back to meet hers again.

She still hesitates. "Yes," she admits finally. "Yes. Lebanon, Syria, Transjordan, and Egypt attacked this place the Zionists call Israel today."

I must still look unsure because she continues, finally explaining something I understand. "I am worried we will not be able to procure your sister's medications."

I gasp. "She must have her medicine! She may die without her medicine!"

"Do not worry, habibi. It is far away from us, and that is where it will stay," she says to me. Then, "In'sh'Allah -- God willing, I hear her mumble under her breath.

"Israel?" I question. "Israel? Where is this Israel?"

"Haifa is right across the border. You know that."

"But that is Palestine!"

"The Jews have authority there. For now." She ruffles my hair. "Children have no need to know about this. The war will not come here. I promise. I need to find a way to get Leila's medicines." She picks up the herbs she has been chopping and stores them away.

I can't imagine having to leave my home—ever. If Islam means "peace," why must we fight at Ramadan? Why must we fight at all?

***

In answer, my mother's voice comes through, ringing in my ears, so strong I half believe she is really there. Touch. She always told me that you knew what was real by touching it. Only through touch did we know we were here at all. I reach my hand through the air, and she is gone.

FINDING HOME

"Lovers don't finally meet somewhere. They're in each other all along."
—Rumi

CHAPTER TWENTY-ONE

Art of the Possible

Dianna squirms in her seat. Qasim exchanges one crossed leg for another. The only things Dianna knew about Eva Peron before this play was that she married a famous Argentine and died young. This play starts with illegitimacy, weaves itself into a brothel, and is on its way to a woman writhing her way into Argentine politics because she attached herself to the "right" man. Dianna prays Qasim does not think she brought him to this play as some sort of hint that she too is destined for this sort of infamy.

All she wanted was a night with music and magic. Instead, they must listen to Evita explain the rules of war that exist between conniving lovers--what tricks they play on each other to get their own way, tricks that they seem to get away with. The actor seems to be pointing her finger directly at Dianna when she slings the last line out across the crowded theatre, as though she's no different from Eva Perone, that even the most committed partners are exactly like Evita.

"Want to go get a drink?" Qasim asks at intermission, and Dianna nods. Eva Peron is only on her way to fame and then death in the second act.

"I'm sorry, Qasim."

"Sorry for what?"

"Sorry that I asked you to take me to a play with these sorts of morals."

He hums "Don't Cry for Me, Argentina" a little off tune. "The music was catchy."

"The libretto left something to be desired, though."

"Li—"

"Libretto. The lyrics," she translates.

"The woman left something to be desired."

"So you knew of her?"

"She was dead before I even began," he replies, helping her on with her wrap. "I was a toddler when she passed. Her reign was brief. Yet she left her country in an awful mess."

"What do you think he saw in her?"

"That gold digger? What everyone else saw in her, Dianna."

She's about to say she doesn't want Qasim for the wrong reasons, that she's not anything like Eva, when a tall American man comes up and claps him on the back.

"Enjoying yourself?" the man asks.

"Not our cup of tea," Qasim responds and takes Dianna's hand. "May I present Miss Dianna Calloway, Michael. Dianna, please meet Mr. Michael Presston, an attorney at JP Morgan."

"My pleasure, Miss Calloway." The man's nod is almost a bow, and his suit is almost a tuxedo.

"See you on Monday, then?"

"Yes, see you Monday. Enjoy your evening."

Qasim directs Dianna down the steps and out into the street. A light freezing rain has washed the streets, and the clean smell of water hovers around them. The colored reflection of lights on wet pavement reflects on the low hanging clouds.

"So how about that drink?" he asks. "I know of a place a few blocks down."

"Do you know him well?" Dianna asks.

"Michael? No, not well. He comes and goes to give us advice on loans."

"He didn't seem very nice," Dianna posits, "though he was profoundly formal."

"He isn't very nice, Dianna. He has to say no all the time. Even when he wants to say yes."

Qasim and Dianna walk hand in hand across the street to a narrow, dimly lit lane. Their silence is comfortable. He swings her hand back and forth as they walk. A burst of lightning and an answering clap of thunder interrupt their stroll. A front has moved in. He pulls her forward to walk faster, but she is wearing her open-toed heels. She pitches forward. Raindrops begin to splatter on the pavement, and she is not able to keep up with him. She turns an ankle. She tries to let go of his hand, but he will not let go. She tries to tell him she is in pain, but another thunder boom mutes her words.

"Two more blocks to the bar," he calls back to her. She searches for their destination, but she can't see very far.

She catches sight of a figure in the distance, standing in an alley. Qasim puts his arm around her and propels her forward. Her heart quickens as the dim figure comes closer and his outline becomes more discernible. He is Arab but with much darker skin than Qasim's. He wears faded jeans, a polyester shirt, and his hair is oily. The man yells something in Arabic as they pass him, and Qasim turns abruptly on his heels. Dianna is reminded of two male alley cats. She can almost see the arching of their backs, their hair standing on end.

Qasim slings words back in Arabic, and the alley man yells again, advancing, until almost face to face with them. Qasim pulls Dianna into him and forward once more. Her ankle throbs as they advance. Then the man turns and walks in the other direction, calling out some final aspersions as he departs.

"What did he want?" she asks as Qasim guides her toward the bar. "What did he say?" She can feel the distaste the man held for her, even though she didn't understand a word. His look had been vulgar, lewd, and yet disdainful.

"He is an animal," Qasim says. "One should not pay attention to what animals have to say, right?"

How is she to get to know this man? How can she love a man she does not know? Drops of cold rain saturate her hair. Had this man been Shiite? Could a Lebanese determine if another was Shiite, Sunni, or Christian, and did their animosity from other lands extend to America, following them years after immigration? She shivers. She knows it's not the right time to ask him questions about this menacing stranger, but the time is never right.

A man in a dark raincoat comes up behind them, almost bumping into them. He, too, looks vaguely Arab. He looks as if he is going to say something to Qasim, but then moves on.

"Who was that?" Dianna asks. The man looks over his shoulder, and Qasim stops and looks after him.

"Someone from my country. I will tell you more about him soon," Qasim says. He opens the door to the restaurant, full of light and the smell of booze, and gives her a light kiss.

"We made it, you risk taker." He shakes the rain pellets off his drenched sleeves.

"I hope so," she replies.

CHAPTER TWENTY-TWO

Vows

Dianna gazes with some dissatisfaction at her reflection in her mirror. She applies eye shadow, then wipes it off, deciding on another shade that matches her eyes instead of her dress. She hates herself for caring so much about her appearance. She takes one last look at herself before answering the beep of a horn outside. She pulls open her window and yells, "Be right down!"

She's decided not to invite Qasim. The night of the play left her jarred, and she hadn't wanted to make him feel she was hinting. His recent silence makes her feel she's done the right thing. Besides, bringing him to a wedding would have pulled on her heartstrings more than showing up solo. Her colleague is to be married at an exclusive country club in Long Island. The union is one of economic convenience as much as mutual affection. Dreading the false chatter and painted smiles she will need to muster, she squeezes herself into a dress that is a smidgeon too snug in the hips.

Her car is leaking oil, and Leah is coming late from work as Dianna's plus-one, so Dianna asked a co-worker for a ride. She hates asking him, halfway hoping he doesn't interpret her request as an overture, embarrassed he might be interested in someone squeezed into a dress a size too small for her. She rushes past a woman goading her child with an ice cream cone, past a man in a tattered, baggy coat, a coat that is as large on him as Dianna's dress is snug on her. The homeless man flips Dianna the bird as she opens the long, low-to-the-ground car door. She slips into the narrow bucket seat and rests her knee on the gearshift.

"Careful," her colleague warns her. "That thing is sensitive. You might shift us into neutral by accident. A big mistake in this traffic."

She smiles her apology and tries to think of something other than the sunny day to converse about.

"So, Dan," she begins, "Are you doing any business travel lately?"

"Going to Italy soon. You know they found another town buried by Vesuvius: Herculaneum."

"Yes, I've been reading about that." She typed a letter for her boss about the dig the day before.

"It's yielding more archaeological and anthropological finds than Pompeii," Dan continues. "Fascinating stuff."

Dianna tries to be interested, but bones and dust do not interest her as much as the suffering of the living. She loses track until Dan mentions a woman found at the site. Her attention pulls up short, like a car about to rear-end another car's bumper. The scientists are analyzing the remains chemically to ascertain whether the young woman was a slave or a mother.

"She was found huddled over and shielding a child's face. It happened too fast for anyone to react. They were doomed." Dan's eyes dart around the road as if he's imagining the scene. His foot presses down on the accelerator.

Dianna gropes for a response. "How sad," she finally replies.

"For them," he sniffs. "Probably the find of the century for us. One human's pain is another's gain."

At least he said human. Dianna gazes down at the gearshift, at Dan's long fingers that resemble the spokes on a spinning wheel, searching for another topic of conversation.

"So, did you watch the game last night?" Dan asks her.

Dianna rolls her eyes and recoils away from him, the doorknob catching her in a rib. She's in for a play-by-play account.

***

Cold in its elegance, the country club reminds her of a three-tiered rectangular wedding cake, wrought forever in marble, with green icing spreading out on every horizon. She can feel her lungs expanding, contracting, as she anticipates climbing the stone steps to the grand porch above: a plump Cinderella without a fairy godmother to transform her for the ball. The valet is opening her door, so she takes a deep breath and advances toward the terrace. Her ride waves and advances in the opposite direction, probably happy to see others who are more interested in yesterday's game than Dianna is.

Dianna searches for a familiar face. The couple beside the door is sneering into each other's eyes and discussing their psychotherapy. Dianna walks in the other direction. She's not a fan of therapy. She imagines sitting for hours across from a skeletal Freudian with a beard and glasses, sucking on his pencil, writing down observations about how she acts, how many times she crosses her legs, how she refers to her mother. She spies a colleague with long, raven hair and black eyes. Carolee. Her hair is wrapped in a bun today, and she is dressed in pink. She advances toward Carolee, hearing snippets of a conversation along the way. Two men to her right chat about "Beemers." A man and woman to her left talk about bakeries. Dianna longs for champagne to dull the boredom creeping up her spine.

She plasters a smile on her face. "Carolee!" she exclaims. "Isn't this a lovely setting?"

It is a beautiful place, with floral décor surrounding a huge marble fireplace and seasonal fruit. White and yellow table bouquets in gold vases are everywhere the eye can see.

"I'm in absolute *awe.*" Carolee's eyes glisten. "Awe! I mean, have you *ever* seen such a place? I feel so lucky to be invited. I mean, do you want to look around, or go sit down and wait for the service to begin?"

"Isn't the service about to start?" Dianna asks. "We'd better beat the crowd in there." She leads Carolee to the ushers, who wear yellow roses in their lapels but have whiskey on their breath.

The service is sedate enough. The bride's hair still looks wet, and Dianna focuses on a spreading water stain gradually ruining the tapered neckline of an otherwise exquisite satin bridal gown. The groom recites his vows in a sonorous voice, more like a ringmaster at a circus than a groom at the altar. Carolee fishes for a handkerchief in her purse. As the best man hands the wedding ring to the groom, it glints in late afternoon winter sunlight before rolling to the floor. A bridesmaid runs after it and catches it seconds before it can disappear under the rows of seating. Her dress rustles and sways as she rushes to return the ring to the groom. The bride looks down at the ring as the groom slips it on her finger. There!

Dianna wonders at her ability to remain unmoved. The magic of nursery rhymes and operas didn't translate into lasting reality. She has never pictured herself on an aisle in a white dress. She wants love, not legal wedlock, with the emphasis on *lock*. She wants to partner and journey with a kindred spirit who wants to help the world with her. Then again, her apathy at a gold ring and a legal document may be a touch of resilient denial at not having a chance at marriage, especially a marriage to Qasim. She'd admitted that marriage to an Arab diplomat was unlikely. Her parents' uneasy, distant marriage had been simple compared to being wed to a diplomat. "Twinkle, Twinkle Little Star" as opposed to "The Magic Flute." Look how Mozart's life had turned out.

The reception is as grandiose as the chandelier it takes place beneath: caviar, smoked salmon, vintage champagne. Some sort of mystery meat everyone raves about. Most people are in long gowns, and Dianna pulls her skirt over her knees. She decides to stand in the corner nearest the ladies' room, in case she needs to beat a hasty retreat. She pastes a cheerleader smile on her face and sips her drink. She hopes to fade into the shadows of the hallway, but a man soon approaches her and puts his arm around her, spilling champagne down her back.

"You have great teeth," the man says.

"Thank you," Dianna replies. She backs into the hallway toward the restroom, but the man takes no notice. He follows her.

"You don't work at the museum, do you?" he asks.

"Yes, but you wouldn't know me. I work off the main floor."

"I know I would have noticed you if I'd seen you, with those teeth." The man moves in for a better look.

"I never thought much about my teeth." Dianna backs further toward her refuge.

"You should smile more often," the drunken man says.

"Yes, I've been told that," Dianna replies. She turns away.

He wedges her between the door jam and the wall, slants his arm over her head, resting it on the wall above her. "Want to get some fresh air?" he asks, and she can smell something besides the champagne on his breath, a chemical smell, like formaldehyde.

"Yes, thanks," she says and slips from under his arm and into the safety of the ladies' room.

Dianna licks the sweat from her upper lip. She turns toward a mirror for the second time that day, ready to assess the damage wrought. Instead, behind her reflection, she sees Leah and hears the announcer calling the bride and groom to the dance floor.

"Leah?"

"Hey, Dianna." Leah sidles up to the sink, runs her hand under the water, pumps liquid soap out in bulk. Dianna opens her purse and digs for lipstick.

"How's the party going?" Leah pouts into the mirror, puckering her lips. "A little lipstick wouldn't hurt, but I didn't bring anything but my driver's license." She points to her bra.

"Here, try mine." Dianna hands Leah her peach lipstick, thinking it will be too subtle for Leah's darker skin. How Leah can have a tan in December when she can't have one in August is a mystery.

"I'm having a blast." Leah sighs. "Never the bridesmaid. Never the bride. Never the one with a hunk on her arm. She smiles her one-sided, sarcastic smile. "What a bunch of stiffs, huh? Qasim waiting outside?"

"No," Dianna winces. "I didn't tell you. He wasn't invited."

"Look, Dianna. You don't need him. Come out drinking with me next weekend. We'll have a good time." Leah rubs hand lotion into her hands, wringing her fingers like a dishtowel.

"Thanks, Leah. I'll see what I'm doing." Dianna ducks back out into the hallway and waits for her eyes to adjust to the bright light of the reception. The man with the teeth fetish is mercifully gone.

Dan is dancing with a redhead with a pixie haircut. They bump their hips together periodically in the dance of the moment. They laugh each time their hips collide.

Dianna wonders if she can afford a taxi. She pulls crumpled bills out of her wallet, and then digs deeper into her purse. She finds a quarter, a dime, and her penny minted in 1903. Nowhere near the amount a taxi would cost all the way back into Manhattan.

Leah follows her. "Come on, let's blow this joint. The food stinks and the music is making me hard of hearing."

"Are you a mind reader?" Dianna laughs. No matter their differences, Leah always comes to her rescue. Dianna forgives all her previous comments about Qasim. She forgives too easily, she's been told. Leah speaks before she thinks, but she does have to live with her. She remains Dianna's friend.

"I'll tell the guy who gave me a ride I'm leaving," she says.

"Screw him," Leah says under her breath and holds out her arm. "He won't even notice. He has his eye on that bump-girl with the big nose. Her nose is even bigger than his."

Dianna links her arm through Leah's, and they almost skip from the room to the valet parking below. The valet is holding open the door of Leah's weathered Oldsmobile like the door to a carriage.

"We should party like this more often, Amiga," Leah says, and Dianna hears the tipsy slur of her verbs. "What about this weekend?"

Dianna leans over and hugs Leah as horns protest behind them. "We both need to get out of the city and use our cars more. We'll see, Leah. I might be busy."

Leah throws her hands up. "What, with Qasim? Come on, Dianna. You know that ole Qasim is no good for you. They're all no good, if you ask me. Use them if and while you can; then get out. That's my advice, but it's your life."

CHAPTER TWENTY-THREE
Stand by for Zone Inspection

Mr. Grant holds the slides in one hand, her typed green cards in the other. He takes his time getting to the point. He stands red-faced, his mouth puffed in a stutter, until Sophia prods him.

"Can we help you, Mr. Grant?"

He's standing by Dianna's desk. It's obvious he wants to speak to Dianna, but perhaps he doesn't want Dianna to realize he knows her name. He walks back to Sophia.

"Miss Diane Calloway, she is in your employ?"

"I supervise her directly, yes." Sophia doesn't get up, but she does take her hands from her typewriter.

Dianna turns around. "I am Dianna Calloway, Mr. Grant. Is there a problem?"

"Miss Calloway, who authorized you to type these cards?" Mr. Grant moves back toward her desk. "Was it you, Miss Leonard?"

Sophia pushes her reading glasses up the bridge of her nose. "I put them in her stack, yes." Sophia doesn't look the least bit concerned. Dianna feels sick to her stomach. She hasn't been paying attention because her mind has been flitting through possibilities of romance and career. Future travel and adventure. Destiny.

"Ladies!" Mr. Grant puffs his chest like a penguin. "These photos are from Herculaneum."

"Yes, I'm aware of that," Dianna says. She won't call him "Mister."

"Miss Calloway, Herculaneum is our most significant project. How long have you worked here?"

Dianna looks him straight in the eye. "I'm sure you already have looked at my file in Human Resources. Two years."

Mr. Grant's puffy cheeks become puffier. The middle button on his tweed jacket looks like it will pop. "Any typist with two years' experience and the word per minute rate you say you have does not make two typos on a card!"

Dianna realizes her typos must have been seen by someone outside the museum, and that he's been embarrassed. "I'm sorry," she says with genuine concern. "I'll fix them immediately." She reaches for the cards.

"No!" Mr. Grants yells, jerking them away from her. Everyone turns toward him, though they all pretend they can't hear. They're afraid he'll start yelling at them next. "You will not touch this project again. It was out of your job description in the first place! Miss Leonard, look through her desk. I want all materials to my office in the next hour!"

Peter Fox smirks at Dianna as Mr. Grant marches away.

"Don't worry, love." Sophia comes around and puts her hands on Dianna's shoulders. "He's always like this. Let me have the remaining cards, and I'll take them to his secretary now."

Dianna looks down on the cards she's typed today lying on her desk blotter. She's aware of some remorse, but that man had no right to berate her in front of her peers. She remembers the ad section folded in her purse, ready for her lunchtime search. She can't stay in this prestigious place much longer. She squeezes Sophia's hand in gratitude as she hands over the cards.

CHAPTER TWENTY-FOUR

Friends and Foes

Qasim and Dianna sit next to Heather and Leah at a jazz club in the Village. It's the first time Qasim and Heather have met. The female performer sings in a plaintive voice. Sporting an Afro and a maroon, sequined, off-the-shoulder gown, she sings with passion, her lips touching the mike, reminding Dianna of her own solos in high school. Her eyes mist over.

Qasim doesn't notice. He's busy humming along with the melody, slightly out of tune, like he did the day they met. Earlier this evening, he presented her with a gift from his travels—a plastic bag filled with flight paraphernalia—a sleeping mask, slippers, and nondairy creamer. She wonders if he's one of those people who take the shampoo after every hotel stay. His gesture, to him one of goodwill, exasperates her, even though it's the thought that counts. After all, he will be leaving again next month. Despite her desire to relish the moments she has with him, tonight's gift seems an afterthought. His mind is not with her. He has been distant all evening, and he hasn't wanted to tell her about his travels at all. It's as though he thinks the nondairy creamer should fill in the gaps those three weeks away created between them.

"You're a native New Yorker?" Qasim is asking Heather.

"Born and bred," Heather replies. "My parents moved to Florida a couple of years ago, but I like the seasons. My boyfriend and I both work in the arts. We plan on settling down here."

"Mmmmm." Qasim turns his attention back to the music.

Dianna can tell Qasim is uncomfortable with Heather, a red-haired beauty with dark circles under her eyes who is on antidepressants. He won't look her directly in the eye, which is very unusual for him, and he fiddles with the napkin on the table when she looks at him. He has told Dianna he is troubled about Heather before this meeting. He doesn't approve of her medication for mental illness, but Dianna suspects he's also wary of her

Jewish background. Dianna decided not to listen to him; it's his problem. Dianna would never abandon a friend. She's glad they're finally meeting.

Heather sits with her head in her hands, soaking up the music in silence. Leah, tall with long legs and longer hair, and Heather's complete opposite, wants to discuss her visit to Palestine with the mayor's office. Dianna listens off and on, tapping her glass to quell the swell of envy that threatens, until she becomes caught up in the topic of conversation.

"But why don't you think the Palestinians deserve their own homeland, Qasim?" Leah asks.

"They never had their own homeland. They have always moved from place to place."

"Why do you keep calling it 'Palestine'?" Heather comes out of her fog to ask.

"He's right. There's never been a Palestine."

Leah's face goes from bright red to pale yellow, before returning to its usual healthy tan. "Just because Israel has occupied the territory doesn't mean it's never existed. Look in any Gazetteer. For that matter, look it up in the Bible."

Qasim grimaces but says nothing.

Heather doesn't seem to have enough in her to argue. She settles back into her fog.

Dianna wishes she knew more; she wishes she'd been to Palestine. She hesitates to contribute to the conversation; she lacks important information. Dianna vaguely remembers a mention of Palestine during her research on Lebanon, a "former" country of the Ottoman Empire and a British mandate until 1940-something. Empathy had won over, diverting her attention from the facts. These refugees had to belong somewhere. She can't imagine not having ground underneath one's feet to call one's own. She is a progeny of American Civil War stories, told by a great-grandmother who lived through the South's reconstruction. Her heritage is one of land, and the earth is almost like a family member. The Palestinians are in the same predicament the Israelis were before they reformed their nation in the forties: no land to call their own.

"Why can't they go back to their homes?" Dianna asks, and realizes from the looks she receives this is a naïve question. Feeling a blush on her cheeks, she is quiet once more. Still, it makes no sense that families could be driven from a land in which they had no home. Dianna imagines them crossing desert wilderness, with keys that no longer fit locks gripped in hands that waited until wrinkled. Yet, if they were wanderers, they would have had no keys. Where did they come from? She shuts off her confusion and listens in again.

"You wouldn't believe the bloodshed." Leah shakes her head, and Qasim nods.

"It is sad, really." He sighs. "But you know these people are not like you and me."

Dianna disagrees with a vehemence that overcomes her feeling of ignorance. "No!" she says. "They are you and I! We are interconnected, made of the same cells, the same organs, the same sinew. We are all born, we all suffer, we all have moments of joy, and we all die. Our hearts pump our blood, and our muscles push out our babies, and our spirits long for love and peace. We all deserve a place to call home."

The table is silent. She hears her pulse beating in her ear. Qasim stands up, overturning his chair. His face is stone. He brings his palm down flat, hard on the table, sending the liquid in the glasses swirling. Even Heather stares up at him.

"You can be so nice, Dianna," he says. "And then there are times like these." He draws a breath to continue, searching the rapt faces that encircle him. "Aren't you a citizen of the country where 'all are created equal'? Do you venture to think they are each *treated* equally? I think not. Yes, I want peace. If you must know, it is they who do not want peace. I used to think like you, but have you seen my countrymen's pain, sitting here in your cushy little bar on your safe street in your peaceful nation? Stand in my shoes for a day, and you shall see. Yes, you will see things anew. Really, you will." Qasim picks up his smooth cashmere cardigan and turns on his heels. He never glances back at her.

Leah turns to Dianna with a wry smile. "Boy, he's a real winner, Di. Told you so." She pushes her long waves behind her shoulder, sloughing

Qasim off like a bothersome gnat. "Doesn't anybody want to go find some real men?"

Dianna frowns at Leah, then smiles at Heather. "No, Leah. I'm fine, really. I'd rather be alone." Her mind is already taking an inventory of her freezer, full of frozen desserts.

CHAPTER TWENTY-FIVE

Outside the Wire

Dianna runs up the steps two at a time to her apartment, not bothering to take the rickety elevator. She pauses at the landing, turns, turns again, and descends to the street once more. The scene at the club two nights ago has her craving something salty, and she's finally giving in. It's Saturday night, and she's home early–alone. The refrigerator contains two beers, some lettuce, fat-free salad dressing, and a couple of eggs. She is on a mission to the corner market for one thing and one thing only: a box of chocolate-covered peanuts.

Qasim called her yesterday as though nothing has happened between them, and Dianna decided to play along. She didn't mention the tough time hailing a cab in the rain at the club or her last few coins spent on the ride home. Nor does she tell him about the half-gallon of chocolate marshmallow ice cream that is no longer in the freezer nor her digestive tract.

If the night in the jazz club does not make her confront him, it makes her even more curious—mystified, in fact. She has so many questions to ask him, but she has learned from cold experience that timing is everything with inconsistent people. He calls himself "a diplomat." Dianna is uncertain what a diplomat actually *does*. He surrounds himself with paper, just as she does little green cards. Do his piles of documents change anything? She does know a diplomat cannot be prosecuted by American law, no matter what the crime—hence, all the illegally parked cars with "DPL" plates blanketing the city.

In her sparse spare time away from her museum typewriter, Dianna continues her attempts to discover more about Qasim's country, one of the world's oldest civilizations. She finds facts instead of substance. More than three million people live there, though no census has been taken since 1932. Most of the populace lives in Beirut, the Middle East's banking center. The Lebanese are savvy in business and value education. The country exports citrus fruit, potatoes, wheat, and wine. If she wants a more personal viewpoint, she must speak to Qasim.

The market is a few blocks away, and she decides to walk. It's a warm night, and she unzips her jacket. The street isn't as busy as usual; a couple of homeless men stand in the shadows, blowing on their fingers to warm them. One of them has been hanging out here a lot lately; he's the one that gave her the finger. He gives her a glare as she crosses to the other side of the street. She wonders if the guy in the market is giving him a daily handout. She turns the corner. The market is two blocks ahead, and its awning is still out, beckoning. She sets her sites and quickens her step.

The door jingles when she enters. The cashier looks up, then back down at his comic book. She can smell the half-rotten bananas and the detergent that lingers on the dull floor. A string of chewed tinsel extends from one corner of the ceiling to the cigarette case behind the register. Faded boxes line ancient shelves that sag under their weight. The man she usually pays is not there tonight. She will probably never see the boy behind the counter tonight again, so it's safe to get more than a box of candy, something that will go down easy. She decides to add chocolate marshmallow to replenish her ice cream collection. The boy smiles or grimaces when she hands him her five dollars; she can't decide which. His eyes seem to say he knows her secret as he hands her twenty-two cents in change.

She hugs the frozen groceries against her chest and leaves the shop. Her heels echo on the sidewalk. A wind blows some litter around in front of her. It picks up a white paper napkin and sends it from one side of the street to the other. The near-deserted street has cleared in the time it took her to decide on an ice cream flavor. She decides against zipping her coat. She can already see the lights of her apartment building.

She reels abruptly to the right. Something, or someone, has hold of her pocketbook. Her knee wrenches as she is pulled backward, and her head feels as though it is falling off her shoulders. It collides with the pavement. Dianna cries out in pain and struggles to see what has pulled her in this direction. A hazy face swims in front of her, reaches out, and clasps her neck. She recognizes his clothes. She gasps when his face closes in on her; it has always been hidden by shadows before. He has a scar. It is as though a blade has cut off his cheek, or a chemical has burned it off. The skin is not skin but hide. His odor and her head wound almost cause her to black out, but she knows if she does, her odds of escape are next to none.

"Well if it isn't the 'fuck you' girl," the man spits into her face. "Bet you won't give me that 'fuck you' look anymore after tonight. Bet you'll remember me after tonight." He fumbles with his pocket, pulls out a glass pint of some foul-smelling liquor, and takes a long swig. She tries to get up, but he slaps her hard, and her head explodes with pain. His grasp is back around her throat. He strokes her neck with the tip of a jagged fingernail. He runs the bottom of his mud-caked bottle over her hair. She can feel his breath getting quicker. Then he throws the bottle against the brick wall behind her, sending shards flying. He picks one up and advances toward her, grasping her neck again.

She can't breathe. Her mind races through the possibilities: a mugging, a rape, a murder. *My God, is he going to rape me?* Where are the people in this city that isn't supposed to sleep? She tries to turn her neck to see if anyone is approaching them. He clasps it tighter, cutting off the air entirely. He seems to take pleasure in this action. Drool runs out of his mouth, and she sees he's missing most of his teeth. She can feel blackness pouring over her again. She's going to pass out. Her mind races, then slows, making any strategy to escape disappear.

He takes his hands off her neck to rummage in his pocket again.

She gulps in air. He must have a knife or a razor.

He comes back toward her, and the full weight of him engulfs her, his ragged, whisky, garbage breath on her neck.

That's when her father's training, straight from the military, kicks in.

She screams at the top of her lungs. She kicks him hard, not knowing what her foot hits. He lets go of her neck and yelps, reaching down to where her foot has met the right mark. She kicks him again—in the shin this time, stamps on his toes—and turns and flees. She runs and runs, past her apartment building, past the next building, onward until she can run no more. She will have to go back; she doesn't have a choice. Where else will she sleep tonight?

The street seems deserted. Her steps echo her heartbeat, pounding in her carotid, pulsing pain into her head wound. She swallows with every third beat, trying to catch her breath. The man is nowhere, a phantom, like the napkin that was flying in front of her before he appeared out of nothingness. She runs up the steps to her building and presses all the buzzers, not taking time to put the key in the latch. "It's Dianna from Number Thirty-Two," she yells into the intercom. "Let me in."

"Okay, okay," replies a deep, disgruntled female voice. "Bring your key next time, stupid."

The buzzer unlocks the door, her entry back to a safe world, and she slams the door shut behind her. Her legs shaking without cease, Dianna takes the elevator even though she only has two flights of steps. First, she searches all four corners of the tiny lift to make certain she is alone. It creaks upward, and Dianna's racing mind imagines the cable straining, pulling its cargo inch-by-inch. She turns her key in the lock, then the double lock, repeating the process on the other side of the door. She searches the closets, grabs a knife from the kitchen, and searches the closets again, behind doors, under beds.

It is only then that she realizes she still has her pocketbook and ice cream. She begins to laugh, but then she stops short. She walks to the kitchen, returns the knife, and walks to the bathroom. She turns on the shower to get warm. She has been crying but hasn't known it. Her mascara runs down her neck—where the man's hand touched. She traces the mascara run with her finger, wipes her cheeks with the palm of her hand, and heads back to the kitchen.

Dianna takes a tablespoon from the silverware drawer, opens the ice cream, puts it on the counter, and leans over it. She brings the spoon up to her mouth again and again. She brings it up to forget the man, to forget the day. She brings it up as many times as it takes to forget Qasim. The ice cream slides down her throat; it fills her stomach. There is her solace, her secret, her strength.

She closes her eyes and rests her head against the kitchen cabinets, shutting out all of the lights she has turned on during her search. When she opens her eyes again, she is calm. She walks to the bathroom, lifts the lid of the toilet, and lifts the seat. The bathroom smells of Leah's bath beads and of her own shampoo. She's not sure she can stand such a light, fresh scent, the scent of spring. She places the toiletries outside the bathroom, shuts the door, and turns off the light. She gropes her way to the toilet again. She pulls her hair back and tucks it into her ripped dress. Then she sticks her finger down her throat, once, twice, to get the hang of it again. The third time, she meets with success. She brings it all up, gets rid of it, gags, coughs, and gags again. The last time she flushes, she is once more in control.

CHAPTER TWENTY-SIX

Parry and Retreat

On Thursday, Qasim calls her unexpectedly.

"What's up?" he asks, an abruptness in his voice that leads her to think he is sandwiched between meetings.

She hesitates, debating how to tell him. She doesn't want to reveal how afraid she'd been. She doesn't want to burden him or make him uncomfortable. She tries to make her voice sound carefree and airy. She needs to relate facts alone. She must omit how her skin burns with dryness from shower after shower. She won't tell him that nothing will ever erase the memory of the smell of the homeless man's lusty hatred and her stark terror. Whatever happens, she won't cry. Qasim isn't hers enough to try to elicit any figment of responsibility from him. It wouldn't be fair, especially after his outburst the last time they met.

"Mmmm..." she begins.

"Come on, Dianna. Snap to it. You're too bright to give me any of this 'mmmmm' business. Give me your thoughts."

She imagines him pacing. She can hear the phone scraping one way, then the other on his desk. Tears prick, but she continues because he has attacked that very place she was trying to hide, her vulnerability.

"I had a little run-in with a would-be mugger. Got a tiny bump on my head." She succeeds in making her voice sound light until it hits the word 'mugger.' Then it becomes noticeably softer, and her ex's voice pops into her mind shouting, "Wimpy voice!"

She hears Qasim's intake of breath on the other end. She reminds herself she is speaking with Qasim, not Danson.

"Are you okay?"

"Yes, I'm fine. I screamed. He ran."

"I regret that you had this happen and..." It is his turn for silence.

"And...? No silences allowed!" She laughs.

He chuckles. He knows she has caught him. "Touché!" he replies. "It's that…it's that you need a man to protect you. I cannot allow this sort of danger for you ever, ever again."

She glances up at the mirror, no longer trying to find the right words, sees her cheeks flush, half-flattered, half-piqued. She wonders if he wishes he had been that man. "I'm fine," she says. "There are millions of women walking unaccompanied around the city."

His voice is barbed wire when he replies. "I am sure you are perfectly capable of handling yourself. You've certainly proven so. What could a man possibly add to your attributes and abilities?"

"I didn't mean I wouldn't want a date every so often," she parries, making her voice heavy with honey. She looks deep into the mirror and fidgets with her hair. Now, she doesn't even want to see him, to have him see her body, not like this. She jiggles the skin flap under her right arm. Maybe after the holidays, when she's thinner. Five more pounds, a new one-size-smaller skirt from the consignment store.

Yet it's already too late. His voice softens in return. "Shall we meet then?"

"I'm not sure. I'm going to my…my family's to check on them." She wants to invite him but decides not to. He isn't ready for what "family" means to her. Besides, she'll lose a lot of weight while she's there.

"Then it is all the more important that we meet before you leave," he says, his voice even softer, like a caress, which probably means he's already mentally undressing her.

She sighs, tries to blot out the image that comes to mind of her nude white body, and relents. She never thinks about nudity when he's with her, but these phone conversations make her too aware of all her imperfections. When they're together, her body takes over; when telephone lines separate them, her mind takes over.

They decide to meet for a quick drink on Friday evening before he goes on to a reception. She finds herself anticipating seeing his face, holding his hands, feeling his skin against hers. After all, she's attracted to him because of his passion for his work. If she accepts his ambition, his hours, his travel, his country, things will improve between them. Hard experience tells her she can't change him; her father never changed his workaholic tendencies. When Qasim becomes taciturn, unavailable, she is all too aware of the resemblance he bears to her unavailable father—in diplomat's clothing.

She doesn't want to admit she needs someone to protect her, but she does need someone to care. Dianna will have to get used to Qasim's absence if the relationship—her mouth curves up when she thinks of what they have as such—is to continue.

CHAPTER TWENTY-SEVEN

Zero Dark Thirty

She'll never do it again.

Dianna works, sleeps, works again. She thinks she has regained control. She sits in front of her typewriter, filling up little green cards, not paying attention. The last time she didn't pay attention, she made a mistake, and Mr. Grant almost fired her on the spot. She realizes she just made a typo. She's making too many mistakes, and lots of people want her entry-level job. She needs to concentrate.

She's ashamed of going back to purging. She'd bid that coping method farewell before she graduated college. She tells herself she does not need to resort to that—or more drastic measures. She has lost two pounds drinking smoothies, though she will never go back to over-the-counter diet pills. Anything is better than pure caffeine. She shakes her head as she remembers how loathsome she felt the morning after getting rid of that food. How she stood outside the kitchen door, the smell of Leah's coffee making her vaguely sick and altogether hungry. How her head reeled as it did after consuming an entire six-pack. How her eyes were red and sore, her fingers so swollen she couldn't put on her ring. How she was afraid she stank even after a shower last night and a bath this morning.

Why is she making herself throw up? What is she trying to get rid of? Her feelings? Her memories? Her very DNA? Part of someone else that has lodged within her?

It is a paradox.

Oops. Another typo. Dianna takes out her green correcting fluid, blows the card dry, and revises the text. Shouldn't it say "glass vase" instead of "glass-like vase"? She makes the correction, an executive decision.

She needs to count her blessings. She has a prestigious job, is starting to make a decent living, and is safe in her bed each night. Besides, she has someone in her life who cares for her, who calls her, who needs her. Right? She's seeing him tonight after a long week of waiting.

Then why does she sometimes feel nothing but emptiness inside until she lifts a spoon of something sweet to her lips? Emptiness so cavernous no amount of food can fill it?

It's more than a convenient way to claim her body and her cake too, to possess a self that isn't too big for the space she's allotted in life, a self that wants to float to the stars. She looks down at her thigh, touches her underarm to see how much fat hangs there. What will it take to get rid of it? Her need for food disgusts her. Her need for anything disgusts her.

No! she shouts inside. Her stomach is almost flat again. She doesn't need to binge. She has conquered it this time. She can lose weight the normal way. She can do without food. She needs to pay attention to her work.

That crazy alley dweller who precipitated this relapse has probably gone on to some other corner to bother some other woman. Maybe she overreacted. If she had ignored him, he may have gone away.

Dianna's memory takes her back to the first time she was in this city, job-hunting with two of her college roommates. A man with wild hair, wilder eyes, and torn clothing rushed up and sniffed the air around her. "Tampon!" he yelled. She completely overreacted. She dashed ahead, like Peter Rabbit in Mr. McGregor's garden, not looking back to locate her two friends, both city dwellers, until she was three blocks ahead.

When she stopped and looked behind her, her friends were doubled over with laughter. "You're going to have to get used to the city, Di," one said when she finally caught her breath. "This kind of person is on every street corner."

She had gotten used to the homeless. She gave most of them a quarter when she passed them, until she realized she didn't have enough money left for her own groceries. Perhaps she had even given this alley man change on occasion. In fact, that might have been all he was doing, trying to frighten or shame her into giving him money. Still, she looks both ways before she leaves her apartment building. She hasn't ventured out at night all week.

Sophia is bent over her typewriter changing the ribbon as Dianna pulls her satchel from under her desk and begins to pack to start home. "How are you, Love?" she asks. "Are you meeting Qasim tonight?"

Dianna detects a note of wistfulness in Sophia's voice along with her obvious concern. Sophia doesn't look like she's made to sit in front of a typewriter. Rather she looks like she belongs on a throne: perfectly coiffed, her make-up minimal, her attire understated. A white silk blouse with a generously knotted bow swathes her long aristocratic neck, turned to one side like a question mark. How could a woman of such beauty and culture remain alone, barely able to make ends meet?

Sophia wipes the ribbon ink off her long fingers. "Well?"

Dianna squirms in her seat. She has been confiding in Sophia over these last few weeks. Sophia has listened, nodding, repeating her words back in different cadence and phrasing, never judging. Even so, Dianna does not want to admit to Sophia that she wants to continue her involvement with Qasim. Sophia might have the same opinion of Qasim as Leah does. If only she could read Sophia's mind, determine Qasim's intentions. "I'm seeing him tonight, Sophia."

Sophia claps her hands, and Dianna almost jumps. "Wonderful!" Sophia beams.

"You're happy?" Dianna queries. "You don't think that he might be using me? He seems to come and go. Do you think he might be here for the long run?"

Sophia looks down for a long moment at her elegant onyx ring. "I knew a man like Qasim in Paris during World War II reconstruction. He was more devoted to peace than he was to me. I was young, oh so young—and accustomed to war."

She looks down at her long hands and even longer fingers, rubs at the only evident age spot. "The older I get, the more important those moments are, Love. Go to him. Enjoy each other. Enjoy the time you have, no matter how long it may be. Make a little peace midst this world of war."

CHAPTER TWENTY-EIGHT

Call to Action

Qasim strides toward Dianna when she enters the bar and embraces her so tightly she cannot return the embrace. "So how are you, Sweetie?" he pushes her back to gaze into her eyes. "How's your head? Are you certain you weren't concussed? A concussion is serious business. I've been worried—very, very worried."

His compassion touches her. She has seen it before, but not to this magnitude. It is strange not to see him smiling. It exhilarates her that someone who usually glosses over the surface of things is frowning over her welfare. She returns his gaze for almost a full minute. "I'm fine, Qasim, really I am. Ancient history already," she assures him. "That homeless guy wanted to intimidate me, and we both know I'm not easily intimidated."

His eyes glisten, though she notices a darkness underneath them, like hints of artist's charcoal. His arms encircle her again, crushing her, making her squirm. "Okay, okay. Qasim, I can't breathe in here," she laughs and softly pushes him away. "Let's sit down." He takes his time letting go and directs her to a corner table where he has already ordered drinks.

"You see? I arrived before you." He helps her with her coat and pulls out the chair for her. He pushes her seat in for her in one graceful rhythm.

She has noticed, and she smiles a relaxed, wide smile. She takes his hand, a public declaration, a gesture that seems right for a change. He squeezes each finger on her hand and never takes his eyes off hers.

"Don't worry me like that again, okay?"

His words beseech her, and she wants to nod in accord. Instead, she shakes her head right to left. "Can't promise that," she teases. "You know me; I'm always getting into some sort of trouble. I can't lock myself up in a tower away from big, bad New York City."

His smile is tight-lipped, but he does not let go of her hand. "I want you to have fun, Sweetie. I know you're American and used to your freedom. I'd never ask you to forsake that. Yet please be careful. Look around the next corner before you run round it. Please. Do it for me."

He has touched some innocent part of her she had long forgotten, and it hurts her to acknowledge it. She turns her head slightly away, takes her hand away, and feigning thirst, picks up her glass. She can see his own hurt in his eyes, but she can't be certain if it stems from a macho sense of rejection, a loss of control, or a deeper sense of risking his affection. She immediately regrets her action and feels her hand growing cold. Dianna telegraphs a silent apology, when, shoeless, she slides her foot up and down Qasim's trouser leg. Under her lowered lashes, she can sense his arousal—and his forgiveness. She's taking Sophia's advice.

"You've been working too hard," she murmurs, brushing the circles under his eyes with her fingertips. "How is your country?" She's almost afraid to hear the answer. His work is one lover she must compete with, along with his family, along with his country.

"I'm not certain I can even talk about it."

"Sorry. I've read the front-page news, but American newspapers don't give enough detail. And my sense of Lebanese geography..."

"No, no, of course you have trouble keeping up. You're a world away. I have trouble myself. I continue to try to get back into Beirut, but it's impossible at the moment. They call a cease-fire in the evening, only to have shooting start in another part of the city before morning. Another embassy, another airplane hijacked, another bomb. It never ends." He shakes himself, and the crease between his eyebrows disappears. His eyes brighten, and he rubs his hands together. "But I have hope," he sighs. "I always have hope."

This is the Qasim she loves. She wants his hope to rub off on her. Still, she cannot let his optimism go unchallenged. She remembers a phrase her parents' Lebanese friends mentioned once, and she repeats it. "There's been violence there since before the Crusades."

His eyes dim. "There are so many factions—faction upon faction in my country. I have nothing against any of them. My realtor here is Jewish. You are Christian. There are jokes about the hostility between Arabs and Jews. In my country, even Christians hate other Christians. If we are to move beyond it, we will need to educate them."

"It's been that way here, too," Dianna affirms. "Not that long ago. We've only come to a peace in the U.S. in this last decade. I guess in a way that was through education. Through a man who taught Americans about what it was like to walk in another person's shoes. Yet, he didn't use formal education. He used speeches, sermons, and prayer to teach peace."

Qasim's frown lingers, but he takes her hand in his. "Martin Luther King had a doctorate, my dear," he says. "Without formal education, he wouldn't have had the podium he did."

"I'm not sure I agree totally," Dianna ventures. "Even the most educated societies have violence."

Qasim squeezes her hand and then releases it. "True. Why we cannot live together in peace is beyond me. Bullets and bombs never solve anything." He rubs his hands together again, hunches his shoulders, shrugging off burden. When he looks at her, his eyes have the old light in them. "Your people and our people have a long history of cooperation. Maybe your people will help. Maybe they can be there long enough so I can get a plane in, assess the damage to my buildings, check on some friends." He takes her hand in his again. "Let's not talk of conflict any more tonight."

Dianna wonders what Qasim means by "her" people. The voice of the recently murdered John Lennon croons his newly released song "Woman," then Bill Haley and the Comets belt out "Rock Around the Clock."

"Bill Haley died just last week." Dianna says, though she is still thinking of John Lennon, which makes her think about all the shooting in Beirut.

Qasim mouths the words along with the melody. "What else did he sing—wait, I remember—that 'letter song'?"

Dianna strikes up the rest of the lyrics to the song on Qasim's lips.

They gaze across the bar, their eyes moving away from each other, active, but not seeing, back and forth, trying to recollect the title. They grasp it simultaneously.

"I'm Gonna Sit Right Down..." Dianna shouts—and Qasim finishes with "...And Write Myself a Letter!"

Dianna clutches his arm, sharing their mutual victory in this little game. He hugs her and kisses her on the cheek, then looks around as though he might see someone he knows.

"Let's go," he whispers.

Qasim drives straight through the city, not bothering to try to bypass the stop-and-go traffic that is routine every hour of the day and night. Dianna slides over so he can put his arm around her, and she puts her head on his shoulder. His hand moves back and forth on her opposite shoulder in time to the radio's music.

"Did I ever tell you I spent my summers on my grandmother's farm?" she almost whispers.

"Tell me," he answers.

"There was a barn and a pony. The barn was white, and the pony was red. I would go on hikes in the morning, picking blackberries. I would read in the porch swing all afternoon. The storms would come at night and wake me up from a sweaty sleep. They were warning me that the summer would not last—that I would have to go home soon. I would get up and play the piano badly, unable to get back to sleep. My mother would come and whack me on the head, yell at me to get back to bed."

"Was home so bad?" he asks, caressing her cheek.

She shakes her head, not a negative gesture—one of baffled wonderment. "Home wasn't always the safest place to be. Home isn't always safe for anyone, is it?"

"Dianna," he chides. "Don't be so melodramatic." He taps her shoulder harder, but she feels warmth in his hand instead of judgment.

The radio station disc jockey seamlessly changes record after record with an invisible hand. She barely notices what's playing in the background. She watches the traffic lights change from green to yellow to red in quick succession, down the street as far as her eye can see.

He has noticed something, though. She can feel his grip tighten, can feel his jaw clinch where the crown of her head rests. She wants to wake from her trance and ask him what is wrong, but she cannot. This is the first time she has known her own real peace in years. She holds still; she hopes he will not spoil this precious moment.

"Do you know the lyrics to this song?" he asks her.

It's difficult to discern what song is playing. This rendition is twangy with a Muzak quality. She breathes out, she breathes in, and finally, she recognizes a phrase. It's a song popular when she was in school. His body tenses against her, and she knows he is waiting for her answer; she also realizes her answer is somehow very important to him.

"Yes," she breathes out slowly, still unwilling to destroy her peace. She searches for the lyrics: Something about holidays. Holidays of the West. *What's he trying to say?* Then her mind latches onto the refrain as the wordless tune drones on. She realizes that it's a song about calling to tell someone you love them. It's a song about true love that comes from the heart.

"Listen carefully," Qasim says.

She is afraid to move a muscle. She knows better than to ask what this means. If she asks a question, in her usual way, he will retreat, and her peace will evaporate. She stays where she is, her body leaning tense against his tense body. And says nothing. Instead, she caresses his hand as she watches him navigate the final few blocks to the twinkling lights on her building's awning. She pecks him on the cheek, gets out of the car by herself, and shuts the door behind her. She knows he's watching her go up the steps to her door. She doesn't ask why he's not staying the night. They both need space to ponder his silent statement.

She turns, tilts her head to her shoulder that was only the moment before touching his. Smiles. Blows him a kiss.

CHAPTER TWENTY-NINE

Forward Observer

"Remember the man we saw after your play?" Qasim sits across from her on her love seat. She brought him water and offered to rub his shoulders, which he declined.

"It's not '*my* play,' Qasim," she replies.

Qasim readjusts his back against the sofa cushions. "I am attempting to explain something significant to you, Dianna, and you not only refrain from listening, you take the conversation in a different direction entirely. Grow up!"

Dianna sits taller in her chair. He has wounded her pride, but if he has something to say at last, she will surely listen. "Yes?"

"The man you saw; he was from my country."

"Yes." Dianna is piqued. She will listen, but she will not contribute to this conversation. He's been keeping things from her, as she suspected.

"Most of the men you've seen are immigrants, refugees, taking shelter in your country. They are from poor countries in my region, and they do not understand our relationship. I personally do not understand them. They are rigid people who only see the world one way. They never see people as people. They see them as pawns, game pieces, to be moved around a chessboard. They especially see women as such. They are violent and abusive to their own women. I will not give them the time of day. I try to shelter you from them."

Dianna relaxes, leaning back to mirror him. He is opening up. "Thank you," she says. "I didn't realize."

He smiles for the first time tonight. "You had no reason to." He reaches out across the room for her, and she kneels at his feet.

"The other man," he begins, and his smile fades. "I know the other man. He was a bodyguard in Beirut for my family."

Dianna gasps. "Who *are* you?" She moves her shoulders away from him but stays seated.

"I am just a person," he answers. "A person who has liked you from the beginning. A man who knew that you had to get to know me before I shared this information with you. We all have bodyguards back home because of the war."

"*All* Lebanese have bodyguards?"

"No, Dianna, I suppose not all. Government officials, those of us who have big businesses, people from good families."

"Which group do you belong to?"

"A little bit of all three."

"But why here, Qasim? Why did this bodyguard follow you here?"

He's smiling again, but she sees pain in it. "At first, my family was worried about us in a big, foreign country. My mother did not want me to go, for many reasons. My father sent the bodyguard to calm her. I sent him back."

"You sent him back after the last time we saw him?"

"No, he is Stateside for other reasons now beyond my father's concern. I'm unable to send him back. As long as he's here, I thought he could ensure your safety, too."

Dianna twirls her hair, trying to make sense of what he is saying. "You're scaring me, Qasim." Memories of *The Godfather* flit through her mind.

"It is completely normal, Dianna. My father wants me back. My relatives want me to return. My son wants to be with me, even though he wishes we could all live here. Now my country wants me back."

Dianna feels sick, giddy. "If your family and country need you, you must return, Qasim." She pauses. "Why is that man following you?"

He clears his throat and shifts his shoulders into alignment. "To keep me safe."

She laughs. "From me?"

"He sends word back home about everything I do, Dianna. It's normal for me. I hope it's acceptable to you."

"Are you going back?"

"Not now. The time is not right. Perhaps not ever. I will leave when I decide to, not they."

"Is your family visiting you here?"

"No." Qasim sneers.

"Qasim, are you married?"

She sees the storm cross his face. For an instant, she thinks he might hit her. "Dianna, you and I have been over this matter. We have talked it to death. My marriage is over, the contract broken."

"Even if you return?"

"Especially if I return."

She sees his doubt.

CHAPTER THIRTY

Interrogation

"Mama, how are you?" Dianna speaks loudly into the receiver. She can hear the intercom inviting the residents to their noon meal.

"Dianna, dear! How nice to hear from you!" She hears a raspy remnant of her mother's younger, healthier voice, which is shaky today.

"Did you get that article I sent you?" Dianna pulls a second article on Lewy Body Dementia, along with a beautiful turquoise scarf out of her jacket pocket, hanging over the back of the kitchen chair. Somehow, Qasim hid both the scarf and the article there last night, and she only just discovered them. She smiles at how the scarf matches her eyes. She half listens to her mother talk about her day, half skims the article, which details the symptoms in graphic detail: a fluctuation in cognition, hallucinations, tics, shakes, falls, and fainting. Her mother has all of these symptoms and more.

"Yes…well. I believe so. What was it again?"

"A new medication for your disease."

"Yes, thank you. This disease is brutal, you know."

"Qasim gave it to me," Dianna says.

"That was very kind of him. What was his name again?" her mother is asking.

"Qasim. Qasim el-Kafry."

Silence ensues, and Dianna waits it out. She puts the wooden spoon down in the porcelain spoon rest and covers the receiver, so her mother cannot hear her impatient breath. What would her mother's reaction be if she said he was wealthy, but she didn't know where his money came from? That he was divorced? That he had a child? That he almost told her he loved her? That she was seeing him more often of late? That there were so many unanswered, imponderable questions about him she still asked herself but not him? That lately these unknowns didn't seem to matter as much?"

"Dianna?"

"Yes, Mama?" Dianna runs her fingers over the scarf's smooth fabric, threading it between her fingers.

"Are you there?"

"Yes, Mama." Dianna puts the journal article down. She must pay better attention.

"Why hasn't your father come to visit me?"

"He's dead, Mama."

"Oh. Dianna?"

"Yes, Mama."

"I wish I could see your face. I'm afraid I'll forget what you look like right now."

"I'll be there to see you soon, Mama."

"Is your hair still long, down your back?"

"Yes, Mama." Dianna can hear the nurses talking in the background.

"Like wheat. Like a field of wheat," her mother continues.

"I think the nurses need you to go with them now, Mama. I'll see you soon."

"I love you, Dianna."

"I love you, too, Mama. I hope you're okay."

"Oh, yes. I'm having my hair done tomorrow. Are you coming to take me home soon?"

"I'm coming for a visit. So I'll be bringing you a treat next week." She makes a mental note to pick up body lotion and a box of chocolates at Bloomie's.

"Okay. I love you, Dianna."

"I love you, too, Mama. Bye."

"Dianna?"

"Yes?"

"Did I tell you I'm having my hair done tomorrow?"

CHAPTER THIRTY-ONE

Interloper

Dianna squeezes into her office chair, wedged between her desk and her suitcase, packed and ready for the all-night train ride to her family. Sophia offered to drop her at the train station tonight after work. Her bag is heavy, laden with all the gifts she can afford. She's even bought a gift for Qasim, a silver pen with the word "Peace" inscribed in seven different languages. She's inserted a card she's written in calligraphy: "Amor Omnia Vincit." It's a fitting, oblique answer to his Stevie Wonder confession. Someday, maybe they'll say the real words to each other.

The clicking keys of Sophia's typewriter fill the otherwise empty office. Dianna sips her coffee and picks at a bran muffin, turning the pages of the newspaper, trying to find the energy to begin typing. Her mind is already traveling to what her siblings call home, though it's more cage than home for her. These days she wonders if she has a home or needs a home. She saw an adage in the corner market today when she bought her paper. "Home is where the cat is." It's a pithy turn of phrase for cat owners, who certainly have their hearts invested in their feline pets. Where is her home? Where is her heart?

She stops with a jolt. She's seen something on the Society page. It's an embassy party photo. The depth of field causes the photo to blur in the gritty grain of newsprint, but it's Qasim. His hands are extended in a familiar Qasim gesture, and he chats with a younger, stouter man. The man looks Egyptian, but of course may live anywhere, even New York. What catches her eye next, though, causes a sharp intake of breath, so loud that Sophia looks up in concern. A woman has hold of his arm; it seems he's escorting her.

"Sophia, Qasim is with a woman in this photo. He's at an embassy party."

"Don't women attend embassy parties?" Sophia smiles her tranquil smile, the corners of her lips barely turning upward.

"Yes, but he said they are boring. This party doesn't look boring. He doesn't look bored."

Sophia extends her hand, and Dianna hands her the newspaper section. "Well, he does seem animated." Sophia raises one eyebrow.

"He seems positively exuberant to me," Dianna says, snatching back the page and looking at it again.

"Dianna, dear, he may have very good reasons for not inviting you to a business event." Sophia pats Dianna on the shoulder. "You're young; you need to realize that sometimes men need strategy in business. They have to kiss the hands of a few frogs."

"That woman looks more princess than frog. Why can't I be part of that strategy?" Dianna's voice echoes through the quiet.

Sophia looks back at her typewriter and adjusts the page in its carriage. "Stop jumping to conclusions. All in good time, Dianna, if that is what you desire."

Dianna throws the newspaper in the trash bin and gets to work. She needs to type fifty-six little green cards before day's end.

CHAPTER THIRTY-TWO

Family Bonds

"Thanks for the check for my books," her brother T.C. mutters once she gives him a hug.

"I'd forgotten what it was like here." Dianna turns to hug younger sister Mary Ann, peering beyond her to the room's full, cluttered bookcases. These days she feels younger than Mary Ann, though she's the eldest sibling. Mary Ann has taken on the family almost entirely alone. "How are you both?"

"We're alright. T.C.'s workload is tougher this semester. Not much time to help out."

"Yes, I remember. He needs to keep that average up so he doesn't lose his scholarship. That's the trick."

"Alright already. I know. I know."

"You still have no desire to go to college?"

"Stop it. Dianna. Somebody has to take care of our mother."

"Okay." Dianna puts her hand up calling a truce. She's barely home, and the conversation has already turned toward their mother. "Dating anyone?"

"Oh, I have an occasional dinner date. The boys are sweet, but..."

"And Jim?"

"He hangs around. I don't know...." Mary Ann's voice trails off, and she shrugs. They walk on, playing a game of break-the-silence. Finally, Mary Ann speaks. "I'm happy at the library. Someday Jim will come around. Until then, I don't need much. The land. Nature. You know."

T.C. stuffs his hands in his pockets even though it's warm. "You okay Dianna?"

Mary Ann hauls out her suitcase. "I could use some help here, Bro'."

"I'm okay." Dianna can feel her heart beat faster, like it wants to admit otherwise. "I had a good conversation with Mama last week."

"Oh?" Mary Ann's voice rises in cadence enough to show she's surprised. "I take care of her, but we don't have any dialogue. I can't talk to her. I'm still so angry. She practically killed Daddy."

"Don't say that, Mary Ann."

"You're the one to talk, Dianna. *You* were always the angry one."

"Stubborn. I was stubborn, not angry."

"Oh, no. I would call it angry."

"So you deserve your turn?"

"This doesn't have anything to do with turns. It has to do with feelings."

"I've worked through most of mine. Daddy always said it was her disease. How can I be angry at someone who needs so much? Besides, Daddy always had choices. He chose to stay."

"I wouldn't describe what he did as staying. He was gone more than he was there."

"You can't walk away from the military, Mary Ann. It's called desertion."

"And what do you call what he did to us?"

She's steaming now. It makes her angry that Mary Ann is angry. Or maybe it makes her feel guilty. She should be here for these two; they shouldn't need to do it all alone.

"How's work?" Mary Ann changes the subject, and Dianna smiles her gratitude.

"Fine. As long as you like typing descriptions of artifacts on little green cards. I'm ready to try something else. Would you and T.C. be alright if I left the country for a while?"

She hears Mary Ann's intake of breath. "Left the country? Where would you go?"

"I don't know. I'm applying for English-as-a-Second-Language positions."

"But what about that guy?"

Dianna blushes. Mary Ann has caught her in her own confusion. "Sorry," she says. "I shouldn't have brought it up before I had definite plans. It's only an idea. I need a change, and I want to effect change, somewhere."

"Change begins at home, Dianna."

"Where is home, Mary Ann? This has never been home for me."

Well, go then. I'm fine. Mama's as fine as she'll ever be. T.C. is happy."

"T.C.'s always happy."

"I guess that's true…mostly. Myself, I can't imagine wanting to leave America. I mean, our ancestors went through so much to get here and make this our home. Why would we want to leave?"

"I don't know. I've got wanderlust in my genes—maybe the same wanderlust our ancestors had that moved them to colonize the U.S. I want to see the world. I want to see if I can help it."

"It'll be weird here without you."

"Well, I'm not gone yet. I'll always take care of you. No matter what."

"No matter what," Mary Ann replies as though she doesn't believe it. Then, "Why would you leave before you know what's happening with that guy? If Jim ever comes around, I'll be barefoot and pregnant before you know it."

Dianna nods though she doesn't want the same things as Mary Ann. She isn't sure she wants to wait around for love to be returned in equal measure, and she can't love someone whom she isn't sure returns her love. If she waits around for Qasim to declare himself one way or another, she could miss out on life.

"I've got to make my own future, Mary Ann," Dianna says. The sun comes out and shines on a leaf dangling on an almost bare tree, showing its veins.

"We'll be fine," Mary Ann repeats, slamming the car trunk.

Dianna looks down the street and breathes in the fetid smoke from the nearby mill. The lampposts still have their worn Christmas decorations months later. One star hangs, precariously, halfway between heaven and earth, its tinsel unraveling in the sunny breeze.

CHAPTER THIRTY-THREE

Allegiance

I speed toward the family's old office headquarters, ignoring the militia groups around me, until I am forced to screech to a halt. When I got into Beirut, I thought this would be my opportunity to accomplish something, if I avoided the Green Line, dividing Christian and Muslim sides, East from West. I am shocked at the rubble, the pockmarked buildings, everywhere, in every arrondissement. I can see my decision to travel here was flawed from the outset. Things are not improving; indeed, they are much worse. Work, even checking on the buildings, is not meant to be part of this day.

A large crowd surrounds what seems to be a demonstration. Shouts come from all directions amid the acrid smell of burning tires. I gaze above me to ensure the tops of the buildings are empty, without snipers, whom I've heard are coming out in the daylight, not even waiting for nightfall. I look into my rearview, hoping to turn around. A Palestinian, holding his semiautomatic by his side like a lover, motions that I better think twice. He thumps the hood of my car with his rifle butt. My bodyguard keeps moving through the checkpoint. Stopping would reveal that I am important enough to kidnap. He slows and stops on the other side.

Two men ask to see my identity card. I roll my eyes, but pull it out of my inside jacket pocket. "Can't a man go to work?" I say rather than ask, frown, and I immediately know I've said too much. Another soldier, chewing on a cigarette stub, points the butt of his rifle at me and motions me out of my car.

"What is it, Sir?" I demand. "My papers are in order. I am a simple businessman on my way to my office. And, I might add, I am quite late." I hesitate to tell them I'm a UN representative. That might give them permission to detain me, or worse, and I am certainly not in Lebanon representing the UN.

The lead Palestinian, in tattered, sand-colored garments that could only loosely be described as a uniform and the standard black-and-white kaffiyah, sneers at me. "A simple businessman?" he scowls. "El-Kafry is your surname? Said your prayers today, simple man?" He eyes my watch and my rings out of the corner of his eye.

I choose to ignore this remark. My prayers with my God are no concern of his; it is written. "Everything is in order?" I ask instead of state this time. The soldier reeks of sweat, sand, and something I choose not to even imagine the source of.

Both soldiers step away from me, my papers in hand. I heave a sigh of dismay. All I'd wanted was to get to work in peace. I watch with guarded eyes while the Palestinians shout over the din of horns in a dialect I cannot completely decipher. The only time I allow myself to smoke is in the Middle East, and this scenario is reason enough. I reach for a cigarette, but I drop my hand when they point the rifle in my direction again. I cannot tell whether they are watching me, but they are definitely too casual with their artillery.

They take their time; they probably are mindful of my inner disdain. The sun beats strong on the top of my head and the roof of the car when they finally return. "You are free now to proceed," the lead man says, and motions me back toward my car.

***

When I arrive at our Egyptian offices the next day, late but full of news, my father and brother are in deep conversation. Having the impression it may be about their desire to have me back on this side of the ocean, I skirt their outer offices and make a beeline to the desk they've loaned me. Saif catches a glimpse of me and calls me, most likely to make an example of my belatedness to my father.

"Qasim, we were wondering what was keeping you." Saif's snide grin, full of narrow teeth, turns my way.

I pretend not to hear his condemnation.

"Wait, come here, I have a box to show you," Saif says. Our company designs the small display boxes for jewelry. Every ring must have its perfect container, leather for diamonds, crocodile for topaz. Only the finest fabrics line these boxes. We work closely with the jewelry crafters to ensure each box accents its bijou to its best and brightest extent. This has been our business for several generations, and we only get better at it. It is a lucrative business—we display fine jewelry as far away as Geneva and Paris. Yet the war has taken its toll on us.

The current design lies open on my brother's desk—a bonded calf leather with an emerald green velvet interior. Nestled inside shines a classic ruby necklace, one the Greek gods would have been proud to wear as adornment. I finger the necklace to make it dazzle, open and shut the clasp to make certain it works properly. What people see in jewelry is a mystery to me, but I must say this presentation is pleasing to the eye.

"The necklace design is from the Armenian artist?" I ask. "I would add some azure blue to the box lining to accent it."

He gets up in a huff and takes the box from my hands. "Qasim! What do you know of our business?" Saif shoves both hands in his pockets, swivels back into his chair, takes a pen out, and stacks some folders. "You are never here! What brought you back anyway?"

Nonplussed, I wonder why he asked me to examine the box in the first place. I suppose he wanted my praise and devotion, or perhaps he gave me the box so he could continue his tirade. I concentrate on the traffic noises coming through the window, the familiar smell of leather and machine oil.

"If it please God, you are always welcome, Qasim! But we must make decisions as they arrive." My father speaks this time, in his usual firm, steady cadence. "Did you get to headquarters?" he asks me, his gaze penetrating.

"I had to turn around," I admit. "Militia everywhere. I don't have high hopes that our buildings are vacant, if they are indeed still standing."

His gaze does not waver, but it does register his displeasure with me.

"I am sorry for my delay, Baba. I was unsure if the plane would even make it out today." I feel my blood vessels warm, pumping in my tense neck. My humiliation seeps down into my legs, and I am rooted to the spot. My father's displeasure turns to incredulity. "They asked to see my papers. I stood by my car for half an hour at least."

"What? They made you stand beside your car!" my father shouts, adding to my exasperation. "But you are Lebanese!"

"That seemed no matter to them," I grumble, more than ready to move on to another subject. I can still remember the beat of the sun's rays on my head and shoulders as the Palestinian tossed his gun around, not caring if it fired, let alone whom it might hit.

"Get on with the taxes, then, Qasim," my father directs me.

"These problems will be our undoing!" Saif rises again and paces the room. "They follow us. Those damned homeless migrants!"

"But we have always taken in refugees. We are a benevolent country, a democratic country!" I stand up straighter and cross the room toward him.

"Even if the entire Arab world has been trying to rid themselves of these Palestinians, they are not our responsibility! They are a political and economic burden. They are nomads." Saif's eyes meet mine, and they are hard.

Even after my experience of the morning, I remain a champion of the underdog. I remember Dianna saying humans are humans at the jazz bar. How angry she made me. I judge them because they have destroyed my homeland. Yet she has taught me they are human, seeking a home of their own. "They have become nomads because they have no homes."

"They had no homes before. They roamed the land." My brother returns to his desk but leans toward me, places his hands on his knees, ready to lecture.

"They are here for the time being. We are a welcoming country. We will have to deal with them," I interject.

"Dogs! They are putting our country in the middle. They are displacing Lebanese citizens. They are creating tension. Making us their scapegoat."

I shake my head in sadness. "We cannot blame one group for this mess."

Saif bites his lip for a moment before he speaks again. "Why do you think the Israelis are shelling the South? The Palestinians. It is the perfect location to continue their insurgency over our border. They care not about whom they hurt. We have no place in our country for hundreds of thousands of armed refugees. They are not ours! They do not belong here!" Saif's laugh has a crackly, bitter sound. "They hide inside Lebanese homes, and then those homes are bombed to rubble."

"Someone must invite them in," I retort.

"Not true. Not true. They force their way in. They must go back. Most Jews who emigrated to our South haven't lived here for centuries either. Let them all go and leave our country at peace. I would like to go home, too, even if you do not."

I have never been one to defend or to prosecute the Jews, but I play the devil's advocate. "The Jews have never had a place where they felt safe. Look, Israel has been there for almost four decades. Can we not forgive the past and get along? All I am saying is the Palestinians need a home."

My brother's face is in mine. "Jordan is not their home. Lebanon is definitely not their home. Palestine is their most recent home. Arabs and Jews lived together there for thousands of years. Yet today our region's stability has been upset in an unprecedented manner, not only in Lebanon."

He points his finger at me. "We finally have our freedom, but we cannot be free. We are a country of many ethnicities, many creeds, and many political beliefs. The Palestinians are destabilizing the balance put forth in our National Covenant. It must be put right."

He has a point, but he has riled me. The balance in our country has always been fragile. We are a country of many persuasions, jostling to gain dominance. Yet I cannot let him win this argument, not with Baba listening. "Balance! What balance? There are more factions here than in the rest of the countries in the world combined!" I say.

He walks away, clenching his fists. "I do not speak of harmony necessarily. I speak of restoring our delicate equilibrium. It was working, until Britain decided it knew what was best for the Middle East, until it decided to renege on its conquest when the going got too tough in the forties, when the rest of Europe used the Middle East as its personal trailer park—to assuage itself of its guilt by association to the Nazis."

Saif has forgotten I'm here. He flails his arms and shakes his head like a donkey, and his voice volleys off the walls. "The Middle East became a prestigious token in the Cold War. We can fix our own problems if they would unbind our hands. Every time we try to arrive at a solution, outsiders invade and tell us what's best for us. If our leaders were our parents, they'd be chiding themselves for not allowing us to accept responsibility."

I let him stew before I speak. When I do, my voice is low. I imagine my father is straining to hear. "What of the Cairo Agreement? Our leaders, the *zu'ama*, are buying into the Palestinians' scheme. They could not do this without our country's complicity," I say.

"What do you expect them to do, Qasim? How can our feeble, fractured army stamp out foreign aggression?" Saif's voice is still loud, and I know I have won by being calm. My father does not like hotheaded arguments.

"We are a strong and noble people. We have seen worse." I try to reason with him. This is an old region, full of conflict, divided loyalty, mistaken transgression. We have always survived it.

Saif's fists come down hard on top of the dark wooden desktop between us. "Watch what you say, my brother. We are still at war with those aggressors. You are already making it uneasy here for our family. Traipsing off to wander overseas with harlots." My father takes a step forward. His face is leaden.

I wave my hand through the air and backtrack even though I seethe inside. For Saif to bring up my life in the West, I must have struck a nerve. "Listen, all I say is that the situation is complicated. I wonder at times if the Jews have anything against Lebanon. We've tried to stay out of it; we should continue to do so. Neutrality has long been our salvation."

"No, you listen, my brother, and listen well!" Saif's tone echoes my father's earlier one, except in Saif's voice I hear a coldness that only the hottest white anger could render. "We will not be able to perpetuate that fantasy much longer. The Jews are already retaliating further into our country, usually against civilian targets. We will need to act sooner or later, or our country will be destroyed, too."

He is correct, of course. No one has a right to attack our land, and this I know in my heart.

"You think you know everything, Mr. Professor," Saif shouts. "You went to all the best schools. You think everything can be analyzed and theorized. You think reason will prevail. Your head is in the clouds." His mouth forms one thin, bitter line. "Or elsewhere. What I am saying is this: why are so many women and children being killed? Shiites, true, but

Lebanese, not refugee nomads. You have the audacity to come in here commenting on *our* homeland? To believe our countrymen would sacrifice their only sons for the Palestinians?"

I have no answer for this, and I turn my head away from him to think. My face burns, but I do not take issue with his statement. All I say is, "A life is a life." I stop short; I see a rage like molten fire spewing from my brother's eyes.

"You, Qasim? You would betray us? You sound like a Jew—an eye for an eye. Or is that the teaching from that luxury Quaker pacifist education you had? What is that American mistress teaching you while you leave Baba and your Lebanese wife to care for your son? Surely, there is some argument to be had that some eyes are better than others. Surely unarmed people trying to live in peace deserve to live, without fearing for their lives each day?"

"I am divorced," I remind him. "Watch what you say, Brother."

"I need this fighting to cease!" my father calls from the other room. "Qasim, get to your work!"

"Brother? Brother? What do you know of brotherhood? You would betray your Muslim brothers for sake of your neutrality, Qasim? The Palestinians have created a state within a state, and it will be our undoing. The Jews will lose not one night of sleep taking an Arab's home, his livelihood, his very life. The Palestinians know this; why not you?"

"Enough!" my father interjects, but Saif keeps going.

"If you drive away from Beirut, you see their armed guards at camps ranging from Sabra all the way to Bourj al-Barajneh. People are taking sides; we all are called to take sides in this life. You will not get by on strict neutrality if you live in Lebanon any more. Maps of alliance are already being drawn – the National Movement, the Phalangists, other private militias too numerous to even count. Mark my words. You will one day take a side. It will be soon. We need you here."

My father is standing next to us, his hands knotted into fists. "He is correct about most of what he says, Qasim, even if he says it in anger. We need you here. We need you in Beirut. Come home."

My shoulders sag. True, I have too little time to spend with my father while I'm here. I leave tomorrow for the States. "I have taxes to do," I say. I go over to his desk to pick up some tax documents, and I notice a traditional Damascene box with red velvet lining, yet smaller, more delicate, refashioned, and updated to hold jewelry. "There's a tear in the fabric here," I rub my finger across the seam.

"You've damaged it!" Saif throws up his hands like a priest dispersing incense to a misguided, sinful following. "Take it with you, then! So be it, Qasim! So be it. You go ahead. Go ahead and put your nose in the taxes. Go ahead and live your neutral, hedonist life."

I pick up the box and retreat to the piles of paper on my desk. It will be a long day.

Later, much later, my father comes in to bid me farewell. I had not noticed how stooped he has become. He leans on the desk, his breathing labored. His words come out with force, though.

"You must watch yourself, my son," he says, and he raises his head so his eyes meet mine over his glasses. I know this look well. "Your actions have consequences. Your words reflect on your family. You say you want peace. The young woman will only bring war upon us. No matter the places you travel or the company you keep. Watch yourself. Do not ruin the name you were given. It is as old as this ground on which we stand, older than the cedars of our beloved country, and I will not have anyone, especially you, defame it."

He marches out, and I return to my papers. I will worry him no more, but I was never the savior for whom they pray. Perhaps I do no longer belong here. Perhaps I never did. I think of Dianna—her smile, her radiance, her kind soul. I have an early flight.

CHAPTER THIRTY-FOUR

Love Conquers All

I wish to buy it for her, but the shop is closed. They close early in the Middle East, and many take a luncheon siesta to boot. I will not have time tomorrow before I head out into the long threads of traffic heading for the airport.

I cup my hands and stare into the polished reflective glass of the jewelry shop. The lights inside the window collide with the street lamps. I wandered the streets tonight, thinking. I wish I'd come across this store earlier. I fish for a slip of paper, after all that paper I dealt with today, but I find only my handkerchief. I pluck it from my inner jacket pocket and jot "Khoury Brothers. Antiques, Consignments, Treasures." I list the address and phone number underneath. My pen is leaking, and I hope the ink won't blur my handwriting so much I can't read it later.

The hair barrette must be antique, Victorian in fact. Probably English. I can imagine it in the folds of the box I am bringing back, wrapped with a gold ribbon, and Dianna's mouth opening in that evocative O-shaped exclamation of surprise and pleasure. She would pull her long, wavy hair back behind her head, and the crystals would make the highlights in her hair shine every time the light hit it. I want to bring it back for her.

My eyes lock on something beside the barrette box. "Family ring. Consignment only. 2 cts./18k." Its design is chaste, but the diamond exquisite. Like her. If she could only know what others saw in her, but I won't be the one to tell her. It would go to her head. It's too soon to think like this, but my collision with family makes me long for my house, my office, and Dianna. I admire the diamond's quiet beauty. It would look at home next to her proud university ring. A ring like that belongs on her finger. Such a shame we met at such a time, a time I no longer possess the right to make my own decisions.

I shake my head because it must rule my life for now. I cannot be certain she and I will work. It is too soon, and we need more time. She is too adventurous, too ambitious. They would frown on her here; hell, they already frown on her, without ever seeing her. It will take my every negotiation skill to convince my male family members. Would that my sister had lived! Would that my mother were still here! Yet perhaps they would not have seen her as I do. They never saw anything in Marie-Amelie, save a threat. Rasha brought us safety, prestige. They saw her as the personification of abundance. Now that abundance is all but rubble. Must I continue to sacrifice my life for their beliefs, my peace for their war?

For the moment, yes.

I must wait until the war is over. It is much too early to purchase anything at all, even the barrette. I trudge toward my family's home away from home, hoping my father is asleep. If he is awake, he will have me cancel my flight and visit Rasha. I am saddened to have missed Tariq who is in school, but I will return here soon. They'll see to that. They've been in Egypt too long. They want to go home, and they think the only route is through me. More than likely their home in Beirut—my home—does not exist any longer.

I pat the box under my arm. I must think of another gift to place inside it. I enter a newsstand, still open at this late hour and buy tomorrow's *Al Bayrak*. I glance at the headlines, always of another battle waging there. I tear the border from the paper and write a sentence expressing my love. I hide it beneath the torn fabric.

She will find it one day soon. By then, perhaps the war will be over, and we can live in Beirut together in peace.

CHAPTER THIRTY-FIVE

Borders

"Thank you, Sweetie. I love my new pen. I needed a new one." Qasim taps his breast pocket. "But what does it say? I possess seven languages, but not Latin."

Dianna smiles and looks down at her hands. "Love Conquers All."

Qasim smiles and squeezes her hand tight.

"Qasim, will you teach me Arabic?"

Qasim laughs and pulls Dianna as close as the gearshift will allow. "We need to work on your French first, Sweetie."

"And your Latin! No really, Qasim. I want to work in the Middle East." She missed him while he was gone, but his time away gave her time to think about herself, her future.

It is a morning in the earliest of summer. Windows rolled down, the scent of a rose bush wafts on the morning air, an intoxicating counterpoint to her thoughtful mood. Qasim points to a high rise with some large letters on it: "*Le Pavillion.* Tell me what that means," he demands.

Dianna thinks at first it is a trick question, and she hesitates a long time. Does he really think her French is that bad? That she is that dim?

"Well?" he asks, the professor glinting in his eyes.

"Well?" she echoes, adding, "Pavilion" in English. "It's the same word."

"Right," he says. He smiles at the road and whistles a song without a melody. She thinks she may have noticed some fear cross his features. "Why are you so fascinated with the Middle East?" Qasim asks with a dry laugh. "I'm not sure you know what you're getting into."

"If we can make peace there, we can make peace anywhere," Dianna says, and then giggles. "As 'old Blue-Eyes' says, the conflict has always been there, and we all come from there, in one way or another, don't we?"

Qasim smiles and pats her hand. "Good arguments. I repeat, you do not know what you're asking for. What would you do once you got there?"

The sun shines into his eyes, momentarily blinding him, and he readjusts his visor. Dianna compares this light to that of this translucent pre-morning, how it filtered into his bedroom from the rising, sleepy sun, illuminating the room like an old television screen with too much static. Is he reproaching or patronizing her?

Hours hence, after coffee and shower, and a glance at the morning paper, here she sits beside him in his Buick, wondering where those eyes that dart under smudges of lids are taking him. They do it when he sleeps, but they do it even when he is awake. Back and forth, crafting something. But what? *Is he going home? Does he want to go home?* She may never know the answer to this question, even if she asks him.

"Shall I call you tonight?" He smiles.

"I have to work tonight," she replies.

"I probably do, too," he says. "But not as late as usual."

"Qasim." She laughs. "I can't wait up for you until midnight. I didn't get enough sleep last night."

"You slept poorly?" he asks, and his eyes drift off the road in concern.

"Must be work," she lies. She wants him to believe she is doing something as important as he is, and she does not want him to know how uncomfortable his bed is for her. She thinks of his wife and his son every time she lies down beside him there. *Qasim bouncing his son on his knee on the mattress, both of them giggling. What would his ex-wife have been doing?* "What will you do today?"

"Meetings, meetings, an embassy event, more meetings. We talk, but we make no progress." He pulls his car to the curb. "Here we are. Shall I drop you at the corner or the door?"

"Corner," she says. "I need the air to clear my head." Pecks him on the cheek. Turns toward the stone building with the columns. Wonders if she has enough energy to make it through another day of little green cards. She turns back toward the car with an afterthought. "Take care," she calls through his window. "Don't work too late. *You* need more sleep."

He nods and drives away.

A familiar man sits by a pillar that supports the robust museum roof. He is there often and has earned the fond moniker of "Map Man." He may be homeless, yet he's not in any way threatening. He seems to be fabricating his own world out of the array of maps he carries around. Dianna and her colleagues wonder how long he has been in the city, wandering with his canvas bag of maps. They have made up stories about his past: He is actually very wealthy but has an incurable psychosis. He is a former spy. He is a disillusioned world explorer.

Today is only different from the other days she has seen him in that she has gathered up her pluck and walks up to ask him what he's doing. He hunches and pores over a map with an oversized magnifying glass. He is a slight man, though his hunching may have diminished a once taller physique. Under his red ski hat, his face is grizzled; he seems neither to shave nor to grow a real beard. He mumbles to himself, and Dianna overhears place names, some of which she knows, some of which are probably fictitious.

Dianna has been afraid of Map Man ever since her last encounter with the homeless man who attacked her. Sitting here in the sun, he seems much different today from that man, even the other homeless who cry out for her money. With caution, she approaches him, and stands gazing over his shoulder. He glances up but quickly returns to his research. The map he is working over is beautiful. It seems to have been drawn with India ink on a kind of parchment. She notices that underneath it is a book that contains cartography that is more current. The magnifying glass moves from one to another—first to the ancient world then to the space age world.

"Where is this place?" Dianna asks him, her left hand pointing out toward a large expanse.

The Map Man pulls the more recent map out, and Dianna sees that it is indeed frayed and aged, if not ancient. "See here?" He points a tapered but grimy fingernail to a broad expanse with little topography. "This is the Sahara—the Libyan Desert. The Allies bombed and mined this desert. They would have bombed it into a million smithereens—if it were not already in a million pieces." He pulls the ancient map out. "Look here!" he demands, his voice rising, his gaze darting from one map to another. "This is the same place. This is exactly the same place! Why does it look so different? They have not changed the borders. They have not built anything. No earthquakes. No tornadoes. No water to whittle away the mountains in the distance. Tell me," he says in a musing voice, now gentle as the breeze blowing around them. "Tell me why it looks like a different place."

He pulls back from her with a sudden ferocity, and she is thrown off balance. Dianna feels her eyes widen, and she's wary he will lunge at her. Instead, he glares at her, and then begins mumbling again. "Must be the bombs," he mutters. The rest is indecipherable. The Map Man has returned to his own world, and she cannot follow him there.

Dianna resolves that she must return to the real world, too. She trudges up the few remaining stairs and walks through the exhibit halls. It is rare that she does so; she usually uses the employee entrance. Yet it seems fitting today to walk through so many pieces of culture from so many different worlds. She passes through the Great Hall. Before she descends to her basement office, she takes the time to walk past the rooms on the right: a Dior dress, knights in armor, and her favorite, "Seated Female Figurine."

Though the one-inch statue is the oldest in the museum, and its features are weathered by years of sand and sun, it is still distinctively a woman, a woman with a full figure. Dianna has lovingly dubbed it "Female with Full Figurine," and she likes to visit it often. Its rotund antiquity, its enduring beauty help her keep her resolve not to purge herself of food again. This time, though, before she starts her circuit around the Medieval Art gallery toward downstairs, she gazes into an elaborate vitrine, studying her face. It seems she may have gained some weight this week. She passes the side of her right hand along her belly. No, it's still flat.

She stows her satchel with her clothes from last night under her desk and settles in to work. She is later than usual; everyone else is already busy with indexing duties. She will need to skip her break. She does not feel much like routine chatter anyway. If she remains at her desk, she will be able to look up the word "pavilion" in a dictionary.

Two hours later, she finds herself flipping through the pages of *Webster's*. She wishes she had an *Oxford English Dictionary* at her disposal, but this one will have to do. She finds the word she is looking for:

pavilion \pe-'vil-yen\ n [ME pavilion, fr. OF paveillon, fr. L papilion-, papilio butterfly; akin to OHG fifaltra butterfly, Lith peteliske flighty] 1: a large *often sumptuous tent 2: a part of a building projecting from the rest 3: a light sometimes ornamental structure in a garden, park, or place of recreation that is used for entertainment or shelter.*

So she was correct. She muses at the definitions, though. Why had he asked her that question? Again, she has learned a nuance, a cadence from him that she has never glimpsed before. About a word from her mother tongue, no less. *Pavilion* was derived from the French, *papillion*, for *butterfly*, but she has never connected the two words before. True to form, he was trying to tell her something without telling her. Was he alluding to himself, her, or their relationship as a pavilion, a shelter, a retreat? Was he thinking about how butterflies renew themselves, become completely different beings, at different times in their life cycles? No, maybe she was reading too much into it.

Are there butterflies in Lebanon? What color would they be? She shuts the book and determines she has pondered a single word enough for a single day. The thick dictionary closes on itself with a resounding clap as her coworkers come back from break, telling jokes and complimenting the nice weather.

"Hey you." Peter Fox gives her a wink as he sits down at his desk. "You're working too hard! Smile!"

She gives him a cold stare and returns to her cards. She forgets about butterflies, shelters, and maps for the moment, files them away in a rear memory compartment, and focuses on her work at hand. She shuts the night before away as well, in its own silent cocoon. What she doesn't want to ponder is this: Is Qasim flitting away from Dianna, or she from him?

CHAPTER THIRTY-SIX

Boxed In

Every time she sees Qasim, Dianna remembers the song from the radio. In fact, they are spending more time together. Tonight, when he greets her at his door, before she knows it, he has picked her up, and they are turning together in a full circle, 365 degrees. They are both laughing, from their bellies, when he puts her down.

"Now we know I can pick you up," he says. "Always good to know for the future." They laugh between kisses, and the sound carries down the street. Dianna hunches over, aching from laughter, but not wanting the laughter to stop.

She admires his beautiful box every time she sits on his living room couch, and tonight is no different. He brought it back with him. The box is carved and inlaid in the Damascene style, like a mosaic. She opens it, touches the lush, hand-sewn red interior, and recloses the lid to appreciate the handmade brass hinges. Qasim returns, carrying a soda he poured for her and a glass of Scotch. Dianna loves boxes—how they encompass a set parameter of space, how they can hold one's most treasured possessions or nothing at all, how they can sit or stack, always adding dimension and design.

"You like that box, don't you?" he asks in a low, gentle voice.

"I love it!" she answers without hesitation. The next instant, she thinks better of it. She's read that you never admire anything in a Middle Eastern dwelling, or the host will feel compelled to offer it to you. Til now, she has never complimented him on any possession, though she's quick to praise him. She tries to hide her reddening face.

"Here! Have it! It's yours," he vows with obvious enthusiasm.

"No, no," she objects, but he is already thrusting it toward her. She keeps her hands to her sides. He walks over to her satchel and places it inside.

She debates whether to accept or to make more of a fuss. She decides not to demur. It will only embarrass them both. She is secretly pleased he is giving her something he obviously values, something that merited the prime position on his coffee table. "Thank you." She kisses him on the cheek, then relaxes back into his couch.

He follows her lead and leans back into the sofa with outstretched arms. He brings her feet into his lap. She pulls back for an instant, unsure of what this means, worried about soiling the loveseat's delicate velvet fabric. Her toes brush against the decorative tassels that hang from the sofa when she relaxes into his lap. He smiles at her and pats her leg as he would a child's. He slips her sock off and rubs the white skin covering her foot. Lately, it's been customary for them to spend Friday nights together alone when he's in town. It's nice spending time in his domain, but she is still ill at ease. In fact, she's uncomfortable. She's bored at being stuck inside on a weekend night, and she's ill at ease that they haven't talked about much. Their caresses always lead straight to the bedroom, leaving little time for conversation.

"I've been interviewing," she comments. "In Washington."

"Ah?" he chortles. "Some senator's looking for..." Her stare stops him short. "I was teasing," he says.

She removes her foot and sits up straight. "Is that all you think I'm good for?"

"No, Sweetie. Honestly, I was teasing."

She gets up, pours herself some more soda, pours him more Scotch, and comes back and sits for a moment before she continues. She knows this isn't the best time to discuss her life plans, but she can't help herself. Her mother always told her she has no sense of timing her requests, which is why she was always sneaking out of the house behind her parents' backs. She would ask, the timing would be off, they would say no, she would do it anyway.

"I went to an employment agency. They gave me some leads. I have an appointment with Save the Children tomorrow. They have an entry-level position, but I'm not sure I want to stay in New York. She pauses, waiting for a reaction that doesn't arrive. "I'm thinking about teaching positions overseas. I'd like to teach the young women how to build homes."

"You? You, a teacher, with your patience? Or are you a construction worker?" His eyes crinkle at the edges.

"I have patience—with most people."

He gives her a sardonic smile.

"I was thinking that it might be easier to get a humanitarian position overseas," she comments.

The soda bubbles fizzle in her throat, threatening to come back up. She hates to ask anyone for anything, and him most of all. This is the third time she has inferred she'd like to live abroad. Now she must do it directly in spite of the strain this may put on an already tenuous relationship. She's been wondering about his intentions, but she hasn't shared hers. If the relationship is to progress, they need to talk about the future. Right now, her desire for some movement in her life overshadows her feelings for him.

She knows she's opening Pandora's Box. He must have realized it, too. He is silent, staring across the room. He finally puts his drink back on the coffee table coaster.

"Maybe Zimbabwe," she continues. "Maybe Nicaragua." She pauses and shifts her eyes to the floor. "Maybe Beirut."

He is still as a stone.

"Maybe with the UN."

"I don't recommend that presently. Really," he replies. "You take a position with the UN at your age, and you'll remain a secretary forever."

"But Leah isn't a secretary, and she's younger than I am."

"She's not with the UN."

"Maybe there's a position open at another nongovernmental organization."

"Beirut's a very dangerous place, Dianna. They're kidnapping Americans."

"I can take care of myself!"

Dianna comes from a past that was highly charged with danger of its own, and if she is truthful, she longs for her childhood's volatility to continue in some way. She wants to appease this emptiness she's been filling with food with someone else's problems. She wants to fill other people's lives in a way she hasn't been able to nurture her own. Besides, she can help. She identifies with and wants to help people who carry a legacy of terror and despair. Lately, with all Qasim's talk of peace, she's carrying around the image of herself as peacemaker like a secret locket. She wants him to realize that hers is a logical request—the chance to use her gifts to help others, to join him someday. Yet the times she's tried to explain her childhood, he has moved away from her, and he's been distant when she brought up training or travel.

"I'll have to check and get back to you." He stirs the ice in his drink.

She forces a laugh. "I'll wear a wig and speak French."

"Come now. They will know you are American. Your eyes…your skin." He touches her cheek with tenderness. "Come now, Dianna."

She looks down at this cursed skin, her skin, a barrier between her and the world from the day she was born. Ivory skin, porcelain like a doll's. It is skin that the "in" teenaged crowd of her childhood had pointed to and laughed at. Skin that prohibits her wearing a bikini, that sometimes necessitates a parasol, or at least a wide-brimmed hat. Sensitive skin that has erupted in rosacea and eczema. Skin that allows her only one hour on the beach between three and four in the afternoon and will allow even less time under an equatorial sun. Skin that brands her a WASP. Skin that may keep her from her dream.

He takes her hand in his and caresses it, tracing its veins with his beautiful fingers. His skin, tan even during winter, is a dark silhouette resting on hers. "Dianna, listen. I thought about you when a place opened up with an agency last winter. I thought better of it." The gall rises in her throat, and she turns her head away from him. He keeps his hand locked over hers. "You must understand…"

She backtracks. "It doesn't necessarily need to be in Beirut. I'll go anyplace where there's a need." Perhaps he thinks he's the reason she wants to go overseas. The kernel of this truth gnaws at her heart, but she thrusts it aside. This is her life, and she must keep it on course, not throw it away for a romance that may not ever yield results. She misunderstood him. He might have been discussing that wordless tune about love in a philosophical way. "You think your judgment is clouded because we are dating. I'm not asking you to hire me. I'm asking for an entrée; then I can handle the rest."

She searches for more rebuttals for his reservations. He doesn't want to put his reputation on the line for her. He is becoming too attached. He doesn't have the connections to get her a job outside the UN.

"No," he is saying. "Our dating wouldn't prevent me from helping you. Perhaps at the UN, it's true, but not elsewhere."

"You don't have enough confidence in my ability," she says. She pulls her feet from his lap and walks toward the kitchen to refill her glass.

"No," he calls after her, and she turns back toward him, waiting for more explanation. "That has nothing to do with it. I don't know that much about your ability, Dianna, but I know you well enough to tell them you are smart and hard working. That may not be enough." He rattles the ice in his empty tumbler. It is his second glass of Scotch, and she knows that his guard is down, so she presses on.

"I knew I'd have to make my own way," she says. "I'm thinking of applying to the Peace Corps, too." She comes back and sits down beside him, drink forgotten.

"You?" His breathy laugh is full of disdain. "You, without a hair dryer?"

She draws a breath, deep but quick. She feigns a smile. "How could you possibly know my hair drying habits? You almost never spend the night."

"Come, Dianna. Let's save this discussion. Come sit beside me."

"No! No! It must be now! If not now, when? If I keep all my words inside me, I'll burst! You talk of peace! How can I be at peace if I never speak my truth? How can we wage peace if I cannot speak my truth?"

"You can speak all you want. I was just joking."

"It didn't sound like a joke to me." She clenches one fist then the other, pacing the room.

"It's only a metaphor. I can't imagine you away from the conveniences of life." He shrugs, but she's hurt him.

"Is that why you never take me with you? Then you don't know me very well. I got sidetracked because of family challenges. I had to go with my second choice in careers. The college I attended wasn't a road to international work, and I needed to help support my family. I finally have a chance to do what I want to do, to work overseas, and be paid for it. I'll even be able to save some money." She leans forward, her head down in thought, pressing her hands together, moving her feet up and down on the smooth silk of the carpet. Why can't this man see her for who she is? She grimaces; the answer is obvious. They have shared much, are intimate, yet there is so much they do not know. Each time one of them has opened a window, the other has closed one.

Perhaps he notices her grimace. "Then more power to you." He raises his empty glass.

"So before I apply, you won't do anything for me?"

"No," he looks down his long, Roman nose at her. "They're only hiring secretaries. They wouldn't use your ability. You need to go somewhere else, where women are appreciated."

She doesn't know what to say. His words ring of truth. So she holds her tongue, something she must do too often with him. She curses herself for her skin, her womanhood, even her intellect. For instead of paving a way for her, her unique qualities seem to hold her back.

She despises what geography has done to them. The blazing Mediterranean sun he grew up under and the snowy winters of her youth resulted in these unbridgeable, stark differences that somehow have destroyed their trust. Like magnets, like poles, their opposite sides move close, pulling them together. When their negatives sides touch, they repel each other, each time further away than the last, across an infinite, divisive sea.

She's resolute. She'll find that job. She needs to work on herself, not him. How can she expect him to want to help her, to love her fully, unless she loves herself? Can she and Qasim ever actually achieve love, when they have moments when they are at such odds? How can they mend each other before they mend themselves?

Her insight saddens her until the pragmatist takes over—the part of her that shuts emotions away until they can be dealt with. Destiny has pulled her toward him, but she is used to doing things on her own. She knows her course. She swears she will never ask him about this matter again.

She walks over to her satchel and takes the box out, fully intending to return it to Qasim. Then she thinks better of it. It was a gift, after all. She holds the box in her hands, opens the lid, gazes at the red felt lining inside, and snaps the box shut.

CHAPTER THIRTY-SEVEN

Epithets of War

Dianna has dressed with meticulous attention, trying on three outfits before deciding on a belted royal blue dress that looks like silk even though it's polyester. She's excited about meeting more of Qasim's inner circle. Jamal has invited Dianna to a posh Italian restaurant for Qasim's birthday. He told her it's a surprise. She shivers as the harbor brings in a gust of wind as she turns a corner and heads toward the restaurant entrance.

Jamal is already seated at a small square table in the back, and Qasim is nowhere to be seen. Nothing unusual about that, yet Jamal is the only one at the table. He glances up when she enters, then back down at his menu. Some old photos lie next to his seat, probably for a trip down memory lane.

He keeps his eyes averted as he helps her off with her coat, then sits back down and beckons her to do the same. She wonders why his usually polite, approving nature has disappeared. He seems stiff and remote. They are going to celebrate, after all.

He picks up and gazes at a photo of a shell-shocked building, full of rubble, in stark contrast to the beautiful photos of the Middle East that line Qasim's office walls. Then he holds up a silkscreen alongside the photo for her to view.

"See this painting?" he asks. She feels his eyes searching her face as she gazes down at it, but his face looks noncommittal when she looks up at him, as curious as she is uncomfortable.

"Beirut?"

"Yes, my dear mademoiselle." His smile is sardonic instead of wistful. He points out the places in the painting, most of them landmarks. His touch is gentle, as a violinist would pluck the strings of his instrument. "Here is where a cousin of mine sang in concert. Here, the cinema Qasim frequented, as did I. The coffee houses where we would sit for hours, toking, what do you Americans call them? Ah yes, water pipes. The trolley that churned round and round the palm trees, taking us back home to Achrafieh or down to the water to stroll along the Corniche. See what remains of Beirut's Martyr's Square? Only this rubbish and a painting." He tosses the photo toward her, and it glides through the air.

She picks it up from the floor and glances back at him before she looks. The painting is in muted pastel colors. This black-and-white shot of a gritty, dirty Beirut is quite the contrast. The pixels are too large, and the photo is out of focus. Thin Corinthian columns hang from demolished walls. Neon signage is obliterated, and where the trolley tracks ran is a pile of rubble. Electrical wires hang like spider webs. A young girl, no more than twelve, already in hijab, gazes from a building that would be condemned in the U.S. She's already turning away from the camera, back into her tomb that she calls home.

"I am so sorry," Dianna says. She knows this is the Green Line that divides the city, yet the extent of the devastation leaves her knees wobbly. "I had no idea, even with the coverage in the papers here, that it was this bad. Does the whole city look like this?"

Jamal does not answer, and it takes her a beat to catch on that he has changed the subject.

"I must admit to a small deception," he says, his penetrating gaze resting on her neck. "I wanted privacy to share the entire story with you. Qasim will not be joining us." He comes around the table toward her.

Dianna's muscles tighten, and her throat constricts. She has wanted the whole story since she and Qasim met. "Yes." She picks a daisy from the bouquet on their table and plucks its white petals one by one. *He loves me.*

He takes the flower from her hand, and when she tries to draw away, his grip tightens. "Qasim's family felt he lacked ambition when he was young, but he was a student even though he loved the seaside and the cinema, and... romance. They sent him traveling, as he was the youngest, and they had other sons. Socially, he shamed them even while he brought them commercial success. It is quite the unexpected paradox that he brought them fame through his business dealings, and thus is poised to help his country more than anyone else in his family. Everyone in the Middle East knows the El-Kafry name because of his father, and Qasim himself. Yet when he shamed them, they knew he must marry at once. They found him a suitable wife who could expand their place in Lebanese society."

"Shamed them?"

"Oh, so he hasn't told you about his torrid little affair with that French girl? He's not spoken of the need to hide his attempt at taking his own life? A rapid marriage was the only way."

Dianna takes a breath in. "So he is still married?"

"All in good time, dear." Jamal traces one finger along the veins of her hand, and his very ruddy skin almost makes her pale skin glow as the overhead light hits it. She looks down at the traffic outside, people coming and going. Happy people leading happy lives.

"This alliance keeps the business going, and it has certain political will at its core," he continues. Qasim is destined for great things. He needs to get over his youth. He has remained immature for far too long. It is time he thought of his country."

"So he might run for office?" Dianna jerks her hand away and begins plucking petals. *He loves me not.*

Jamal's dark eyes flutter, then turn even darker. "He *will* run for office."

"And does Qasim know of this plan?"

Jamal spreads his arms wide. "Look at you, my dear. How could you ever understand his joys, his burdens, his life? His life in Lebanon. Of course, Qasim knows. This is his last hurrah, so to speak." His smile is back, imperious.

"So he remains married?" Dianna repeats.

Jamal runs his fingers over her hair, another reminder that he owns this conversation. He snatches the daisy from her hand and throws it to the floor. "Even in this country, Dianna, dear, do you elect an unmarried man for high office? A divorced man?" He lets the strand of hair drop. "I doubt it."

Dianna's eyes pierce through him, and she can't seem to move a muscle, frozen to the spot.

"Enjoy him while he is with you. Treasure the moments. And know that he will one day return, to his rightful place."

The server passes with a huge platter of food, leaving their table in shadow. "I understand," Dianna tells him. "I don't yet know if I will comply, but I understand. I thank you for filling me in on *your* 'whole story.'" His words ring true, deep down beyond her body, even beyond her mind, but she does not want him to know she believes him.

"Let his country live," Jamal murmurs, his voice less sinister, though his eye twitches. She picks up her coat and turns to leave, but he does not assist her. "What you know, you know," he says. "I will say no more. I leave it to you. It is your decision."

Her arm catches in her coat sleeve, but she keeps moving toward the door. "By the way," he says as Dianna reaches the threshold, "do you know how Martyr's Square got its name?"

"It certainly seems to have been some sort of massacre," Dianna replies, pulling on her gloves to erase the memory of his clammy fingers.

"Yes, martyrs executed during the Ottoman rule that time. We Lebanese argue about the statue there. It truly matters not why they were martyrs or even their affiliation or creed. One of the statue's arms was recently blown off, a fitting symbol, no? Whoever these young people were, they were trying to overthrow the bondage imposed by the Turks. All we have ever wanted is our freedom. The Turks only brought us war and hatred. This square stands for division. This is where it began and where it continues."

"And peace?" Dianna raises one eyebrow.

"That will come at a price."

"I need to figure out if I'm a martyr or not," Dianna tells him. "I'll let you know when I do." She turns on her heel and walks into the restaurant's vestibule, walls covered in blood-red wallpaper, already letting the dark of another winter night in.

CHAPTER THIRTY-EIGHT

Crisis, Escalated

At first, Dianna turns away from the newspaper. The front-page photo is too disturbing. It shows a battle scene, although she doubts that either the Israelis or the Palestinians in the photo would call it that. Then her curiosity gets the better of her. The dust, and perhaps cloud cover—she can't tell—obscure the action. A man on horseback has a rifle bayonet drawn in a blur over the head of a scarfed woman. Her children cower behind her flowing skirt. The headline states in black bold letters: "Israel Invades Lebanon." Dianna wonders what happened next, after the shutter opened, then closed again. Sitting on the marble steps of the museum, she watches traffic thread outward in every direction, and men and women in New York business attire–anything basic black—stroll past on their lunch hour, while vendors sell T-shirts proclaiming "I Love New York." Every so often, she spots a jet plane in the distance, climbing hard to break its ties to *terra firma*, bound for who-knows-where. Dianna wishes she were on it.

She holds this unfolding front-page tragedy with trembling fingers—a moment caught by chance, yet the seconds that followed are never to be recorded. She wonders if anyone else who gazed at the photo this morning had these thoughts, possessed these feelings. The photo brings the Middle East straight to her doorstep here in the United States, more than a country, more than a war zone, more than a mythical place she's heard of since childhood. In this moment, staring at these faces, it is as though these two worlds are superimposed on one another, each one its own reality, but creating a third world, full of subtle shading and layers. She shivers despite the warm day, and a breeze ripples the page back. She takes this as a sign she should put the newspaper away and get on with her day. What has happened has happened. What good can she do sitting here staring at this picture?

CHAPTER THIRTY-NINE

What's Not Said

The meeting ripples with tension. The men around the table slump forward, their faces inscrutable. Everyone knows this resolution will not fly today, though. Too many people at the table, all with separate agendas.

I adjust my headset, hoping my eyes do not betray my frustration. These meetings continue today even though everyone here realizes the stalemate happened yesterday. Nothing will occur here other than the usual formalities in tomorrow's General Assembly. They will draft something flimsy, and everyone will walk away from the table to catch their breath.

I feel pride at being pulled into a meeting immediately preceding the General Assembly even when every nation knows this war will go on for a very long time. As much as I feel honor being at the table, I know I could effect change more on the ground back home. If I sit here long enough, someone may ask me to travel to Uganda. No one in his right mind would want to do that now.

This war in Uganda has just begun, and the ambassador won't admit genocide is occurring even though everyone sitting here knows it is. Child soldiers, guerrilla warfare, atrocities. Yet no one here today will hold Amin accountable because he might lose all his chips at the bargaining table. If that happens, he will go home and lose his head. The more these bush wars change, the more they stay the same.

I hand my boss the document of the moment, and the chief whispers in his ear. His boss nods, and hands me a stack of papers to take back for review.

I head out the door with some relief, documents thick under one arm. A stern Jamal waits for me in the hall, hands in his pockets. He crosses them over his chest when he catches sight of me.

"I am heading over to deliver these documents," I tell Jamal.

"Let me walk with you."

Jamal has something grave to say, then. He usually wants to speak behind closed doors.

"Yes, Jamal? Is everything alright back home?" We begin to walk down the red-carpeted hallway.

"Qasim, you would have done well to listen to my advice."

"About?" My neck stiffens though I play ignorant. I know what Jamal is hinting at.

"I told you to keep out of the public eye."

He and Dianna have been seen, then. "I doubted anyone would see us at a play like that. Look, Jamal..."

"No, you look, Qasim, and look well. That flirtation is now all over the UN, and if here, it will soon be abroad. It must end."

"I am sorry, Jamal. I wanted to please her while I am able to be with her. I owe her that much."

"You owe her nothing! Nothing! She is an American!"

I stand hangdog in front of my mentor. I have no rebuttal.

"It is no matter, now, Qasim. Gemayel has asked for you."

I stop dead in my tracks. "Now?"

"He asked me to inquire about your interest in a position. If the answer is 'yes,' he will telephone you tomorrow. If your little escapade were not Lebanese news, it would have been a Cabinet post. He probably wants you out of here before you can do more damage." Jamal rolls his eyes.

He wants me there to sway the Sunni side to his line of thinking. Jamal cares little about what I do with Dianna. He's had more affairs of the heart than I can count. Jamal's concern is Rasha's opinion. She is the wild card in this appointment. He wants me to pacify her. "When?" I ask.

"As soon as possible. I suggest you begin packing tonight." Jamal starts to walk away but thinks better of it. "We may need to send someone to sell the house for you."

"You know what this means to me personally," I say, loud enough for others in the hall to hear.

Jamal swings around, his face ruddy with rage. His bushy brows reach up toward what remains of what used to be a thick mane of hair.

I back up two steps. I have never seen my friend in such a fury. "Jamal, all I ask is a few weeks."

"You would betray your family, your country, for—an American?"

I know I have lost this battle, though I have much more to say. It matters not. The only choice in life is to live rather than die. I have faced death once. I would rather live.

CHAPTER FORTY

Preparing for Battle

Dianna wakes in the wee hours not knowing where she is. At first, she thought she was in her bed. Lately, Qasim has been too busy to come her way. Lately, even his bedroom seems to have a revolving door: initiated, spent, done. Rote. Qasim has been too busy to stay, and she, too, is busier, having taken a second job in a boutique to make ends meet and send more money home. They ended up falling asleep, but she's thinking of going back to her place, even at this early hour.

Last night, Qasim and Dianna methodically sipped their drinks and watched the evening news. There was no report datelined Beirut. It's been three days since Israelis crossed the border into Lebanon, and late last month, she read about UN reports of Israeli "large-scale tank and infantry training in Southern Lebanon." She asked Qasim about the border skirmishes, but he told her they'd talk about it once the news was over. Then he was too tired.

They drifted in to his king-too-big-sized bed, and he wrapped his arms around her, nuzzled his nose in her neck, her breasts, laid his head on her shoulder. She felt his body relax and decided to let him be, but then he surprised her, kissing her with more tenderness than usual.

Dianna was going to tell him about what Jamal told her, but his tenderness took them in another direction, bringing back memories of their first night in this bed. He looked exhausted, so she stroked his temples. He moaned, his kisses became firmer, and his leg locked over hers.

She responded, her mind drifting, letting him take her where he wanted her to go. He sent his hands gliding up the muscles of her legs, and she moved her body in tempo with his. They kissed, and kissed again. No words needed. And then it was finished, and she was left alone in darkness, his gentle breath drifting across the bed.

Sleep eludes her. His fingertip grazes the curve of her waist, tickling her. She sighs and shifts her weight, trying not to wake him. Where is this half-fulfilled passion leading? To his swift exit? To hers? She curls up against him, but he moves away—into his own space, his own dreams. At times, she feels she is sleeping with a part of her heart, other times with a total stranger.

She traces the ever-darkening circles under his eyes; she can't help herself. He looks much older when he is in repose, unaware. His body seems smaller and more vulnerable, strange without his usual frenetic energy and charming smile. She wonders what project he is working on that is taking up so many night hours, or perhaps it is Project Beirut. She watches his chest rise and fall, then runs her fingertip down to his chest, ever so lightly, until she can feel his heart beat pumping through the skin and thick yet fine black hair. Funny how this chest, which one year ago seemed as mystical as a map of the Orient, is now part of her world. Perhaps this is how a relationship evolves after a year: comfortable, familiar, routine. Should she trust him or Jamal?

***

"I hope you don't have to travel soon," she ventures the next evening perching on the edge of her bed.

Qasim laughs. "What do you mean?"

"It's getting too dangerous even for you."

"It will get better." He pats her back. "I'm here for a while anyway."

"And how long is 'a while'?"

"I don't know, my dear." His smile is tight. "I never know."

She takes a deep breath, plunges in to make her heart known: "I worry, you know."

"There's no reason for you to worry about me." He laughs again.

"What about the Israeli invasion?" she ventures.

"Someone is always trying to claim my country for their own," he says with a deep sigh. "The Ottomans, the French, the Palestinians, the Israelis. Once they take hold of a piece of land, they all fight amongst each other. Everyone always thinks that the land, the trees, the sea can be owned." His eyes grow narrow, and she can feel his anger. "Really, truly, I tell you. I have always, *always* believed that violence solves nothing. It is not even a last resort."

"That's your Quaker education," she teases him.

"Everyone should feel this way. Everyone! The world would be a different place."

She grows serious. "I agree with you." She puts her hands behind her back and bending her elbows, leans back. She wants him to relax, too, to realize that she is open to his ideas, that she is not the enemy.

He shakes his head like it's full of cobwebs. Then he smiles again and rubs his hands up and down his thighs.

"Qasim," she says, and she looks straight into his stark black eyes. "I will worry about you until I am no more." She takes another deep breath, not believing she has mustered the courage to say this. "That does not mean I will ever prevent you from doing what you were put here to do, that I will ever ask you to give up your freedom, your convictions, and least of all, your country."

He tentatively touches her face and wipes away a tear that has not fallen. Her eyes fill with water, and when she looks up, she realizes his have, too. His kiss is tenacious, different somehow than the kiss he gave her at their last meeting, hearkening back to their first night together. She stiffens at first, uncomfortable with his ardor, but returns his kiss. He unbuttons her blouse, unhooks her bra, and they recline in one smooth movement. She closes her eyes and loses herself in his caress. He lifts her skirt and runs his hands up as far as the waistband will allow. Never will she be able to resist his touch when he is totally with her. She moans and wills him to continue. She rips at the button impeding his progress. They linger in this moment, a mutual reciprocity, like flowers opening petal by petal to the sun. Drunk with desire, Dianna abandons any remaining vestige of control. Qasim, staring directly into her eyes, matches her passion in kind. She gasps, and it is too much for him. Responding to his release, she catches the wave and rides it with him to the end.

"Stay," she whispers.

"I cannot," he replies. "I am so tired, and I have an early meeting." He lays his head for one precious moment on her shoulder, and her hand runs distractedly up and down from the hair on his head to the hair on his chest. He almost nods off to sleep. She notices that his ankles are swollen, even more than the last time they were together. Then he sits up, and she gets up abruptly too, pouting.

"I have to use the bathroom," she says. "But when I come back I need to tell you what Jamal said."

She flushes the toilet before she even closes the door, looks at herself in the mirror, dabs at her smudged mascara. When she sits down, she gasps. There is blood on her leg, bright blood, yet she has no injury. She jumps up and leans against the wall. She can feel her heart pounding, but it does not seem to be in her body. She counts to 100. Then she flushes the toilet again and walks back into her bedroom. Already dressed, Qasim perches on the edge of her mattress, as though waiting for school dismissal. She smiles in spite of what she needs to tell him.

"Qasim, there was blood when I went to the bathroom. It's not my time of the month. Are you injured?"

He grips the mattress but does not reply. He just stares at her.

She goes over, inspects his arms, rolls up his pant legs, inspects his legs. "I don't see any cuts. It's not my blood. It has to be your blood."

He opens his mouth as if to speak but doesn't.

"Do you understand?" She moves in closer to hear him.

"Yes...yes."

"You need to see a doctor." She sits down by him and clutches his hand.

"I guess I should." He looks at the floor, then at her hand on his.

She wonders what he is feeling. She cannot determine if it is shame, fear, or if he is peeved that she knows there's something wrong with him. She catches her breath but knows she must continue. She must convince him to be treated. "No, Qasim, it is essential that you go see a doctor. This is not normal."

He nods his head, first north to south, then east to west.

"Are you in any pain?"

"I suppose. A little." He is frowning in concentration.

"Where does it hurt?" Her hand moves toward his abdomen, but he pushes it back and gets up.

"My back," he says back in a clipped voice and opens the bedroom door.

"Promise me you'll call the doctor tomorrow morning."

"Yes, yes, I will."

"That's not a 'maybe,' is it?" she asks. "It's a 'yes'?'"

"Yes!" he shouts. He rushes out of the room and down the hall.

She pursues him along the narrow hallway, down the stairs. Before he can open the door, Dianna hugs him, not wanting to let him go. "You'll be alright," she says, trying to believe it herself. She has no idea what this symptom could mean—to him or to her.

"Yes, yes, of course I will be," he murmurs in her ear and turns.

"Call me!" she shouts after him, but only the night air hears.

CHAPTER FORTY-ONE

Wounds

The phone jars Dianna awake. She hopes it's not about her mother; then she remembers the evening.

"Qasim!" The word is out of her mouth almost before she picks up the receiver.

"No, it's Heather," says a bleary voice on the other end.

"Heather? What's wrong?" She reaches for the clock. "It's two in the morning."

"I took some aspirin, and then I took some sleeping pills to help me sleep."

"And?"

"Well, I guess I took a few too many aspirin." Heather's laugh is disconcerting.

"You need to call 911!" Dianna says with all the force she can muster.

"You think so?"

"Yes! Hang up and call. I'll meet you at the hospital, okay?"

"If you really think I should."

"Yes, yes. Do you want me to call?" Dianna rubs her eyes with vigor, willing herself fully awake, trying to make sure this is no dream.

"No, I'll do it. If I don't fall asleep."

Dianna hangs up and calls 911—they have already received Heather's call. She dresses and realizes she is leaving the house without buttoning her shirt. She grabs her purse and flies to her battered Toyota. She notices a man crouching in the shadows across the street. Dianna is fumbling with the key when Leah sticks her head out the window.

"Hey, what's going on?"

"Heather swallowed some pills."

"What?" Leah leans further out the window.

Dianna cups her hands around her mouth for more volume. "Heather swallowed pills!"

"Oh my God! Do you need me to drive you to the hospital?"

Dianna hesitates. "No," she says eventually. "You've got work in the morning. I can handle this."

She gets in the car, revs the engine, and screeches out of her parking space, narrowly missing the car in front of her. She grimaces; she won't find a space near her building when she returns.

Heather lies on a gurney when she arrives at the Emergency Room at nearby Beth Israel, and her face matches the sheet. Her long, curly hair trails over the corner of the gurney. The freckles on her nose have all but disappeared. Her deep green eyes emit sparks of fear, a good sign.

"Thank you for coming," Heather almost whispers. "Please, please, don't call my parents." She bursts into jagged sobs and grips Dianna's fingers so tightly her ring leaves a red mark in the fleshy part of the lower knuckles.

"Has the doctor seen you yet?" Dianna tries not to flinch in pain and keeps her hand in Heather's.

"Yes, he says they're going to have to pump my stomach." Heather begins wailing again.

"Heather...why? Why did you do this?"

"Mark and I broke up." Heather's voice cracks. Her hands shake over the crisp white linen.

Dianna catches her breath, trying to convey calm. "It'll be okay, Heather," she comforts. "I'll be here when they're done. You can come to my house."

"Thank you," Heather whispers again, and they whisk her down the hall.

CHAPTER FORTY-TWO

Under Siege

I wake gasping and covered with sweat. The pain sears through the left side of my back, but it takes me an instant to realize where I am and that I need more pain medication. My swollen eyes cannot make out the hands on the clock. I know it is deep night, a night with no moon, and the clouds let in little light. I begin to make out the margins of bedclothes, wrung together at the foot of my mattress in a knot. I hope I have not screamed loud enough for the neighbors to hear. I prefer to bear my pain alone. I have not dreamt this dream since I reached American shores, but I carried it with me all through my marriage. I would wake screaming then, everyone rushing to my bedside but fearing to touch me as my arms flailed in fury.

In fact, it is no dream, but a retelling of what happened, and what might have been—had I not driven from the cliff on Mount Lebanon the night before I was to be wed, or had I succeeded. The dream always begins in hospital. I wake, the bandages covering what little sight I have through swollen eyes and brain. They call my name, and I try to answer, but the tube down my throat prevents it. Instead, I hear an ugly grunting that seems to come from someone other than me. A guttural, animal noise, an animal in pain. The dark takes over again, and I am glad of it because, in the blackness of this coma, I see the moon above me, as I did that night I sped over the cliff, instead of harsh lights and peering faces. The blurry profiles I see when I am conscious are ever worried. Yet, instead of concern for me, I hear snippets about what will happen after I wake.

"What shall we tell Rasha?"

Andromeda begat a nation with Perseus, who rescued her from his parent's sacrificial hand. St. George, or al-Khadr as we in Beirut call him, slew a dragon to save both Beirut and his fair maiden. They found glory in love. I risked death for love and found hell instead. I have no maiden, no love, no life, only the concern that my actions have not brought the family honor, prestige, and wealth through a sham of a marriage that neither Rasha nor I want. We do not even know each other. I suspect, when I can claim enough wits to do so, that there is someone else she prefers. I am cuckold before I am wed.

"Will he live?"

The time shifts, as it does in every man's dream, and I am sitting in my bed, my broken leg bound and strung up like a slaughtered lamb, when they begin to speak beyond their circle, and then to me, of their worries, of their renewed hope for my wedding plans. I feel nothing but shame. I could not even do the family honor by exiting this life. What they believe will lead to my happiness will lead to their misery.

"Qasim, you lay there a month! We thought you might join our beloved sister."

I am fully awake now, sitting here with pain once more in 1982. I sit on the corner of my bed, feeling the ache from my kidney, feeling the sharp tingle of a ruptured disk that plagues me still. Feeling doom cast its shadowy carpet, dropping its pall on my passion. I must stand strong, bear this pain, end this sorrow for Dianna. How little I can do for the women I love. A strong man does what he can to protect those he cherishes. I can at least, no, at *most*, save Dianna from my own wretched fate. I can keep the sad weight of Lebanon that rests on my shoulders. I chose duty over love. When I could bear it no longer, I chose myself over family. I can no longer choose my heart over my honor or my country, but that does not mean I do not sit in sorrow.

I struggle up and pace, slinging open the blinds to let in what little light exists. I will survive this pain, just as I always have. I must return to work, pack, prepare to respect my family, save my country, and salvage my career.

The pain seers through my back, into my abdomen. I double over and scream. It is finished. I feel the stone pass.

We must live our lives as they were written. She will remain written on my heart.

CHAPTER FORTY-THREE

Friendly Fire

The next two days fly by in a blur. Dianna fears another suicide attempt if she sends Heather home too soon. Yet she is bleary-eyed from too little sleep and too much emotion. Heather consumes her few hours away from work.

She has not heard from Qasim. She calls him at close of business, the second day, a Friday. His secretary informs her that he's on sick leave. Her heart is in her throat as she dials his home phone. This same man walked away from an automobile accident and returned to his office immediately following oral surgery, even before the anesthesia wore off. Sick leave is not in his vocabulary. The phone rings, six, seven, eight times. Dianna slams the receiver down and dials again. She gives up on the third attempt, and she calls hospitals.

The hospitals tell her he has not been admitted. Dianna paces up and down the narrow, redbrick tile of her tiny kitchen, calculating whether to go to his house. He probably isn't there. What would she do, break in? She lets a few tears fall down her cheeks to relieve her sense of desperation. After a few silent sobs, she attempts to focus on the problem again. She decides to call again in an hour's time.

The hour is divided between preparing Heather's dinner and watching the second hand on the kitchen clock. She can hear the mechanism behind the clock's face clicking as each second passes, synchronized with her heartbeat. Dianna finds the bread and makes herself cinnamon toast. One, two, three slices she shoves down into her mouth. Then she calls Heather to join her for dinner.

Heather sits across from her at the table, picking at her chicken potpie and iceberg lettuce. Dianna has finished hers.

"May I have some more water, please?" Heather's eyes wander from the glass to the wall and back again. An hour passes, and Heather retreats to Dianna's bedroom. First, Dianna prays. Then she paces and breathes, *one two three, one two three*. She badly wants to get rid of her two dinners, but she will not allow herself. Instead, she picks up the receiver again. Her finger touches each number with slow precision. She does not even recognize the voice at the other end of the line. "Qasim?"

"Hi," comes a weak reply. She hears voices in the background, or is it a radio?

"What's happened? How are you?" She stands statue still, afraid to move a muscle.

"I have a simple case of kidney stones. A little infection, too. I'll be fine."

She can hear his heavy breath. "I'll come over," she states instead of asks.

For a moment, all she can hear is labored breathing. "No. Don't."

She draws breath to argue but thinks twice about it. His tone has told her that the matter is closed. "Please call me if you need me," she squeaks and hangs up the phone.

She is weeping in earnest. Luckily, Leah has not gotten home from work. She can't run to her bedroom. Heather is occupying it, and she won't allow herself near a bathroom. Dianna throws herself on the couch to stifle the sounds that involuntarily force themselves out of her chest.

"Dianna?" Heather calls.

Dianna tries to catch her breath. She cannot answer.

"Dianna?" Heather calls again. "Are you alright?"

Dianna bites her wrist as hard as she can. When she looks down at her wrist, she counts four red teeth marks. She focuses on them and the slight pain throbbing up her arm. "Yes, I'm alright," she calls back. "I accidentally ran into the furniture." She hears Heather fumbling around upstairs, trying to get out of bed. "No, Heather, you're too weak," she says. "I'll go to the bathroom and run some cold water over it."

"If you're sure," Heather calls.

Dianna marches toward the hallway. She needs to calm her reeling stomach. She places her teeth on her other wrist but does not bite down this time. Then she takes the hallway with quick, measured steps, to avoid any questions. She locks the bathroom door, turns on the water, and gazes into the mirror for a second only. She makes the decision before she can pick up Leah's toiletries and throw them at the reflection staring back at her. She steps back, leans over the toilet, closes her eyes tight, and sticks her finger down her throat. The relief is instant.

Dianna brushes her teeth, walks out of the bathroom, and leans against the wall in the hallway. Her head spins. *This is the last time.* She's made a decision. This demonish behavior cannot continue. And if she stays with Qasim, it will continue. She will leave him. She will take the next job offered.

"You alright, Dianna?" Heather calls.

"Sure, Heather! You doing any better?"

"Yes. Do you want to do something this weekend? I was thinking it might do me good to get out."

'Getting out' is not exactly uppermost on Dianna's list of desires. Still, it might prevent any further trips to the bathroom. She does not know how feelings of relief and disgust can coexist, but they do within her, like Siamese twins. She wants normalcy in her life more than anything else. "Tomorrow night?" she suggests.

Heather's face actually lights up. "We both could use some time away from our men, don't you agree?"

Dianna doesn't ask if Heather and her boyfriend are back together. "Yes!" Dianna says. "Do you mind if I invite Leah?"

"The more the merrier!"

The next night is a beautiful one, spring finally turning toward summer. Eager to enjoy the evening air, they decide to dine *al fresco*, choosing a restaurant in the East Village where they can relax on its rear veranda. A few of the night sky's shimmering stars manage to break through the veranda's roof of wisteria, seemingly to shine on them. The wine flows freely, and the women giggle at each other's jokes as well as their own.

"So how's good old Mohammed?" Leah is asking.

"That's not his name." Yet Dianna cannot help but smile.

"Is he away?" Leah pulls a cigarette out of her purse and places it in her lips but doesn't light it.

"No." Dianna twists her napkin in her lap.

"Why are you gracing us with your presence, then, Dianna?" Leah smirks, and then fumbles for a lighter. "Anybody have a match?"

"Can't I have a girls' night out?" Dianna slides her chair back from the table and crosses her legs.

"I guess so." Leah swishes her wine in her glass. "You seemed a little tense." Her eyes hedge toward Heather.

Dianna shakes her head no. She doesn't want Leah to think Heather is the burden she carries, at least not the bulk of her load.

"Come on, Dianna, 'fess up."

"Yes," Heather echoes. "What happened last night?"

Dianna clears her throat. "He's ill."

"Oh, come on," Leah chortles.

"No. He's really sick. He has kidney stones."

Leah's eyebrows go up, and Heather looks away.

"He's in a lot of pain." Dianna uncrosses her legs and brings her napkin up to her lips, then puts it on the table, staring at the small pink stain her lips have left.

"Oh my God, Dianna. And you're here with me?" Heather touches her arm. Dianna turns it over so the bite marks are hidden. "Go to him!" Heather cries.

"Well, I tried, but he told me he didn't want me to come." Dianna hears her voice choke on the word *want*.

Leah hesitates, but only for a moment. "Look, Di, he's not the person for you. You're too good for him."

Dianna looks at Leah, then at Heather. "I'm not too good for him, but I'm beginning to realize we're not meant to be together. The bridge isn't wide enough."

"Think he's got another woman?" Heather ventures.

"I don't know," Dianna says. "I suspected his work was his other woman."

"Work isn't nursing him," Leah chimes in.

"Well, he's pretty sturdy. I know he's got a high pain threshold." Dianna clears her throat, wanting it to sound more authoritative. She does not believe herself.

"He seems like a little cry baby! I mean, when he stubbed his toe that time I knocked on his door…" Leah purses her lips and stops.

Dianna measures Leah's words, trying to make sense of them. "When did he stub his toe? I don't ever remember him stubbing his toe."

"Well, he was surprised to see me," Leah begins, then changes her tone into her usual convincing, sarcastic one. "You know, I haven't told you this, but he invited me to his office a couple of months ago. I guess he didn't think I'd come, but I was curious."

"And you went," Dianna finally replies. She wonders why Leah is telling her this—perhaps she wants Dianna to step out of her way. She's hinted at it before.

"Well, I thought he could get me back to Palestine," Leah counters. "Pure business."

"A pure business *deal*," Leah puts the emphasis on the last word. "He told me to stay out of Palestine anyway. He said it was too dangerous. He doesn't mean anything to me. Come on, Dianna. I told you that you were better off without him. He's not good enough for you. You want to end up being some rich Arab man's mistress?"

Dianna pushes her chair back completely from the table. She wants to say, "How could you?" Instead, she motions to the waiter and orders another drink. She has no ownership of this man, of anyone. She asks no more questions.

Her mind whirls with the women's names and personalities Qasim has spoken of. All this time, Qasim has been exploring. That's what divorced men do. Hell, that's what all men do. Dianna has been one of his many conquests. He was probably speaking with women on the phone in Arabic. Leah realized this months ago, perhaps from the moment she met him.

Dianna has been in denial. If she had looked more closely, she would have seen his intent wasn't at all serious. She was worried that she was breaking up a failed marriage, while he was playing the field. When had he cooled toward her? January? February? That was probably when he found someone and began to get serious. He probably has his real girlfriend there, tending to his every need. What a fool she's been. It's difficult to feel irate at Leah when she has merely shown her the truth. Dianna wants to ask if they actually slept together, but she blushes at the thought of spreading her pride on the table like a bad hand of poker. *They must have. Look at Leah. She knows how to please a man, how to keep him coming back for more. Stop!* she tells herself. *Stop these thoughts before they consume you. In the end, none of this matters. It is already the past.*

"Oh, great, an Irish band!" Heather says, with a little too much exuberance. "My favorite!"

A band is setting up in the corner of the veranda. They pull mandolins, fiddles, and a guitar out of cases. It's time to cast out her demons.

"You can't believe anything Leah tells you," Heather whispers to Dianna. "She's always wanted him for herself."

The drink comes, and Dianna takes a gulp. It smooths her parched throat. She takes another gulp and looks toward the band. A man with curly blond ringlets tunes a fiddle. He looks over at the table and smiles, brushes his hair from his eyes. Dianna knows what she must do.

CHAPTER FORTY-FOUR

Ceasefire

Dianna realizes tonight that heartache is more than a metaphorical cliché. The pain that extends under her ribs, a pounding, physical grief, surprises her, but she recognizes it for what it is. She turns half her attention to the Irish band and taps her foot but misses beats. When the band finishes the set, she watches the lead singer approach her table. His name is Connor. His wavy, mussed hair and lithe body would have once turned her head. She looks at him in appreciation, but without any interest, even though he directs all his jokes toward her, waiting for her laughter. She is hard-pressed to produce even a smile to amuse him.

He buys a round of drinks for all three women and chats amicably in his Irish brogue. "You know we still have fairies in Ireland," he says, winking at Dianna. "Some say they follow us around, waiting to steal our cow's milk."

Dianna can feel her brow arch in interest in spite of her gloom. "Fairies?" she repeats.

"Oh yes, wee fairies and some dressed up as lasses," he continues. "Don't ever let a neighbor girl milk your Kerry cow."

Dianna furrows her brow. "What's a Kerry cow?"

"Woman! You never heard of a Kerry cow?" Connor glistens with glee to have caught her attention. "Only the best milking cow in all of Ireland, if not all the world."

"We have pretty good livestock right here," interjects Leah.

Connor pretends to choke on his beer. "What, you call those butterballs on four legs livestock?"

Leah folds her arms on top of each other and sits back in her chair. She doesn't answer.

Dianna laughs under her breath, and she can tell he notices. He sits with them long past time for him to play again. His band members motion a couple of times before he finally joins them on the stage. When Connor's session ends, he offers to drive Dianna and Heather home in a beat-up

Volkswagen. Leah looks as if she is going to give a standing ovation when Connor leads Dianna out of the restaurant. When the three of them reach their destination, Heather and Leah quickly say good night. Heather averts her eyes while Dianna turns the key in the lock and lets her inside, and Leah waves and flutters her eyes as she goes upstairs. Then Connor and Dianna sit on the steps and look up at the night sky, which is clear and dark.

She lets him kiss her. The Irishman's golden ringlets brush against Dianna's cheek as his lips meet hers in a lingering, almost familiar way. His breath smells like fresh pears despite the beer he has been drinking. Dianna remains unmoved.

Even so, she says she'll accompany Connor to Central Park for a bike ride the next day. He seems gentle, harmless, and sardonically melancholy, and she longs for someone with whom to share her own grief. Too fatigued even to shed a tear, she asks Heather if she might sleep in her own room tonight. Stripping away her clothes, she throws them into a ball on top of her covers. *This is the bed that we made love in last week*, she thinks as she drifts into sleep.

Dianna wakes shivering, the sun shining in an early morning slant that infiltrates her dreamless night. She showers, dresses, and walks resolute to retrieve a pen and paper.

Dear Qasim,

We've left many words unsaid. I've held my tongue. I didn't want to ruin the little time we had together, and I was afraid of revealing my feelings. I was afraid of losing you, and instead, I'm losing myself. I was trying to keep the peace, but I started my own little war inside. I don't understand your life, and I fear I'm more burden than joy to you. You've reawakened some demons that I felt I'd slaughtered when I moved to New York. It's time to keep moving, to love myself first so I won't be afraid to love at all.

This much I know is true: Heaven sent you to me in answer to my prayers. I was praying for someone who would lift me up and make me alive again, and you did. You lit up my life that night, and you will continue to shine in its corners even after you are no longer with me.

Your country needs you. Please remember our similarities instead of our differences. It's not that I didn't love you. It's that I loved you too much. I can't risk having my life swallowed up by that love.

Dianna

She takes care folding the letter and seals it in an envelope before she can change a word. Then she stows it in the box he gave her, waiting for him to get better so she can send it.

The next day is warm, the sun bright overhead as she waves at Connor, who waits for her outside her building. He stands grinning beside two bikes. "I borrowed this one for you."

"They say once you learn, you don't forget how," she quips.

"That's what they say about other things, too."

She laughs, but her heart is not in it. The day goes by in spite of her thoughts being elsewhere. It is brisk for summer, and the park is green with possibility. Dianna has forgotten how much she enjoys propelling herself through space with the wind beating her hair back. Her memories trace themselves back to riding without a saddle at her grandparents' farm, the smell of hay and grass and dust in the breeze made by horse's hooves, the feel of the horse beneath, the sound of its breath, and the pounding earth underneath them.

Connor is cute and compact, sinewy, and his golden hair matches hers. His words tumble from his tongue like poetry. She finds herself gazing at him and trying to figure out why a man with this much appeal should leave her heart cold. This kind of outing is exactly what she has dreamed of doing with Qasim. If he were here beside her, she would be blissful.

Connor taps her shoulder, and she jumps. He has brought along some water, beer, and soda bread. They sit under a large tree, watching diners go in and out of the Tavern on the Green, trying to see through the glass once the customers are inside. Their view affords them a panorama of park life—children tethered to their balloons, runners dodging traffic, a mounted policeman overseeing all from his sixteen-hand high steed.

"So you're from which county?" Dianna nibbles on the dry piece of bread.

"County Cork." Connor shrugs, as though there is nothing else to be said, as though he is from Paradise.

His shrug shows her his homesickness, his pride, and his determination to make a living. Here is a man with a home. His cover is blown, and she can see that melancholy wedge its way forward in his face again. She's reminded how difficult it is to live in one place if your soul is somewhere else. She wonders if he has a girl back home.

"And you've been here how long?" She picks up the water bottle but doesn't drink, waiting for his answer.

"A little more than two years."

"Touring?"

"At first. Then the band decided to settle here. There are lots of pubs 'round." He shrugs, this time with his other shoulder. His eyes go blank and far away, but not in a vacant way. As though he is dreaming.

"I know. I have my favorite."

"Favorite what?" His attention is back on Dianna immediately, but he has lost the thread of conversation.

"Favorite pub... O'Leary's."

"Oh? Don't think I know that one." She cannot tell if he is playing along with her joke or not. Then he says, "You'll have to ask Mrs. O'Leary's cow to give me directions. I need a new gig."

They laugh, really laugh, with one another. He twirls a lock of Dianna's long hair around his finger and hums a little tune. It is beautiful. Even if her heart doesn't stir, at least she has found someone whose music brings her solace. She decides she'll see him again if he asks. Dianna lays her head back against his arm, enjoying the moment, and falls asleep.

The next afternoon, Dianna sits on her bed, flipping through a women's magazine, one she's never seen before. Heather has gone home today, and she's feeling lonely. Leah's always working, even weekends these days. Dianna asked Heather to continue to go for outpatient visits. She's sure Heather isn't well yet. But Heather was all excuses, saying her insurance wouldn't cover clinic visits.

Dianna is worried about her, wishes she'd stayed, but she is also sad about the route of her own life. Thus, the magazine. She stops at a quiz: "Is he cheating?" The questions amuse her, but she fills in the circles in the multiple-choice questions hoping she might understand Qasim. On still another level, she imagines his Arab ex-wife. She is sure that woman never filled out a quiz in some mindless magazine to try to understand her spouse. A jab of envy shoots down her shoulder and arm, and she tries to squelch her insecurity that he is forever attached to this woman, with or without love, because of the son they share. Then she shakes her thoughts off, feeling silly, putting the tip of the pen into her mouth, pondering how to answer the following question:

You see your guy speaking with another woman at a party. Do you:
a) Go up to them and introduce yourself?
b) Act like a fly on the wall, hoping to hear what they're saying?
c) Find another man to flirt with you?
d) Ignore it, as you know you're better for him than anyone else he could meet?

She wonders what the secure woman would do. She gets ready to write her answer, "b," but she might also do "a," so her pen wavers in the air above the paper. The telephone jangles, and she reluctantly puts her pen and magazine down. The phone is already peeling out its fourth ring when she picks up the receiver. She stands rigid with forced composure when she hears Qasim's voice.

"I thought you were out," he says. His voice is raspy but much stronger than the last time they spoke.

She doesn't know how to answer him or what to say. She is tempted to hang up, but she's never hung up on anyone before. "Are you better?" she finally asks.

"Yes, much, thank you. I am doing quite well."

"I'm glad." Her eyes drift back to the folded magazine and then come back and rest on the box Qasim gave her, how long ago? She traces the straight mother-of-pearl lines, which lead like a path to the geometric rose center, like the quilts her Gran used to make. She runs her finger up and down the triangular shapes that surround the rose. Funny, she'd never realized they were hourglass-shaped before.

"So what's new?" His voice almost sounds like he has a chest cold.

"Not much." She wraps her hand around the phone cord and she can feel her nails digging ever so slightly into her palm. Another silence spans between them like a room divided by Plexiglas.

"I leave for Kuwait next week. I'd like to see you before then," he says.

"I'm going to see my mother," she lies. "I leave tomorrow." She looks down at the bite marks that are beginning to heal on her arm and knows she's doing the right thing.

"Oh." Another pronounced silence spans between them. She hears him fidgeting. "I will call when I get back."

"That's fine," she replies and hangs up the telephone before he can ask questions.

Dianna remembers another time when she felt like this. A college student, she bummed a ride to a fraternity party one lonely Saturday evening. She hated fraternity parties, but she was sick of studying. *What harm could it do to go up the road an hour to a party?* Four young women piled into a tiny silver car and sped up the highway at seventy-five miles per hour. Six hours and a keg party later, Dianna was the only sober person on the return trip. The driver, whose name she's forgotten, was high and decided to beat her own record back to school at 125-135 mph the entire ride home. The highway was deserted.

Trees sped by like blades of grass, and the white lines of the road blurred. No one was saying a word. Dianna realized they were all drunk, but her fear was no less.

"Please stop!" she shouted into the front seat.

The young woman turned her head, startled. The front right tire hit a pothole, and the car almost flew off the road. The night filled with women's screams, one piercing, another shrieking, and another wailing. Dianna did not scream aloud. Her scream expanded inside her, but for some reason, her body kept it locked inside.

Dianna's feeling tonight matches the one of that time. More than disorientation, but not fear. Instead, a numbness, a not knowing. It was being hit in the stomach without wincing, not due to courage or strength, but because one's nerves weren't responding.

She slumps on her bedspread and looks down at the magazine without really seeing it at all, then flips it closed. Then she walks back toward her dresser, in a trance, across her dim, dusky bedroom to the box. The dresser lamp shines directly on the rose and hourglasses, and the box in turn reflects into the mirror. Her face reflects up into the looking glass, too. Geometric shadow patterns dance across her forehead, the box's temporary tattoo. She opens the box and fingers the hinges one last time, takes the letter out, shuts it. She runs to the post office receptacle and lets its cavernous mouth swallow the envelope. It is darkening quickly. Raindrops start to fall.

CHAPTER FORTY-FIVE

Negotiations

The manila envelope arrives at the tail end of a flurry of rejection letters. Dianna weighs the size and thickness of the envelope and holds her breath as she rips it open with a dull kitchen knife. Operation Ready to Read wants her to leave for Zaire in six weeks. The operation is based in Kinshasa. After a brief training period in Nairobi, and a French proficiency test, she will be approved to teach African children English. It's not the Peace Corps, but it is a beginning. Her first instinct is to call Qasim, but her letter has closed that door. He would have called her himself had he cared enough to respond. She calls Leah, who has already left work, and then she dials Connor's number.

"Congratulations," he says in a tone lacking conviction. "What are they going to pay you?"

"I've got a million things to do," Dianna tells Connor and prepares to hang up the phone.

"Don't go," Connor says.

"You know I have to go," she says. She wants to save his feelings. She doesn't know if his dampened enthusiasm is due to real feelings for her or to selfishness. Either way, her imminent departure is only going to complicate any face-to-face good-byes. She bids him an abrupt farewell, then races up the hall and begins emptying her dresser drawers: one pile to give away, another to take with her. The donation pile is much larger than the latter. This is a new start.

Leah gives Dianna a puzzled look as she comes through the door. She looks from the small pile of jeans and T-shirts to the large pile of Evan-Picones and Joseph Bankses. "What's going on?"

"Want some new work clothes?" Dianna flashes a big grin.

"Don't tell me you're going to Africa?" Leah screams and flies across the room to hug her apartment mate. They hold hands and jump up and down giggling like schoolgirls jumping rope on a playground. "I am so thrilled for you!" Leah continues. "I hope I can visit!" She picks up the pillows on Dianna's bed and throws them up to the ceiling, and Dianna sits down on top of her clothes and bounces up and down on her too-soft mattress.

"When do you leave?" Leah asks when she finally sits down beside Dianna, out of breath.

"Six weeks. Do you think you can find someone to move in?"

"I've got some interested people; I'll call them for interviews tomorrow. Will you be able to meet them with me? I've been thinking about that. I knew you'd be offered this position."

Dianna blushes. "You did? I wish I had known."

"Dianna, you're one of those people who can be anything you want to be." Leah gives her another quick hug. "So let's see what fits me here. I've borrowed these two blouses before; I know they fit." Leah picks up the skirt Dianna wore the night she and Qasim met. "I love this wool tweed purple skirt. I can't believe you're giving that away?"

"Don't need it. Here. Take it." Dianna places the skirt into Leah's extended hand. "Try it on."

Leah holds the skirt in midair, a slight frown marring her usual cheerfulness. "I don't know if I should take it, Dianna. It's so nice. Isn't it Evan-Picone?"

"Yeah. Bad memories. Take it."

"Thanks!" Leah hugs the skirt to her and does a little jump, but Dianna notices that both their eyes are moist.

***

Dianna almost skips into the museum the next day. She doesn't even glance at the huge canvas billboards that advertise the upcoming King Tut exhibit. She is finished with exhibitions of any kind.

Sophia looks up from her cards. "Dianna, you look radiant today! I haven't seen you looking like this since..." She cuts herself off, and color floods her face.

"It's okay, Sophia." Dianna smiles. "Everything changed last night. I leave for Africa the end of next month. Do I give you my letter of resignation or Brenda?"

Sophia grins and gets up to give Dianna a bear hug. "I'm so glad you're getting your adventure, dear," she says. "You give one copy to me and another to Brenda."

"Oh my God, carbon paper!" they both mouth to each other. Carbon paper means no typos allowed; they can't be corrected on the copy. Their boss only allows the copy machine to be used for more than three copies. Photocopies are too expensive for small jobs.

"Maybe I'll type two separate originals," Dianna muses. "It'll take me all day if I use carbon."

Sophia goes to her desk and rummages through her bottom drawer. "Here, Sweetie. I bought this a long time ago, and I was waiting for the right moment to give it to you."

It is a simple enough plaque, with a picture of a waterfall on it. "That's Victoria Falls, as it happens," Sophia tells her.

The inscription is the important part of the gift, the photograph coincidentally symbolic:

"If one advances confidently in the direction of their dreams, and endeavors to lead a life which they have imagined, they will meet with a success unexpected in common hours."
—Henry David Thoreau

Dianna turns the framed memento over to find another quotation on the back, written in Sophia's own elegant handwriting:

"I have no place in my life for people and things without passion;
I want my life to burn like a thousand suns."

"That's Hermann Hesse," Sophia explains. "I probably don't have to tell you that, Dianna Apassionata, my friend of a thousand-and-one suns."

Dianna's eyes well up with tears, and she lets them roll down her cheeks. "My ex-fiancé used to say that he was Narcissus, and I was Goldmund."

"You had a fiancé?"

"Yes, many moons ago."

"Goldmund!" Sophia sniffs. "If only he could see you now!" and she is crying, too.

CHAPTER FORTY-SIX

Exit Strategy

"Mama?" Dianna asks when she finally hears her mother shuffle to the pay phone in the convalescent home corridor.

"Dianna?"

"Yes, Mama. I've called to tell you something."

"Dianna, can you bring me my dinner? I'm really hungry."

"You know I can't, Mama. I'm in New York."

"New York City?"

"Yes, Mama."

"How'd you get there?"

Dianna puts her elbows on the table and coils the phone cord around and around her index finger. "I live here, Mama."

"Get these nurses to bring me something to eat. I'm hungry."

"Okay, Mama. Listen, I have something to tell you."

"What?"

Dianna takes a deep breath, hoping this won't set her mother to weeping. She can imagine her mother standing there, shifting from one foot to the other to keep from falling. She really needs a wheelchair, but she refuses one. She broke the wheelchair Medicaid provided, and they won't pay for another one yet. Dianna doesn't have enough money to buy one for her. After Medicaid, her mother's room and board take half Dianna's salary, and she sends her brother money for school whenever she can. Mary Anne picks up the rest, but she makes less than Dianna. Maybe she can send more once she's out of New York.

"Mary Anne is going to be visiting you more than I am, okay? For the next year. I'm going away for a little while. I have a job overseas."

"So you won't be able to come every day?"

"No, Mama. You know I only come four or five times a year."

"You could take me with you. Do they have sweet tea there?"

"Not where I'm going. Don't worry; I'll still send the check to Mary Anne and T.C. I'll get back to see you often."

"I guess your father wouldn't let me go anyway."

"Mama, my father is dead."

The phone goes silent for a full minute, then her mother speaks again, and this time, her voice has that faraway, half-here quality. "Okay, Dianna. Can I stay in this room then?"

"Yes, Mama."

"Well, then, don't worry me like that again. I'll see you tomorrow. Good-bye, Sweetheart." Her mother hangs up the phone before Dianna has a chance to reply.

CHAPTER FORTY-SEVEN

So Long

Dianna wonders how so few possessions can fill a suitcase. She sits on the battered green baggage and attempts to close the latches for the third time. She gets up and digs to the bottom for another book that cannot be taken. No matter, she tells herself, there will be little time for reading where she's going.

The buzzer sounds, and Dianna wonders who can be at her door so late in the evening the week before her departure. She frowns at the lack of consideration, but she goes to the wall and punches the intercom button to find out who it is.

"Hello, it's Connor. Can I come up?"

Dianna puts her hand on her hip. She doesn't know. He'll want to stay, like he asked the last time they were together. She is not up for intimacy with a friend she already considers an artifact from her past. Anything that she has to catalog in her memory is too much to handle at present. If only she could get on a plane tonight. Connor is a nice-enough boy, but the spark is not there for her. She cannot grasp what he sees in her after such a short amount of time. He must have left people before, too. She never wanted another intense-one-month, go-nowhere-the-next-month relationship, and her departure makes any sort of relationship improbable. Has this man thought about the price of a telephone call between here and Africa? How does she get herself in these situations?

His voice comes over the speaker again. "Dianna? Please? I have a little surprise for you, Darlin'."

Dianna cannot resist the little-boy tone in his voice, never could resist men who act like boys. This has been her downfall before, more than once. She sighs, deep enough to make certain he has heard. "Alright, then, I'm buzzing you in."

She holds her arms at her sides as he hugs her. "You know I like you, Connor, but we've been through this twice before. I can't get involved if I'm leaving in a week."

"I'm not asking for involvement. I only want to be close to you once before you leave me here all alone." He grins.

Dianna shakes her head back and forth. "Uh-uh. That's not going to work."

"Damn!" His grin grows bigger, which makes her smile back. "Well, I guess I'll have to give this to you and take my leave, then." He hands her a package wrapped in tissue paper, with wads of tape holding the edges together.

Dianna pulls at the tape, which only reveals more tape underneath.

"Sorry," he says and stuffs his hands in his pockets.

"No! No!" She laughs. "You're so sweet to give me a going-away gift. My office has yet to even mention that I'm leaving."

"I wanted you to have something to remember me by." His brogue deepens, and a chill runs up her spine. "Besides, if you like it, you might sleep with me."

Dianna chuckles again, but she moves toward the kitchen. "I'll need scissors to open this." She can tell Connor's had too much to drink. This is when he is at his most charming. "Don't you have to play tonight?"

"In a wee bit. I have time." He wraps his arm around her waist and tries to kiss her.

Dianna takes an empty glass and pretends to throw cold water in his direction. "Down, boy," she laughs.

"Okay! A lad can only try, right?"

The phone rings. There is laughter in her voice when she picks up the receiver and fiddles with the tape. "Must be our obscene phone caller," she tells Connor and brings the receiver to her ear. "We've been getting weird calls for the past two weeks."

The voice on the other end not only stuns her, it stupefies her. She has not expected to hear it ever again after the letter she sent. Dismay sweeps her up like a wave crashing against an empty bottle. She can't imagine why someone who refused to let her nurse him in illness would want to reconnect in the aftermath of her blistering letter. *Perhaps he likes pain*, she thinks, and stifles a hysterical laugh.

"Who is it?" calls Connor. "Come on, girl, get over here and open that present!"

Dianna ignores him. She wants to ignore both of them.

"I'm going to hang up," she tells Qasim.

"Why?" His voice is startlingly warm, almost teasing.

"We've grown apart," Dianna counters. "How long has it been since we talked?" She wants to ask him how he felt about her letter, but with Connor fifteen feet away and waiting, the timing is inappropriate. She puts up her index finger to indicate to Connor that she'll be off any minute.

"I have no idea." He laughs. "You could have called *me*, you know." Then his voice grows serious. "I want to see you."

It's Dianna's turn to ask why.

"Does a man need a reason to see a woman?"

"In your case, yes," Dianna retorts. She forces her voice to be hard. She is amazed but relieved he has not brought up the letter himself. What difference does the letter make anyway? She is leaving.

"Come on!" Connor shouts.

"Who's that?" Qasim asks. "Do you have a man there?" His voice is clipped. She strains to differentiate if there is an English word between the next Arabic words he mutters under his breath.

Dianna bristles. She has never invaded Qasim's privacy, not once. How dare he come marching back into her life at the last minute, demanding to know her business? Yet for some reason, she's embarrassed, too, like she has cheated on Qasim. "No," she lies. She paces back and forth as far as the phone cord allows, notices Connor's puzzled frown, and crouches in the corner beside the refrigerator. She is annoyed with herself for fibbing, but then she tells herself that he has no right to know. He doesn't own her any more than she owns him. "Look, I've got to go, okay? I've got a friend of the family here."

"When can I see you?" The phone line is full of static, and his words are full of his accent.

Her pulse beats a jagged rhythm in her ankle. She stands up, dizzy. Is this really the way to break up with someone? She's overcome by another hot wave of embarrassment at her cowardice. "Oh alright," she says. "I have something to tell you anyway. The bar around the corner from your office? Seven o'clock tomorrow?"

"I can be there by eight."

"Alright, I'll see you then." She hangs up the phone, and it jingles from the force.

Connor stares at her. "Who was that?"

Dianna wonders if he should know. After all, what does she know of his life before this, his life in Ireland? In the end, her honesty gets the best of her. "An old boyfriend."

"Boy, we're all coming out of the woodwork, aren't we? I'll wager he doesn't have a gift, though." Connor's cute, crooked front teeth show, and she goes over and hugs him.

"You don't have to worry about him," she says. "But you do have to worry about Africa. My mind is made up."

Connor is quiet. He leans forward, closing his eyes tight and putting his hands to his mouth. When he speaks, his words are muffled. "Dianna, I haven't known you long. I have nothing whatsoever to offer you, except this simple gift. I know you're too good for me. I've nothing to look forward to—here or back home. So let's get this over, okay? Open the damned gift!"

Dianna touches his arm and gives him a soft kiss. "You know I'll always remember you."

"And I you," he says, looking up again and straight into her eyes.

She continues to stare into them as she tears off the last pieces of tape. Inside is a chain bearing a Claddagh ring. She's seen it on his finger, and tonight she had not noticed its absence.

"I can't..." she starts to say, but he interrupts her.

"That word is not in your vocabulary, woman."

They stare at each other. Finally, she says, "I must meet him. I was hoping I wouldn't have to see him again, but I should tell him I'm leaving in person. I guess I owe him that much. We'd been dating two years...if you can call it dating."

"Jerk," is all he says.

"Friends anyway?" she asks.

"Friends," he replies, and he places the necklace around her throat. It feels right there.

CHAPTER FORTY-EIGHT

Last Stand

Dianna waits at the restaurant until nine the next evening. She waits until she realizes how ridiculous it is to wait any longer. No one but a fool waited more than an hour for a man to break up with him! She wears her basic black suit, the last suit she owns, but she has reapplied her make-up. She takes a last sip of her drink and stands up to leave.

As she is descending the steps outside, he appears at the bottom, running.

"You were hoping I wouldn't show," he states.

No, that's not true," she says, her voice flat. "I told you I had something important to tell you."

"Let's sit and have a drink." She reluctantly lets him take her stiff arm, and they walk back over to the tiny, intimate bar counter.

"Hey," the bartendress smiles. "Wha'd'ya have?" She knows Qasim and Dianna as regulars.

"Scotch and soda on the rocks, and..."

"Nothing for me, thanks," Dianna interjects.

Qasim touches Dianna's arm. "It is so good to see you."

Dianna leans back when he tries to kiss her. Her mind whips back and forth in confusion. How can anyone be this self-assured? Anger rips up her body like fast-advancing ice. How can someone try to kiss someone else after a "Dear John" letter? She laughs when her mind touches on the name John, her late grandfather's name, a name of endearment, not rejection.

"You're laughing at me," he says and leans back, too.

She does not object.

"Mmmm, this drink is just what I needed," he says and closes his eyes.

"Should you be drinking?" Dianna arches an eyebrow.

"I am fine," he says. "What was it you have to tell me?"

"We can't see each other anymore. I've told you before." She picks up her purse to leave, but he touches her arm to keep her there.

"Dianna, you cannot be serious."

It's rapidly becoming a game of wills. She wasn't going to bring up the letter if he wasn't. "You remember," is all she says.

He looks across the room, tracing back through some distant thread of memory. Dianna tries to rise once again. She does not want this interaction to continue; it hurts. Again, Qasim catches her wrist.

"I leave for Kinshasa next week," Dianna says and looks at his eyes to determine if he cares. She sees nothing at all in them for several minutes. They are both completely silent, a silence she finally breaks. "Well, aren't you going to congratulate me?"

He looks puzzled, and then his face closes down again. "When?" he asks.

"Tuesday. Well?"

"Congratulations, Dianna. I know this is what you wanted."

"Yes." She smiles.

"You've quit your day job?"

"Qasim. Stop. You can't hurt me that way any longer," she says, but her voice is hoarse.

"Well," he rephrases, his voice full of gravel, "you've resigned?"

"Yes."

"Congratulations," he says again and takes another sip of drink, then a larger sip.

"You're not drinking," he adds, and looks for the bartender.

"I already had one."

"Come on, you must drink with me. We must toast your success. What will you be doing?"

"Teaching English."

"You don't need French?"

"I know French."

"You?" He snickers and looks away.

"Yes. You know I've studied French before." She wants to say something demeaning or profound in French, but vocabulary escapes her. She registers annoyance that this man still has that effect on her.

"Dianna, please don't! How can you do this to me?" Qasim asks.

"You need to go take care of your country. I told you all this in the letter," she says.

"What letter?"

"You didn't receive the letter?

"No."

"I don't believe you, Qasim. How can I trust you? You never tell me the real story." She is disgusted now. He cannot even be genuine with her at this last moment, the last time they will speak, the last time they will look in each other's eyes.

"Yes, I do, Dianna. Really, I do. It is you who will not believe me."

Dianna looks away. It's true; she doesn't trust him.

"How's Leah?" he asks, a beat too quickly. "Will she have trouble finding a roommate?" She suspects this is a calculated change of subject, to divert the tension, to calm her down, but she falls for it anyway.

"How dare you ask me about Leah?" She braces for a counterattack but none comes.

"Leah's been anticipating this. She's already interviewed several applicants."

"You know, you haven't made this easy on her," he says.

Her eyes blink, register the strange words, and blink again. She is more baffled than jealous over his concern for Leah. "I have no idea what you mean," she says. "How could you possibly know much about my relationship with Leah? You've not been around enough to know. Who have you been talking to?" Leah immediately pops into her mind, and she pushes the thought away. What difference does it make at this point?

"*You're* never there for her, always gavalanting around, doing whatever it is you do."

"Gallivanting," she laughs, correcting him. This is so typical of Qasim, caring more for someone he hardly knows than for someone who is standing before him, who has waited for him month after month.

"Gavalanting," he says harshly. "That is what I said. That is the word."

"No," she says, "you got the syllables confused."

"You don't know how difficult it is going to be for her, renting that apartment all by herself, with such sudden notice!" His voice is loud, and customers at a nearby table stop drinking and look up, curious.

"Qasim, she hasn't complained." Dianna touches his arm, hoping to calm him down. "I know all about her designs on you, but it can't have gotten far."

"What are you talking about? I have nothing in common with Leah."

"She says you do."

"I don't. I just think you're being completely selfish."

"And I think you're projecting." She hears the shrill noise of her voice echo.

Qasim drains his drink, and his eyes start at one corner of the bar and track around to the opposite corner, a full half circle. She half expects him to turn on his bar stool to scan the rest of the room, but he does not. Instead, he stands, toppling the stool. The glass of ice is still in his hand, but only for an instant. He swings it above his head with amazing agility, and it smashes against the bar counter at a point where no one is sitting. Ice goes flying. His breath is hard and quick, and his eyes scare her. They remind her of a horse her uncle once tried to break but could not. Dianna finds herself thinking a thought that does not fit the intensity of the moment or her previous conception of him: *I'll bet he was an athlete in school.*

The thought leaves as immediately as it came, and she again feels the urge to turn and run. "I'm sorry," she mutters, and does.

She looks over her shoulder when she reaches the exterior door. He is paying the bartender for damages. He makes no move to follow her. That familiar feeling has returned beneath her rib cage, the feeling of tears that need to be shed but can't be. This time, this last time, she allows herself to weep. She knows this is for the best. The setting sun glints over her shoulder on a puddle straight ahead on the pavement revealing a rainbow. Peace washes over her like a newfound world. Her heels click the sidewalk, moving her ever faster toward home. This time she does not look back.

CHAPTER FORTY-NINE

Wheels Up

Dianna's said her final farewells to her colleagues and friends. Leah gave her a high five; Heather wept. She's handed her apartment key over to her landlord, who was standing on the outside steps smoking a cigarette.

Waiting to board the airplane, she bids a good-bye to an absent Qasim, one of forgiveness, affection, and gratitude. She misses him, yet she'll never turn back. She won't give up her goals for him. Theirs was not a fairy tale love, but a love spanning shores and seas, the kind of love an oyster shell gives a pearl, equal parts friction and protection, and only time enough to polish it bright and beautiful.

She wants to call him and tell him what she has discovered, but she can't. Not yet. She'd denied it, couldn't see through her scars, but she'd been searching for true love when she should have been searching for home. They had shared moments of love, more than most people get. She would have to be true to herself first, and he'd prepared her for the next leg in her journey. She'd found pieces of herself with each demon he'd brought to the surface. Demons dispersed, she was ready to pursue her dreams. She hopes he finds peace because that is his biggest gift to her.

Peace in her heart. Love of herself. She smiles as she remembers his beautiful box packed inside her carry-on luggage, a box within a box. Her heart is like that box, a container for love and peace, as a riverbed is to water, or the soil is to a garden, the ocean to continents. She'd never had to look for love at all. Because it matters not where she travels, or whom she meets, she has home now. She carries it with her in the labyrinthine chambers of her heart. She puts her hand on her chest. *There he is.* Running through the vessels, the ventricles, beating out a jazz tattoo, deep in the home of her.

Qasim would feel at home here in this terminal, but she has not flown much. In one corner, some men in somber polyester suits smoke cigarettes and drink tea in cracked white cups. In another, a mother dressed in loose, comfortable bright rainbow colors and uncomfortable-looking high-heeled sandals feeds her baby a bottle. People she assumes are humanitarian workers chat with an occasional outburst of cheer. They all wear cotton, button-down, tailored shirts and faded jeans. Everywhere, noise bounces off the walls in this self-described "state of the art" international airport. She buys some chewing gum, a bottle of water, and postcards—her last remnant of New York. She tells herself she'll send the postcards to family members, but she knows better. *So long, New York City. So long, friends and family. So long, Qasim. Hello, Africa.*

She imagines a balloon in front of her, bobbing, and then imagines it floating upward, away. Her chest lightens at the thought. Peace. She's ready to learn by herself, to take on this new adventure. She gets her boarding pass checked and seat assigned, and the first rows begin to form a line.

A young woman rushes in.

"Madame?" She fishes for her boarding pass. "Can you tell me where this plane is heading?" Her words are half-English, half-Italian. "Have I missed my plane?"

"Nairobi," Dianna says. "Not yet."

The loud speaker finally calls her row. She looks out the window at the morning mist, and it triggers memory.

The night they met in that loud bar. Their nights of passion. The long waits for him when he was late. The shock at hearing his weak, ill voice. One memory lodges, takes its place at the front of the line. Qasim picked her up one night, early on, and she hadn't noticed his car waiting for her. He was waving, a frantic spasm of a wave, as though she might look right through him. He tried to roll down the passenger window as she walked to his car, but he couldn't reach it. He was speaking, but she couldn't hear him. Instead of rolling the window down, he only succeeded in fogging the window with his breath.

She sees him there now, for an instant, before he dissolves into the misted window in front of her. Then her reflection replaces his face, and she looks across at herself.

The final boarding call echoes loud and clear. Butterflies do their transformational dance in her abdomen, and she wonders what waits for her. A bright blue feather, the kind you find on a kindergarten art project, blows around the floor in front of her. She picks it up and blows it up into the air. Now, now, now. She boards before it has time to land.

Addendum

DATELINE BEIRUT

January 1, 1944, Beirut, Lebanon. France grants Lebanon its independence. According to sectarian lines, the president is to be a Maronite Christian, the prime minister a Sunni Muslim, and the house speaker a Shia Muslim.

May 1948, Beirut. The State of Israel is created. Britain withdraws from Palestine, formerly their territorial mandate. Fighting breaks out. Palestinians flee into Lebanon and Jordan.

July 13, 1958, Fort Bragg, N.C., USA. Master Sgt. and Mrs. Robert E. Calloway proudly announce the birth of their first daughter, Dianna Lynn, blue eyes, blonde hair, 7 lbs., 11 oz.

July 14, 1958, Beirut. President Dwight D. Eisenhower dispatches U.S. Marines to the bikini-clad beaches of Beirut to re-establish the Lebanese government. Several thousand Lebanese have already lost their lives in civil war.

September 28, 1961, Damascus, Syria. Syria withdraws from the United Arab Republic after a military coup. An initial step to creating a pan-Arab union, the UAR previously combined Syria and Egypt into one country, with Nasser as its president.

May 29, 1964, Jerusalem. The Palestinian Liberation Organization (PLO) is created.

June 5-10, 1967, The West Bank, formerly the Directorate of Palestine. Following the buildup of Arab troops on Israeli borders and the closing of the Strait of Tiran, Israel attacks. After six days of war with Syria, Iraq, Jordan, and Egypt, Israel declares victory and occupies the West Bank.

November 2, 1969, Cairo, Egypt. Emile Bustani, Israel's commander-in-chief, and Yasser Arafat, Chairman of the PLO, sign an agreement that aims to stop Palestinian fighters from launching operations from Lebanon.

September 6, 1970, Amman, Jordan. After a year of clashes between the PLO and Jordan, Palestinian guerillas seize and blow up three airliners in Jordan in an operation called Black September.

September 1971, Beirut. PLO guerillas and newly elected leader Yasser Arafat are driven out of Jordan and establish a headquarters in Lebanon.

April 30, 1972, Beirut. Conflict claims another 25 lives in sniper attacks. Militias regroup.

April 13, 1975, Beirut. Gunmen kill four Christians during an assassination attempt on Lebanese Maronite Christian leader Pierre Gemayel. Believing the assassins to be Palestinian, the Christians attack a bus of Palestinian passengers, killing at least 26. The Lebanese Civil War begins.

June 1975, Lebanon. At the president's invitation, Syrian troops intervene and occupy all but the south of the country.

June 1976, Saudi Arabia. The Arab Summit approves an Arab Deterrence Force in Lebanon to restore peace and order..

August 12, 1976, Beirut. The PLO is accused of using civilian areas as headquarters for its fighters. The Palestinian refugee camp of Tal al-Zaatar in East Beirut is overrun by Christian militias; its inhabitants are massacred or expelled.

March 11, 1978, Israel. Fatah (a PLO faction) members hijack a bus near Haifa, and commandeer a second bus en route to Tel Aviv. A lengthy chase and shootout leaves 37 Israelis killed and 76 wounded.

March 14, 1978, Southern Lebanon. The Israeli Defense Forces invade Lebanon up to the strategic Litani River, pushing PLO forces north. Talks about a UN peacekeeping force in Southern Lebanon continue.

January 1, 1979, Jerusalem. A bomb explodes in a marketplace. Israeli forces retaliate with their heaviest strike into Lebanon in a year. The war revs up again.

February 13, 1981, Lebanon. Lebanon's leaders adopt security measures to protect its embassies after the kidnapping of Jordan's charge d'affaires in Beirut. Snipers paralyze traffic between East and West Beirut.

April 28, 1981, Beka'a Valley, Lebanon. Israeli warplanes down two helicopters in the second day of a bombing offensive on Palestinian strongholds. Syrians deploy retaliatory missiles. US Arab American envoy Philip Habib steps in to negotiate the crisis.

May 19, 1981, Tel Aviv, Israel. Israeli Prime Minister Begin demands Syria remove its missiles from Lebanon and Syrian-Lebanese borders. US envoy Philip Habib proposes a resolution to the crisis, which seems doomed to failure.

July 10–24, 1981, Lebanon. Israeli attacks flare on Palestinian bases in Lebanon, and the PLO shells Israeli towns. Israeli warplanes bomb PLO headquarters in Beirut, killing hundreds.

September 24, 1981, Saudi Arabian Coast. An Israeli missile boat, possibly bound for Beirut, runs aground. Contact is made with the Saudis through the US, and the boat is extricated.

October 10, 1981, Cairo, Egypt. Israeli Prime Minister Begin attends Anwar Sadat's funeral in Cairo, meeting with Egyptian President Mubarak. They pledge "Peace Forever." Newly elected Israeli Defense minister Ariel Sharon declares he supports the implementation of "Operation Big Pines," an invasion of Lebanon that "includes Beirut."

November 20, 1981, Southern Lebanon. Christian militias lift a blockade on 800 members of the UN peacekeeping forces, permitting a UN convoy to move between their base and Israel.

December 3, 1981, Damascus, Syria. U.S. special envoy Philip Habib meets with Syrian President Hafez Assad as thousands of residents demonstrate in the Damascene streets to protest a bomb explosion that killed scores of civilians.

December 7, 1981, Beirut, Lebanon. Terrorist commando hijacks a Libyan passenger jet at Beirut International Airport, holding 43 hostages.

December 12, 1981, Tripoli, Lebanon. Rival paramilitary factions exchange shots after a car bomb explosion kills 14.

December 14, 1981, Israel. Israel annexes the Golan Heights, which it captured from Syria in 1967. The UN Security Council declares the annexation illegal.

December 15, 1981, Tel Aviv, Israel. Israel's Defense Minister Sharon warns that PLO shelling of Israeli settlements is intolerable and threatens to wipe out the PLO completely.

December 16, 1981, Beirut. A suicide bomb wrecks the Iraqi Embassy in Beirut, killing scores and wounding at least 100 people. Responsible parties unknown.

December 19, 1981, Beirut. A car bomb at the UNESCO building kills 16 and injures 18.

February 23, 1982, Beirut. A Lebanese Druze leader says that Israel's annexation of the Golan Heights has "radicalized" the Druze sect, increasing the likelihood of new sectarian bloodshed.

April 21, 1982, Damour, Lebanon. After a landmine kills an Israeli officer in Lebanon, the Israeli Air Force attacks Damour, a Palestinian-controlled town, killing 23.

June 3, 1982, London, England. Palestinian militant group Fatah attempts to assassinate Shlomo Argovi, Israel's ambassador to England, paralyzing him.

June 4, 1982, Lebanon. Israeli F-16 planes bomb Palestinian refugee camps and other PLO targets in Beirut and Southern Lebanon killing 45, wounding 150.

June 6, 1982, Lebanon. Israeli forces invade Southern Lebanon and Beirut. Shelling continues unabated.

June 6, 1982, Lebanon. Poet Khalil al-Hawi, distraught at the Israeli invasion, dies by his own hand.

June 12, 1982, The New York Times: "Civil war, religious strife, foreign invasions, a crippled economy, disintegration of governmental authority, a scarred and bloody landscape—these are the tragic elements of Lebanon's tortured modern history, elements more appropriate to a battleground than to a nation."

September 14, 1982, Beirut. A bomb assassinates Lebanese President-elect Bachir Gemayel.

September 16, 1982, Beirut. As the Israeli military encircles the area, Lebanese Christian militiamen enter Beirut's Sabra and Shatila refugee camps in revenge for the assassination of their leader Bachir Gemayel. The massacre leaves hundreds, possibly thousands, of innocent civilians dead, the bloodiest single incident of the Arab-Israeli conflict to date.

September 21, 1982, Beirut. Bachir Gemayel's elder brother, Amin Gemayel, is elected president.

September 24, 1982. A U.S.-French-Italian multinational force, requested by Lebanon, arrives in Beirut.

April 18, 1983. A suicide bomber detonates an explosives-laden lorry driven into the U.S. embassy on Beirut's seafront. Sixty-three people are killed and more than 100 are hurt. Islamic Jihad claims responsibility.

May 17, 1983, Naquora, Lebanon. Israel and Lebanon sign a peace agreement on the condition that Israel withdraws from Lebanon.

September 1983. U.S. warships shell Muslim areas of Beirut in support of Amin Gemayel's government.

October 23, 1983. At least 241 U.S. Marines and 58 French paratroopers are killed in a suicide lorry-bomb attack on the U.S. Marine base in Beirut. The war rages on.

About The Author

After graduating from Hollins University, Kathryn Brown Ramsperger worked as a journalist. In Washington, D.C., she became a researcher for the National Geographic Society and wrote for their children's magazine *WORLD*, now National Geographic *Kids*. Her articles also appeared in Kiplinger's *Changing Times*, now *Kiplinger* magazine, the *Gazette* newspapers, as well as online publications.

As head of publications for the International Red Cross and Red Crescent in Geneva, Switzerland, Kathryn lived and worked in Europe and Africa, travelling throughout the Middle East. Her cause-related marketing for the American Red Cross gave a voice to the homeless, people living with HIV, neighborhoods reeling after disaster, blood and bone marrow recipients, and refugees fleeing war and famine.

In 2000, she formed her own communications company, Ramsperger Communications, focusing on global relief and development, multicultural communication, women's and children's issues, and peace building.

A lifelong writer, Kathryn's writing for humanitarian publications received two Hermes Creative Awards and multiple awards from the International Association of Business Communicators. Her first novel, *Moments on the Edge*, won the Hollins University Fiction Award, and this novel was a semifinalist in the Faulkner-Wisdom Literary Competition.

Kathryn lives in the Washington suburbs with her husband, two teens, and two cats. When she's not writing, reading, and coaching, she's travelling, singing, or both.

To learn more about Kathryn and her novels and short stories, visit her web site at shoresofoursouls.com.

Acknowledgments

It takes a village to write a novel, and this novel has become a virtual town. The author expresses heartfelt gratitude to the following:

Brian, who gave me space and spirit, and whispered, "Shhhh! Mom's working!" outside my office door. Sean, who told his kindergarten class, "My mom's hobby is computer games. She's always on the computer!" Aimee, who said, "You don't have to watch me try on prom dresses. I know your manuscript is due tomorrow."

My mother, Sarah Elizabeth, who gave me my first grammar, typing, and revision lessons, and her mother, Annie Lee, who spun stories I continue to tell our children. My father, Harold, who nicknamed me "The Little Engine That Could." My entire Southern family, who thought the best day ended with a porch swing, icy sweet tea, and family sharing the tales of the day.

My best friends, Stacey, the wind beneath my wings, and the late Laura Schimdt, my writing buddy and partner in crime on our "debauched" afternoons, who showed me how to live life in the moment. My teachers, from Mrs. Covey, who had us write a story a week, to Mr. Johnson, who crowned me Desdemona, to Dara Weir, who had me make writing my priority over other work, and Richard Dillard and Greg Pape for believing in my first novel so many years ago.

We Seven (Alice, Anne, Candice, Cynthia, Donna, and Tami), the ultimate Critique Group. Better creative feedback or friends could not be found. Nancy for her devoted historical research and shared wicked sense of humor. Christiane, who helped with names. The Faith United Methodist Book Club who read the whole darn thing before edits and then hosted a reading for me with roses. My Facebook Friends who keep asking, "Where can I buy it?"

A special thanks to Josh Moore, who sent me his beautiful translation of Khalil Al-Hawi's "The Bridge," from *Rivers of Ash*, at exactly the right moment.

Assistant extraordinaire Tina, who answers my every question. My coaches Lynne, Kristen, and Kim, my first editors Laurel and Susan, who suggested intricate, effective tweaks to structure and plot, my first copy editor, the late and much missed Lynn Gallagher, whose edits to the second chapter made 1980s Manhattan come alive, my agent Johnnie Bernhard for her comprehension of my characters and "never give up" attitude, and the entire TouchPoint Press Team, especially my editor Kim. Cathy and Maura, who made sure of last minute details with their eagle eyes.

To you, Reader, who enjoys this novel,

To the Muses who inspired it,

And to the courageous people of the Middle East. May we all see Peace in this lifetime.

Made in the USA
Middletown, DE
01 August 2017